SISTER SWING

SISTER SWING

Shirley Geok-lin Lim

mc **Marshall Cavendish**
Editions

Copyright © 2006 Marshall Cavendish International (Asia) Private Limited

Published by Marshall Cavendish Editions
An imprint of Marshall Cavendish International
1 New Industrial Road, Singapore 536196

All rights reserved

No part of this publication may be reproduced, stored in a retrieval system or transmitted, in any form or by any means, electronic, mechanical, photocopying, recording or otherwise, without the prior permission of the copyright owner. Request for permission should be addressed to the Publisher, Marshall Cavendish International (Asia) Private Limited, 1 New Industrial Road, Singapore 536196. Tel: (65) 6213 9300, fax: (65) 6285 4871. E-mail: te@sg.marshallcavendish.com

The publisher makes no representation or warranties with respect to the contents of this book, and specifically disclaims any implied warranties or merchantability or fitness for any particular purpose, and shall in no events be liable for any loss of profit or any other commercial damage, including but not limited to special, incidental, consequential, or other damages.

Other Marshall Cavendish Offices

Marshall Cavendish Ltd. 119 Wardour Street, London W1F OUW, UK • Marshall Cavendish Corporation. 99 White Plains Road, Tarrytown NY 10591-9001, USA • Marshall Cavendish International (Thailand) Co Ltd. 253 Asoke, 12th Flr, Sukhumvit 21 Road, Klongtoey Nua, Wattana, Bangkok 10110, Thailand • Marshall Cavendish (Malaysia) Sdn Bhd, Times Subang, Lot 46, Subang Hi-Tech Industrial Park, Batu Tiga, 40000 Shah Alam, Selangor Darul Ehsan, Malaysia

Marshall Cavendish is a trademark of Times Publishing Limited

National Library Board Singapore Cataloguing in Publication Data

Lim, Shirley.
    Sister swing / Shirley Geok-lin Lim. – Singapore : Marshall Cavendish Editions, 2006.
    p. cm.

    ISBN : 978-981-261-227-4
    ISBN : 981-261-227-0

    1. Racism – Fiction. 2. Sisters – Fiction. 3. Family – Fiction.
    4. United States – Fiction. I. Title.

PS3562.I459
813.54 -- dc21   SLS2005056308

Dedicated to

Gershom
With the hope that
he may find many sisters.

Acknowledgement

This novel was not written in isolation. It has grown in the presence of numerous readers, friends, and funders.

I thank Hedgebrook, for the initial support of time and place;

The University of California, Santa Barbara, and my colleagues who believe in the creative life, with particular thanks to Richard Helgerson, Barry Spacks, and Porter Abbott for reading the draft;

My amazing students and my friends at the Massachusetts Institute of Technology, particularly Isabelle d'Courtivron and Michelle Oshima;

The English Department staff and faculty at the University of Hong Kong, for their support;

Melissa Heng, my editor, whose work cannot be sufficiently praised;

Aria Ting for her hard work;

The many women whose passionate minds continue to guide me, including Nancy Miller, Florence Howe and others;

And as always my family, Charles Bazerman and Gershom Kean Bazerman, for being family all these years.

One

*I*t was Yen who began calling me "Sister Swing." Yen, my oldest sister, who grew up to become younger than me and who shared the secret of how we came to kill our father. We didn't kill him because he wanted to get rid of Yen by sending her into a stranger's hands. In fact, although she denied it later, she was willing to marry, eager to learn what a man might do to her. She had a notion of something to be gained from an arranged marriage, something more than what we shared at home. Still, we both knew Ah Kong died because of what he had seen us do as sisters, but whether we were guilty my bad dreams could never resolve.

I always liked Yen, even when she kicked and bit me. Mama said she was a no-good eldest sister, but Yen only wanted me to grow up faster so we could play better together. When I was five, she took me to the playground at the corner kindergarten and placed me on a swing. "Swing, swing!" she chanted, pushing the dangling seat into the air, and I felt the rush of a strange animal against my cheeks. It rustled its paws in my hair. I could smell its breath up close — something sharp and sourish — before I wetted myself. "Aiiyah," Yen scolded, "good for nothing, scaredy cat!"

Ah Chee, our amah, grumbled when she changed me out of my wet underpants and skirt. "Not so little anymore, how will you marry if you cannot keep your pee in?"

"Swing, swing," I mumbled, trying to keep the new word in my mouth a little longer.

"Sister Swing!" Yen cried out triumphantly, having gotten me into trouble yet again.

Because of Yen's early teaching, I grew to believe English words were a form of magic. I remembered when she first came home from Methodist School speaking a strange new language which broke in her mouth in ways nothing like Chinese. It brought a different force into the world, and one better for being black magic to Ah Chee, who snapped at us in Chinese as we spoke more and more English to each other, leaving her ignorant of our wicked ways.

Yen carried home different words each day, like colored beads or dried plasticine shapes. Father. Mother. Man. Woman. Dog. Cat. House. Tree. Bird. See. Run. England. Asia. She laughed because they scratched and tumbled when I tried them out, but I liked these sounds pulling me out of Ah Chee's lap and into some place she couldn't follow.

Little wonder when I began school — not Yen's Methodist School, I went to the Government English School —I liked it so much. I liked the playground with its ten swings and the earth scraped hard by hundreds of pairs of canvas shoes everyday. I liked the hot blue sky reeling as I ran with the other children, without Ah Chee or Mama shouting, *Don't be a tomboy! Don't get burned in the sun! Don't fall down! Don't get dirty! Don't sweat!* I liked dancing down a long line, singing, "Here comes the chopper to chop off your head!"

Every recess, instead of crowding into the tuck-shop for hot curry puffs and fried noodles, I planted my feet solidly on the grassless hollow, then pushed off alone on the swing. Once in the air I stood up on the plank seat and pumped the swing higher and higher, till I was soaring above ixora and hibiscus, higher than the young coconut palms by the toilets, almost a bird rushing up through the warm air, if I would only let go of my grip on the chains. Sweeping up, then plunging down, hands fastened tight to the steel chains, wind humming under me, addicted to flying and afraid of falling, I would gradually slow down and stop, breathless and hungry.

Soon, I found English books that carried me higher than swings in the playground. I looked up from Noddy, naughty

Golliwog, and later Wendy and Peter Pan, and imagined them, children in places far, far away, viewed through the other end of a flying telescope, yet seeing them so close, as if I was pressed against them and breathing with their breaths.

Neither teachers nor Mama, who didn't like my rough play, ever reproved me for my addiction to reading, and so I became a very good student. In school, I learned English words and more words everyday. Word lists, spelling lists, vocabulary tests, adjectives, adverbs, synonyms and antonyms, prefixes, suffixes, roots. School was full of eye-words, coloring pictures not in Malacca. Words sprouted vines, branched into pages, rustled in forests of books in which I hid all day.

Of the words I learned to write, I liked my name best, although it wasn't really English. "Wing Su Swee" — the last name teachers read from their roll-books, like a favorite sweet kept for last or an almost forgotten secret. "Wing," the family name for Ah Kong and Mama, Yen and me. For Peik, who was so different from us Yen and I sometimes forgot we had a younger sister. "Swee," for me, or "Swee Swee," Chinese for "pretty," my classmates joked, and sometimes my Malay classmates teased me, "Su-Su," for "milk." And, of course, "Sister Swing," Yen's funny name for me.

With a family name stretching so many languages and meanings, I became more possessive of it as I grew older. Malacca had no other Wing family. It had hundreds of Wongs. Humdrum name. Wong, all wrong, I hummed to myself. Thousands of Tans and Lims, but only one Wing family. An occult name, I daydreamed, conjuring feathers and flight as Malacca turned sooty purple in the evenings. Bird freedom. Starlings, magpies, grackles, crows, fish gulls, the bats and flying foxes swooping in and out of raggedy eaves in the narrow streets, bringing the sun and moon down.

But what was the good of magic in Malacca if it didn't do something for us? By seventeen, I became impatient for something to happen, something promised in our family name.

That was before Ah Kong died. "You are very wicked not to cry!" Ah Chee scolded. She would have cried at his funeral, except she couldn't attend it as it was held at Ah Kong's first home in Singapore. I supposed I would cry monsoon rains when Mama died, but Ah Kong was a different kind of family.

During the memorial Sunday service, Pastor Fung told his parishioners about us. He described us as a fairy tale, Ah Kong's three daughters.

Even what Mama asked us to call our father was part of the fairy tale. Ah Kong. Chinese for king, highness, the grand vizier in *A Thousand and one Nights*, grandfather, all rolled into one note. Or King-Kong, as Yen complained.

And he was old enough to have been our grandfather, the creepy part about being a Wing.

Ah Kong was so aged he had hair growing out of every aperture — nostrils, ears, curling over his lips. I sometimes wondered where else. His hairs grew longer and whiter year by year. They pushed out of his ears like smoke or worms poking out to sniff the air. Mama looked like a girl next to him. He must have been over seventy, and she only thirty-five or so, her skin slippery soft. Whenever she laughed, she looked more like our oldest sister. We must be grateful to the powerful for giving us life, she said.

But we didn't have to love him. Ah Kong came home to us every week, on Saturday nights and Sunday mornings. Although his visits were short, he depended on us for many things. We walked on his back with our bare feet, pulled his toes till they crunched, and read our exercise books aloud until he fell asleep in the evening. "Good girls do those kinds of things for their fathers," Mama said.

Yen was always getting into trouble with Ah Kong. It wasn't that she couldn't get her words right. They were right for her. But she didn't pay attention when she spoke, so speech came carelessly out of her like hot sputtering oil.

Ah Kong stopped talking to her after one evening when he

leaned close to instruct her on something and the white hairs sticking out of his nose-holes tickled her cheek.

"Aiyoh! Don't come so close, Kong-kong!" she cried, slapping at her cheek. "Your hair is so itchy! Itchified!" She was only fifteen then.

He was offended. Daughters must never say their fathers are *itchified*, it means the wrong thing, Mama warned. But Yen said whatever came into her head. Ah Kong didn't speak to her again for a long time, and when he did, it was to get rid of her.

Mama kept saying I was too clever for my own good. I could see and be two ways at the same time, like the little girl in the poem we learned to recite in our first year in school, "And when she was good, she was very, very good, but when she was bad, she was horrid." Whenever Mama reminded me of the poem to shame me, I answered I was better for being two ways than Yen, whom Mama nagged for being only one way. Mama said Yen was horrid all the time, but I disagreed. Yen had many different ways of being, but they seemed only one way to Mama because Yen was forever mixed up.

Ah Kong liked little Peik best because she kept the sweetest tongue among us. When she was just three she already knew how to be silent and what to say to him and when, and Ah Kong praised her for being as quiet and good at sixteen as when she was three.

Take one of the last Saturdays Ah Kong came home. When he came out of the shower, Peik had the tin of Tiger Balm by his chaise-lounge. "Ah Kong, you're so tired, I massage you now," she offered.

Peik was the lightest of daughters. Her little feet pattered on his back and kneaded his speckled body with clean bare soles. Ah Kong lay groaning with pleasure while she pounded his shoulders with her fists. Then she showed him her best class work. "Ah Kong, see, I keep these drawings for you!" She pulled out the sheets, smooth and uncreased, from their pink plastic folder. Peik copied photographs of landscapes and animals from *Life* and *National Geographic*, the only magazines Ah Kong subscribed for us.

Yen and I had to save our pocket money for *Cosmopolitan* and *Vogue*, which we hid under our beds. He hated to see pictures of modern western women, actresses and models with bright lipstick and mascara, who leaned into each other and on the arms of tall white men.

On Sunday mornings, before Ah Kong drove back to his first family in Singapore, Peik would give him his glass of warm ginseng tea. "Kong-kong, come back next week," she'd repeat, parrot-like, a tape-recorder for a mouth.

When the lawyer read his will, Ah Kong had signed off, "To my daughter Wing Su Peik, who gave me twice the pleasure of her sisters, I bequeath a double share." It didn't matter because he left plenty for each of us. He had five other children in Singapore who received as much as we did. They were his first wife's children, the legal family, the Wings we hardly knew.

Later we heard rumors Ah Kong had more than two nests. At Jason's wedding, when we met for the first time our five half-brothers and sisters, the legal Wings, some of them older than Mama, I was told Ah Kong's public name — Tun Wing Pak. On the first day of the wedding, the Singapore Wings were busy greeting guests and ignoring us, so I could wander through First Mother's large rambling bungalow near Scotts Road, where Ah Kong lived during the weekdays. No one stopped me as I walked through the living quarters and even down some unlit corridors to the kitchen where a squadron of cooks and servers were chopping, stirring, and washing up. In a kind of library filled with Chinese newspapers and brown leather-like-bound books I came up to a wall with glass cases in which a stunning aviary of pigeons spread long blue-green wings. Strangely enough, the cases bore English-language labels each with the same message, "Green Imperial Pigeons (Pergam), Borneo forests." I stood transfixed by their many shiny eyes, breasts still gleaming white below the brown heads. But it was their sharp curved beaks that finally made me flee this glass cemetery; so much like Ah Kong's scary beak that grew pinched when he was angry.

Later I asked my second half-brother, Melvin, just returned from Sydney for the wedding and the only Singapore Wing to speak kindly to me, about the pigeons. Melvin said Ah Kong had been known as the Timber King of Indonesia. He had also lived in Sumatra, Sarawak, and Borneo, where he was a famous hunter, and was rumored to have had minor wives. The cases of Imperial Pigeons were all left of Ah Kong's fabulous collection of mounted animals. Melvin remembered standing guard in the living room a giant gray ugly Sumatran rhinoceros, a brown honey bear at the bottom of the stairs, and, posed by the front entrance, a handsome tiger with smooth-feeling tight fur. Ah Kong had gotten rid of these signs of his early manhood when the feng shui master explained these wrathful spirits were why he couldn't have more sons.

What happened to his Indonesian and Borneo families, I asked. Well, Ah Kong didn't marry those women, so Melvin, like us, had never met their children, our probable other half-brothers and sisters.

Later, when I told Mama about Melvin's scandalous stories, she smiled. She had known better, she said. She had held out for a Chinese ceremony even if a civil wedding was impossible, so we were Ah Kong's recognized second family.

At the tea ceremony, we addressed Jason's mother as First Mother, but we kept forgetting to call Mama Second Mother. First Mother was vexed at Mama for raising badly trained daughters.

"Imagine that!" Mama said. "Her youngest daughter living with an American diplomat — unmarried! Imagine her saying my daughters are badly brought up!" Mama didn't like to gossip, but she had a way of getting things known.

I wasn't sad when Ah Kong died. What was the good of being a Wing if you couldn't fly? The strangest thing about our family was the difference between our name and our lives. Ah Kong kept us tied to him, we were his fledglings. But he was the eagle with his hawk nose and white hair feathers, driving his gold Mercedes 450 SL every weekend across the Causeway, between his two homes in Singapore and Malaysia.

Yen and I didn't tell Mama how Ah Kong died. Because Mama was never suspicious she forgot what were secrets and what were not, so she often got Yen and me into trouble by telling Ah Kong stories we had begged her not to tell. After we confided in her about a boy we liked or some poor exam results, she was sure to say it to him over supper on Saturday. One night when Ah Kong slapped me for going to a dance without his permission and I cried out Mama had promised never to tell him, he retorted, "Your mother is simple like rain water. That was why I married her — for her virtue. You should learn from her if you wish to find a good husband." That terrified me.

Because Ah Kong was the only person in our family free to use his wings, we had left Malacca only twice, to travel to Singapore for our half-siblings' weddings. At the second wedding, in December 1979, Wanda's wedding, Yen wore a new red dress. She had hemmed the pouf skirt up without telling Mama, and looked quite amazing, as if she were wearing a tutu and had wandered on to the wrong stage, or as if her legs had suddenly grown in length overnight. Mama didn't show any embarrassment. As the Second Wife, she'd told us, she was accustomed to mean people and coarse comments. And First Mother's children and grandchildren were rude during the wedding reception. Yen was disgracing the Wing family, they sniped.

Next Friday, Ah Kong came home with a dirty face, his eyebrows scrunched up like wrung-out dishrags. Peik showed him the pillowcase she was embroidering with peonies and phoenixes, Chinese-looking figures Ah Kong liked, but it didn't help improve his temper.

"Yen," he said after dinner. We were surprised, as he hadn't spoken directly to her for over three years. "Yen," he repeated, "you are completing your exams this year?"

"Yes, Ah Kong." Yen gave Mama a desperate look for help.

"Do you have any plans?"

"Plans?"

"Yes, what do you intend to do afterward?"

"Afterward?"

"Yes! Don't repeat my words like an idiot! Your mother was already married with two daughters when she was your age. A woman cannot be too careful about her life when the time comes. I was watching you at Wanda's wedding and I think I must make some arrangements for you."

Yen gave Mama another look and opened her mouth. Before she could speak, Mama said, "Goodness, Pak, of course you make plans for Yen, she not yet nineteen and know nothing of the world, and her exam results not successful, so she cannot continue in school. Perhaps a secretary course in Singapore or London? That will be the right thing for her. It is so difficult with three daughters, how to help them in life...."

"I'm thinking of a marriage for Yen," Ah Kong interrupted.

"What!"

"Don't be rude, Swee," Mama said softly. "Say sorry to Ah Kong."

"Sorry, Ah Kong," I mumbled.

Ah Chee padded to the table with a plate of gold-yellow sooji cake. Her sooji cakes were famous among Mama's friends. I bolted a square down to comfort myself.

"Yen, say thank you to Ah Kong," Mama prompted.

Curious I stared at Yen. She'd never liked reading Barbara Cartland and Harlequin Romances. So sissy, she sneered at my taste. She preferred Raymond Chandler and Mickey Spillane. Tough guys. "I want to be tough," she had said one night when we caught each other sneaking into the kitchen for some of Ah Chee's love-letter biscuits.

"Eee, I don't care! I don't believe in love," Yen said to Ah

Kong. "Like you and Mama, uh? You also had an arranged marriage?"

Mama kept her eyes down.

"If not love, what difference does it make? Any one can do."

"We have a family reputation to maintain. Not anyone can marry a daughter of mine." Ah Kong was steaming. "It may not be easy to find a husband for you."

"Will Yen be able to choose?" I had to ask it.

"There will be no time." Ah Kong stared at me with distaste. "I've already consulted the fortune teller at Pure Mountain Temple. He says Chap Goh Mei is the most auspicious time for her to marry. That is a few months away. I have two prospects. The man from Sarawak is more willing."

"What's the hurry, Ah Kong? I'm not going to go bad, you know. Hah, hah! Now I am not so sure. You have already made decision before you asked me. That isn't right!"

Reading so many detective novels, Yen had grown an extra-suspicious mind. "What's behind all this?" she would repeat peevishly, harassing Mama and Ah Chee after they cleaned her room or put her things away. Little would put her off once she asked the question. As if she had just set her mind down, gone on strike. It was difficult to shift her accusations after that moment.

"Right, right? A daughter has no right. You are an ignorant girl. Have you ever done any work in your life? Made any money? You have been a parasite all your life, living off my body, this body that gave you life!" Ah Kong smacked his chest. His face turned red, and liver spots on his cheeks throbbed like purple thumbprints.

"Now, Pak, Yen never wants to disobey you, you know her tongue is in the wrong place. We talk more later. Peik has commendation from her Sunday school teacher she wants to show you now."

Sometimes I looked up to Mama as truly the meek of the earth. At other times I agreed with Yen that what Mama really wanted was to inherit the earth. In Ah Kong's will, he left her plenty of property and money. "To my good and obedient second wife," he dictated to his lawyer, and after he died, Mama continued to obey him, exactly the way she did when he was alive.

But I took my share of Ah Kong's money — blood money, I said to Yen — to go to America. Where else should my wings have carried me?

Mama forbade New York and San Francisco because they were wicked cities — Sodom and Gomorrah, Pastor Fung named them when she went to him for advice. "Swee should leave only to study," he counseled. "A young girl must be protected. In a quiet college far away from big cities."

I had thought America was the same everywhere.

"You see Paul Newman in the East and in the West and he looks just the same," Yen agreed. "Boy oh boy oh boy! You're gonna have fun!"

We tried to talk like Americans when we were alone together. It was a game we began as children after seeing *West Side Story* at the Rex cinema. The actors talked with twisted mouths and the boys and girls rumbled and had sex.

I chose to go to an expensive college in New York, New York State, that is. I had heard about Peps College at Wanda's wedding from Paul Frazer, Weena's American lover, who'd spent much of the time chatting with Yen and me, curious, he said, about "the Malacca outsider daughters." His tone was so humorous we didn't know if we should be offended. The wealthy family that had established the college had made its money out of toothpaste, Paul joked, so it was widely known as Pepsodent, and he was a proud alumnus.

Paul's letter of reference probably got me accepted to the college. Mama told my teachers and her acquaintances about Paul's joke, and everyone agreed it was the funniest thing I could have done so soon after Ah Kong's death. Apparently, everyone we knew had a tube of Pepsodent toothpaste in their bathrooms. "Pepsodent! Ah, she learning to brush her teeth there?" Auntie Mei-chen asked, rolling her eyes. My classmates thought I was

Sister Swing

going to dental school. "Why you want to be dental hygienist?" they asked me. "Lousy job, looking down people's stinky mouths. All those rotten teeth!"

What I wanted most was to get away quick from Ah Kong's ghost. I was afraid it would do me harm because Yen and I had killed him.

Ah Kong had been prowling around the house on Saturday night when we gave him his heart attack. Yen had warned me, "Ah Kong peeking into our bedrooms ever since we babies!" but I never believed her. Until that Saturday, some weeks after he began checking out a stranger in Sarawak to marry Yen.

I was mad he was preparing to ship Yen off just like that, simply because she had worn a short skirt to Wanda's wedding. Weena had been Paul's mistress for two years, even though he'd told everyone he had a fiancée waiting for him somewhere in America, but Ah Kong never made a stink about it. Being mistress to an American embassy consul was just fine with First Mother and her children. They were proud Paul took Weena to diplomatic parties and she got to shake the hands of visiting dignitaries, like the Sultan of Brunei and assorted rajahs. "Face clean, backside dirty," Mama said with delight, explaining First Mother's attitude to us. So I didn't understand why Ah Kong acted as if Yen's mini-skirt episode had tarnished her virtue.

I couldn't rouse Yen to indignation. "Oh, who cares?" she caroled chirpily. "Where am I going to meet a man anyway in sleepy old Malacca? I don' wanna continue studying, so what else to do? So many million women marry and do okay!" Yen still had no idea about herself and what she wanted from life. She was like Mama, but without the check on her tongue Mama always practiced in front of Ah Kong.

When I told my High School English teacher, Mrs Hughes, that Yen was going to have an arranged marriage, she was horrified. "Why, that's like the dark ages!" she exclaimed. "You poor girls. Has your mother told your sister anything about sex?"

Sex? Poor Mama would have turned purple and burst before

she would pronounce the word. I didn't reply, just dropped my eyes in embarrassment because Mrs Hughes had used the word with me.

On Friday after class, she gave me a package for Yen. She had it wrapped in newspaper as if it were a fish from the wet market. "Tell your sister she should open this only in the privacy of her room!" she admonished, a flushed determined look on her face.

My fingers traced the outline of a large oblong book under the newspaper wrapper, but I stifled my curiosity till Yen and I were alone together in the evening. "Can I look?" I pleaded as she opened the package. At first I was disappointed. It was an old book, more worn than even the books I bought from the second-hand stalls along the Central Market alleyway that sold paperbacks the Australian backpackers left behind at the YMCA. Its pages were yellow and frayed, and the bent cover showed a boring picture of women holding up a poster, "Women Unite," and in red the title proclaimed, *Our Bodies Ourselves*.

"It's a book by women," Yen said, turning the pages, "so I guess cannot be a dirty book."

I couldn't talk to Yen about her book through Saturday with Ah Kong at home, but I knew she was reading it in secret. She was unusually quiet, and a silly smirk kept appearing as if she was bubbling inside. I couldn't sleep thinking of Yen reading the book, so at about midnight I sneaked out of my room. Sure enough, when I pushed the door open, she was sitting in bed, knees up, reading.

"Let me read a little," I whispered.

"No, no, I'm at exciting part."

"It's not fair! You only have the book because of me."

"Well, get into bed with me. We read together."

Yen was reading the passage about that part of a woman's body, the vagina. I giggled at the photograph of a mirror reflecting a woman's bottom.

"Hey, let's do same examination!" Yen said. "I have compact mirror, and we can use the reading lamp."

"I get to look first," I said, not sure if she was simply daring me like she usually did.

"Cannot. I'm the one who's getting married, so more important for me to know about labia and all that. Here, you take the mirror. Now, squat on the bed and open legs, and I bring the reading lamp close, so we can both see what we look like down there."

I took off my pajama pants and lifted the blouse around my waist, but the cloth kept shifting and blocking the light. So I pulled the blouse over my head and squatted on the bed. It wasn't as if Yen had never seen me naked before. Ah Chee used to bathe the three of us together till we were ten or so.

The compact mirror was so small it was hard to see anything in it even though I tried angling it in different ways. Yen twisted the gooseneck of the lamp until it turned upward to shine on my vagina, and then it came into view. Two pink things, frilled, and a little tongue, as well as a small opening, an indentation in my bottom. My heart was thumping, seeing that part of my body for the first time. It flashed in the mirror like a strange face, bearded, with lips and a mouth, having hidden down there all my life.

"Let me see, let me see," Yen urged, craning her head down, and that was when I looked up and saw Ah Kong at the door.

How long had he been standing by the door watching us? My nipples suddenly felt hard and cold. I wanted to hide under Yen's blanket. His eyes shone red. I gasped, and Yen raised the lamp to light up his face with the white hairs in his nostrils moving because he was breathing hard.

"Filth!" His mouth was shaping rather than speaking the words. "Sisters sluts perverts no shame no fear . . . I . . ." Ah Kong had one hand holding his pajama pants as if he was afraid they would fall down.

I grabbed my blouse and pulled it down over my head just in time to see Yen sticking her tongue out at him. That must have done it because he left at once, and we heard him stumbling against something in the kitchen.

"Why he cannot mind his own business?" Yen whispered.

"We should explain to him . . ."

"No! What right he has to walk into our bedroom every night? I tell you, he check our rooms when we sleeping. Maybe he won't do it again after tonight. We're big girls now!"

"But what can he be thinking about us?"

I wanted to run to Ah Kong and beg his forgiveness, to show him the book, how we were simply learning about our bodies. But I was hot with shame. Ah Kong would never understand such a book — for him it would be a filthy book. Nothing could forgive what he saw.

"Go away!" Yen said. "If you not come to my room we won't be in this trouble. Just wait. Ah Kong will find a way to punish you too."

I could see a faint light in the kitchen where Ah Kong had opened the fridge door. I thought of going into the kitchen to say something to him but remembered he had just seen me naked, squatting like a frog, breasts tingling with cold, my bottom raised. How was I ever going to show my face to him again? In my bed, I covered my whole body and head with the sheet, wishing I were anywhere but in Ah Kong's house.

Next morning, Ah Chee found Ah Kong lying beside the refrigerator. He had had a massive heart attack as he was standing in front of the open door. The freezing air had been pumping out, so his body was double cold when she discovered him with the little light from the fridge like a spotlight on his face. "He looked terrible!" Ah Chee shook her head. "His eyes wide open looking at the Underworld God. I always say cold water is bad for the body. Why he want a cold drink at night?"

"Ssshh, mustn't let Mama know!" I whispered to Yen. The ambulance, sirens screaming, had carried Ah Kong away. There was no reason for sirens, but perhaps the driver was in a hurry to drop the body off at the morgue. Mama never even suspected, and how were we to tell her Ah Kong died because he had seen Yen and me looking at ourselves in a mirror?

Two

Swee waking up at night screaming like a devil woman. A giant bird with white feather hair and horny claw-hands pecking at her shoulder and chest, she cried. Even in afternoon she complained about a sharp beak rapping against her skull, going to split her head open. So Mama let Swee go far, far away to college first year after Ah Kong's death.

"All this because you didn't cry at Ah Kong's funeral!" Ah Chee nagged Swee to burn joss sticks at Ah Kong's altar and beg his ghost for forgiveness. Then bad dreams sure go away. She scolded, "You must not think of leaving your Ah Mama when she is still wearing black! What are daughters for?"

Ah Kong never came back to punish me, even though I also not cry. I was lucky Ah Kong never liked me as much as he liked Swee.

Swee was leaving for New York four weeks after Hungry Ghosts Festival. "So good for you!" Mary Choo said to Swee. They both studied for final exams, but after results came, Mary still stuck in Malacca. She always beat Swee, got more As than anyone in Malacca history, but now Mary facing two more years of classes because her parents decided she must attend university in Kuala Lumpur.

I make fun of Swee's college choice. Mama told everyone, "Peps College the ALMA MATER of Mr Frazer, US consular officer in Singapore, come out of toothpaste money!" "Whiter than white," I sang to Swee, just as in the radio advertising. "Swee's going to college to become whiter than white!"

To make Ah Kong's spirit happy, Mama invited Abbot

Narasimha from White Elephant Buddhist Temple in Penang to chant Lotus Sutra for us. His temple's papers say he was same world-famous monk once preached at Swe Dagon Pagoda in Rangoon and London Theosophical Institute! Mama paid for first-class air ticket and room at Tanjong Rhu Resort, that one the Malacca Times called Ice-Cube, built with Sultan's money when everyone talking about Japanese tourists taking over Malacca. Tanjong Rhu advertised French brandy, Spanish cigars, karaoke and what-not for anyone with gold credit card, the paper boast.

When the monks first come to our house, Mama gave abbot check (she wouldn't tell how much) in red envelope, and asked Peik to brush Chinese welcome on it. Swee and I surprised Peik was helping Mama in Buddhist adventure. Peik was attending morning and evening service every Sunday at Evangelical Church in Lorong Pinyin. But she only sniffed, "Jesus said, 'Father, forgive them for they know not what they do.' It's too late for Ah Kong, but why stand in Mama's way if she wants penance for Ah Kong's soul?"

"It doesn't matter Ah Kong not Buddhist in life," Mama told us. "Important thing is we must get his ghost into Paradise, not haunting us at home."

Abbot Narasimha started the monks chanting Sutras early morning. I used my detective skills, but still Swee and I couldn't tell how old they were — everyone had only bald scalps. They leave copper begging bowls outside and stand eight hours around the altar, shaking chimes from little bells. Looking at them made me hungry. Shoulders and collarbones bare and brown like our mahogany stairs, but robes blowing in the breeze saffron colored like ripe persimmon. Ah Chee set up lots of standing fans to cool the house. After first morning I got to like rattling and droning, high and low tones, like humming from big bees.

Ah Chee so excited! She prepared wok and wok of noodles, stir-fry with every type of bean curd. Fried, dried, press, bake, steam, salted, spice, season, puff up, shape into balls and squares, sticks, twigs, ropes, looking just like duck-breasts, beef-balls, red meat, pork cutlets, chicken livers, gizzards. But everything tasting like tofu! Abbot Narasimha and monks ate tofu and tofu and tofu, as much as Ah Chee cooked, all day, plates marching up and down the table.

As we watching Ah Chee shape tofu, she became talkative. "I never told your father," she said, pinching tofu into duck breast shape, "I was a follower of the Abbess Tien Hin in Ten Thousand Blossoms Association. In Fujian I cooked for a kong-si owned by Hakka members. We swore to be faithful, never to marry or have children, never to eat meat. We were so contented together! But the kong-si ran out of money, and your father brought me from Amoy to serve your mother. All this was before you were born!"

This was first time I heard Ah Chee having a different story from ours. Wah, it was like she'd gone back centuries and countries.

Shooing us away, she cleaned the altar table, third time in one morning. The monks chanted and rang bells but wouldn't look at us — they cannot look at women when saying sutras, Ah Chee said. She was acting like religious maniac. Lighting joss sticks, pushing them into the big bowl of ash. Dusting the oranges, big pyramid of pomelos and wheat buns. Whisking at fungus, hair, any sign of decay. She wiped the glass over Ah Kong's portrait, Ah Kong as young man, Swee told me, when he was Sarawak timber tycoon, because address at bottom of the picture was a studio in Kuching.

Ah Chee put bananas in front of Ah Kong's portrait, perfect yellow bananas, no brown spots in three days of abbot's ceremony. Swee and I marveled how she keep them so fresh, till we get to eat them on Monday. Each banana painted with mineral wax. I peeled one for breakfast. Wax cracking into white crumbs, and inside the banana was unripe, bitter. I had to throw it out.

"Do you have to go?" I asked Swee.

She was packing for America enough black clothes Mama tailor-made for three years of mourning. Abbot Narasimha consulted Mama — four women alone, he said, frowning — to follow strict Confucianist observations. Mama even got pajamas of black polished cotton sewn for us.

    Ah Kong had not given Mama the name of Sarawakan man he match-make for me, so my arranged marriage now dropped. I didn't know whether to be happy or sad. "Now your oldest daughter has her own fortune, she will have time to decide what to do with her life. Do not rush into marrying her," abbot advised Mama.

    But what did he know about my life?

    What I really wanted was to go with Swee to America, but she was in a hurry to leave. When the rest of the bananas turned blotchy days later, she said she'd seen Ah Kong's liver-spotty face. "He'd been hiding in a brown cloud in front of the refrigerator," she whispered, "his face back-lit by a mirror reflecting off my body!"

    After Lotus Sutra, no one again found Ah Kong's white hairs turning up in strange places. Ah Chee was every day sweeping from corner to corner, picking up, mopping, scrubbing, until all the rooms smelled of caustic soda. Yet Swee still saw the dust of Ah Kong's body shifting around in the house Ah Chee kept so clean. She could not wait for me.

Three

I grieved over Mama's superstitious actions, even though she couldn't help herself, her life was sealed, fated, by her union with Ah Kong. She was not yet sixteen when they married. There were no photographs of the ceremony, no marriage certificate.

We had only Ah Chee's stories about the courtship, how mad Ah Kong was over Mama. She was the quiet, only daughter of a small-time trader for one of his Singapore companies. Her father sourced for wild rattan from the jungle Sakai. Ah Kong had not expected to find passion in the sleepy backwaters of Malacca when he drove up from Singapore one Friday to go boar hunting with his business associate. Mama's papa died before I was born, an unhappy man, Ah Chee said, because Mama accepted Ah Kong's proposal to become his second wife. With her beauty and good nature, her father expected her to be another Yang Kwei-fei, to reach as high as an emperor's court; and Ah Kong, then not so rich although already quite old, was an unending disappointment to Mama's parents. Without a brilliant match to anticipate, they declined, Ah Chee told us with a warning look, and both passed away after Swee was born. They were lucky, she added, not to have been around to see the birth of a third granddaughter.

"The third daughter is like lightning striking three times in one spot," pagan Chinese said to Mama before I was born, "it's not going to happen."

Mama never learned from the fact than none of these superstitions ever turned out right. That time she spent pots of money on playing the numbers because Ah Chee heard an owl hooting in the chiku tree at the back. "Owls add up to four — because they symbolize death, which sounds the same as four — but also eight, because they are birds of learning and learning can only be good luck, which sounds the same as eight." So Mama bought lottery tickets numbered 48, 12 — "the number you get when you add the two numbers," — and 3, "what you get when you add one and two." I was in primary school, just beginning to learn arithmetic, and Mama had me add every kind of combinations of 48, 12 and 3, because I was the most innocent of her daughters. And nothing struck.

"Because you asked the third daughter to choose the numbers!" Ah Chee said. "Third daughters are always unlucky!"

Once I believed Mama and Ah Chee's nonsense. I was unlucky, coming last.

Yen was the fruit of Mama and Ah Kong's folly. "No one in Malacca would believe it," Ah Chee told us after Ah Kong passed away, "but your Ah Mama was as mad over your father as he was for her! Everyone, sour grapes, thought must be his money. But you see how tight your Ah Kong was — he gave only a little money each week for the house, food, all the expenses you girls cost your Ah Mama. She married him for LOVE!" "AI NI!" Ah Chee repeated loudly, "LOVE YOU!" — proud to be the bearer of this shameful history. However, we Christians knew such deceitful stories carry the message of sin. That was how Yen was conceived, in mortal sin.

Like Yen, Swee never took me seriously. I was too young, too small and weak, and I was not permitted to go out in the sun. Mama wouldn't let me follow them to the playground because they pushed and climbed and fell down. "Like bad boys!" Mama said, "and Ah Kong will be angry if he comes home and find you have broken a bone or burned brown like an old turtle."

Instead of being outraged when lightning struck a third time, Ah Kong resolved when I was born that I was to be his talisman. My skin, Mama said, was a shade of pearl, just like Yang Kwei-fei's in the Chinese legends; silky white tinted with the blush of baby blood. Yang Kwei-fei's complexion made her so precious to the Tang Emperor he was willing to lose his kingdom for her. So I was to be quiet and good-natured like Mama, an emperor's queen, to reconcile Ah Kong to his two older daughters, troublesome, stubborn, noisy, disobedient, moody, everything he hated about other women.

"Being good. We Christians know it is hard to be good, how hard to receive God's love with grace. Finding His church here is finding His kingdom even in Malacca. Our home is only a screen behind which God's light shines, showing angelic domains before us." I thought the beautiful language of the church would persuade Swee to join me for regular communion, but she chose instead to spend Sundays with Yen, reading magazines and cheap novels, eating cake, trying on vulgar nail polish, and talking about boys.

That was how it had always been, I inviting Swee, but Swee choosing Yen. Of course, once I found grace and became my own person, it no longer mattered. "Three sisters, although close in age, are after all only mortal sisters. The church gives us everlasting life," Pastor Fung pointed out when I spoke about my hurt because Swee preferred Yen's company to Sunday communion with me. I knew then I was to seek an everlasting family, not cry at being the forgotten last sister.

Ah Kong rewarded me for my filial piety. I told Pastor Fung about the inheritance, wanting his counsel. "It is easier for a camel to go through the eye of a needle than for a rich man to enter heaven." So much money was unclean. But Pastor Fung said I should think of Ah Kong's largess as the gift of talents, to do good with, not to fear, waste or hide away. "The church is rich in spirit but poor in body. Let your sisters use their inheritance for their ends; you can use yours for the church."

Yen's tears when Swee was leaving only proved how I had been saved. Saved from the evil of selfish love, for Swee, I knew, was truly happy to be gone, and I could only rejoice for her.

Four

As soon as the visa came from the American embassy, I bought my air-ticket to New York. From Kennedy, the travel agent cautioned me, take a shuttle bus to another airport, Newark, and board a smaller plane to Albany, where a student would meet me to drive me to Peps College.

"Promise me you wear black until the three years are finished," Mama insisted. "If you put on another color, Ah Kong's ghost will be angry again!"

I was happy to promise Mama. I didn't need Ah Kong to follow me to America.

Mama and I were not the only ones troubled by Ah Kong's restless spirit. The same day the monks came to chant the sutras, Peik gave Pastor Fung $5,000 for the Sunlight Beneficent Old People's Charity in memory of Ah Kong. Our lawyer Mr Chia had suggested, although she was just seventeen, that Peik keep a separate bank account since she was a rich woman in her own right. The check to Pastor Fung was the first one she signed, Peik told us proudly.

"Peik is more advanced than you!" I teased Yen. Yen didn't like dealing with lawyers. She didn't want to leave Mama, and she wished I wouldn't leave either. She had never grown those wings I wanted so badly to use.

"Don't go!" she begged on my last night home, moaning without shame, mucus trickling down her nose like thick tears. "Oh, oh, oh, oh, Swee's leaving us, she'll never come back!"

"What bad luck!" Mama muttered. "To say such a bad luck thing! Rubbish!" Mama was losing her dulcet tones fast now

Ah Kong was gone. Aloud, Mama comforted Yen. "Swee's got a round-trip ticket, and she's coming home same month next year, alright, Swee? Anyway, after you finish your secretary course, you can go visit her. Pastor Fung says Swee's college is in beautiful and safe country part of New York. The two of you can go look-see look-see over America."

I knew Yen would never go. She was terrified of flying. "Gulls and pigeons have pea-sized brains," she said, "that's how they fly. But humans with our big brains can't stay up."

Crying till she shook, Yen wouldn't listen to Mama. With her wet eyes and damp red nose she reminded me of the puppy which, after only three weeks with us, had run out onto the main road and been struck by a Malacca-Kuala Lumpur taxi. It was a shivery thing, born under a scary star, and it never stopped shaking, even in our laps. Peik had proclaimed it a sick pup that should be put to sleep, but Yen hid it under her towels in her bedroom and Mama didn't have the heart to wrench it away from her. Ah Chee had left the gate open the afternoon when the puppy was run over, and I wondered how it had escaped, being too timid to venture out of Yen's bedroom.

Ah Chee refused to speak about my leaving. Whenever Mama raised it, she began to pick books, shoes, cushions, lint, off the floor. Or she brought out the large straw broom and banged it around furniture, or squatted in the kitchen to clean the refrigerator's bottom coils one more time.

When we were younger, Yen and I made up stories about how Ah Chee had been Ah Kong's secret lover in Fujian. Ah Chee had been devoted to turning out his virility dishes every Saturday. Sweet lotus-seed buns, she sniggered, for fathering many children. Bitter melon in rich pork soup for tranquil fornication. Ginkgo nuts and tree-ear fungi fried with liver to enrich the blood before ejaculation. Jellied pig-blood and ginger to heat his lust.

I believed Ah Kong came home for Ah Chee's cooking as much as for Mama's submissions. His eyes turned milky with greed at the dining table, and he was forever complimenting Mama on keeping Ah Chee with the family.

Mama said Ah Chee had arrived from China even before the wedding, and she never asked what Ah Kong paid her each month. After the funeral Yen and I waited for Ah Chee to quit.

The night before I left for New York, Ah Chee arranged for the taxi, ironed my underwear, packed them in the suitcase, baked a sooji cake for me to take on the plane, then padded around the kitchen as if nothing had changed. "You write to your Ah Mama," she said, "and don't make her cry!"

Then I knew it was Mama whom Ah Chee was devoted to for more than twenty years. She served Mama's gliding voice, Mama's dimpled smiles, Mama's slow lazy body. All those virility dishes for Ah Kong were to bring Mama satisfaction. Ah Chee was never going to leave Mama.

Flying away on board the Boeing 707 was a relief. I liked the cool dry artificial air blowing out of vents, the pilot's mechanical voice crackling with static, "We are now climbing 20,000 feet above sea-level." I liked being in the compact plastic and steel machine, so different from the hot moist atmosphere of Malacca and Malaysians. I knew there could be no fungus, no green mold or brown spores fuzzing my seat, no passenger on board like Mama and Ah Chee, demanding I show proper feelings and actions, no Ah Kong nightmares waiting for me in New York.

The white hazy clouds outside the port window were like trailing smoke to my speed, incense to thank Mama for letting me go.

Guilty, sorry, relieved, free, elated, hanging for hours between Mama and New York, I remembered my childish delight in that small pause when swinging, between fearfully speeding higher, higher, and the rushing drop earthward, and wished I could remain suspended between leaving and landing for a little while longer.

But after three breakfasts, two dinners and one lunch, I was scrambling with a crowd of wrinkled strangers for my suitcases at the Kennedy terminal, my new passport and student visa crammed down my jeans pocket so tight a pickpocket would have to peel me like a banana to get to them.

I almost cried when I first saw Albany. Pastor Fung hadn't told me it would seem more dingy and smaller than Malacca. In September at 5.30 pm the sky was already sickly-gray. A sharp air, colder than any wind in Malaysia, whistled in my ears and through the industrial cinder-block airport buildings, the empty oil-slicked runways, and parking lots dotted with abandoned cars like behemoths in a ruined world. I gazed at bottles, sheets of newspapers, empty soda cans, rags, glass shards. Tall weedy strands like shredded ferns poked out of, wrapped their presences around, the buckled corners of lots and pavements.

The plane was an hour late because of bad weather, but the student driver was waiting out on the curb for me, just as the agent had promised, with a cardboard sign on which was scrawled "S Wing." His van had graffiti written in ink over the seats. I read "Bulls charge!" "Go, Bulls, go," "Nice girls give," "Oink," and hesitated to sit on words.

"C'mon, you're late," he said impatiently, tossing my bags at the back.

Should I apologize for the delay, confess it was my first day in America? Instead, as he started the engine, I asked nicely from my back seat, "What day is it?"

He looked at me in the rear-view mirror. "Friday." Then he added, without turning his head, "Don't you people have watches that tell the day?"

I couldn't tell if his question was friendly, if his frown was because he was running late. It was easier to stare out of the window and say nothing.

In silence, I arrived. I'd come to Peps College ten days after the semester began, too late for orientation, welcome receptions, icebreakers, rushes, ice-cream socials, class introductions. I found Americans worked fast, everything was speeded up at

Peps. By the time I landed, students already had courses signed for, boyfriends and girlfriends picked, and sororities, fraternities, and social clubs organized.

I had the smallest suite in the quad, the residence from which earlier roommates had migrated as they checked out other vacancies. It was the suite for absentee students, the freshman who came down with mononucleosis and had to put off college for a year, a student whose father's business had unexpectedly failed and who couldn't make the fees, and another who found herself pregnant in August and had decided to get married to her summer sweetheart.

I learned these stories weeks later, but for the first few nights I waited for my roommates to show up. I longed for real live Americans, some college sisters who knew the latest in pop music and who would teach me how to dress like an American, which professors to study with, what to eat in the cafeteria. Falling asleep alone in the set of rooms, I reminded myself I was the strong second sister. I didn't collapse like Yen when things didn't go my way.

I was alone all that first Friday. The dormitory floor had a shared bath area with three shower stalls and three toilets, but although muffled noises of running water woke me later that night, I met no one.

On Saturday, I convinced the lunch checker I was a real student even without a meal card, but I didn't have enough courage to talk to anyone and ate by myself in a corner of the cavernous dining hall.

I watched the students, boisterous, noisy, strong, and big, like young Northern giants, heap food on their trays. As if playing a game, they piled plates on other plates, carefully balancing saucers and dishes of pies, chocolate cakes, ice cream and rice pudding on top of everything else.

I studied them as they ate, large freckled people who cut their Salisbury steaks, which were only hamburger, in flamboyant gestures. They left green beans strung with white fibers in piles on the sides of their trays. "So sloppy!" Yen would have yelled at them, for the mess they made with their food. Still, they kept returning to the line to pick up more food — apple sauce, mashed potato and gravy, sweet potato sprinkled with marshmallows, chunks of iceberg lettuce, hard red tomatoes. Everything was sweet, including the salad dressing.

At first I thought they must be hungry, they put so much food on their trays. Then, amazed, I noticed they threw most of it away. Even the pies with the lovely gold crusts oozing apple pieces and purple blueberry filling were only picked at, the crisped crusts uneaten.

I did not dare go up for seconds and couldn't finish the mud-brown Salisbury steak studded with lumps of gristle. Anxious I might be hungry later, I put a shiny red apple in my coat pocket. The thought of the apple, hard and sugary, snuggled next to my hip, consoled me through the day, so much so I took an apple each afternoon from the dining hall.

But I was too heartsick to eat them. In a month, I had a laundry basket full of star-bottomed red Delicious. My little room, squashed with scratched Formica-covered built-in furniture, the desk drawers that had to be juggled closed and which reeked of raw plywood and cockroaches, now wafted a heavy scent of apples, like a grocery bin, or like a fantasy orchard brimming with real fruit.

During those nights, while I read in bed, I saw myself as a worm safely hidden in the heart of a giant apple. Fluorescent light jumped off the waxy apple skins, pooling the room with warm crimson spots.

I needed the color. Wearing those black clothes Ah Chee had packed for me was making me sad.

"You remind me of the Hmong," Clarissa said. She was in my American history course and found our suites faced the same corridor. "All that black. Is it something to do with your culture?"

"Yes." I did not want to explain about Ah Kong and Mama.

"You're not Hmong, are you?" Clarissa asked. The teacher was late as usual, and only six of us were in class on time.

"Those people who are coming to America from the Cambodian highlands. You look just like them."

"What do they look like?"

"Like you. My dad works with the Hmong in a refugee camp in North Carolina. They keep dying on him."

"What does he do, kill them?"

I thought I was making a joke but Clarissa stiffened.

"You're not very tactful, are you?" she pouted. "My dad says they're people from the Stone Age. They can't tell the difference between reality and television, so these young men, when they watch Dracula or the Werewolf or some other horror show, they think these spooks are for real. My dad says they're actually dying from fear! In 1980! Imagine that!"

Professor Lopez came in then, and I didn't have time to tell Clarissa I could imagine it very well.

Manuel Lopez. He was a Puerto Rican, Clarissa told me, the only Puerto Rican professor in the history of the college. Clarissa said he was short, but he was taller than me.

I liked his mustache, the black hair on his head twisting in hundreds of tiny fastidious curls, his glossy skin that shone like my apples.

Nervous, skinny, he lectured on American history, dancing in polished leather dress shoes, treading back and forth in the front of the room like the elegant paws of a big cat.

"I guess you can't be Hmong," Clarissa decided, "you're too westernized. I see how you've been looking at Professor Lopez."

By Christmas, although I was still sworn to wear black, I had thrown away the rotting apples and replaced them with bright colored beach balls I found for sale at Woolworth's on a shopping trip to Albany. I had my pick of blue and green and red and yellow and white, each more cheerful than Red Delicious, and non-bio-degradable.

Wandering through Woolworth's every Saturday helped me get over my absent roommates and the dank empty suite. The store, an impressive limestone-faced building, was an emporium of cheap jeans from the Philippines, 90-cent costume jewelry from Guatemala, and gummy chocolates in fancy rose-printed boxes from Brooklyn. In November, when students had gone home for Thanksgiving, the red, blue, yellow, green, white globes behind the toy racks, left over from a summer sale, reminded me of the open market stalls in Malacca. I bought a dozen. The salesclerk rang up the price without taking her eyes off me, acting like I was going to stick a gun in her face at any minute.

Their roundnesses took up almost all the spare space in my room. I could toss them around, but they didn't fly like my nightmare birds, and sometimes after I woke up from a sad dream, I talked to one or the other of them like I would have done to my missing roommates or to Yen. Yen and Mama wrote to me, even little sister Peik, but their letters seemed to echo as if from a place long past. They couldn't fill the silence in the rooms.

Just before Christmas, Pinny came over to introduce herself.

Clarissa had pointed Pinny Hong out to me weeks ago in the dining hall. "Hong from Hong Kong," she said with particular emphasis.

"What do you mean?" I had stared at Pinny who, wearing tight ski pants and a yellow and lime-green striped tee, showed her cleavage of crotch and breasts like a neon-lit bumble bee Venus.

"You know, easy lay."

I was shocked by her language. Clarissa was a prim born-again Christian.

"Harry told me she's slept with everyone who's asked her." Harry was Clarissa's boyfriend, whom she had just successfully invited to accept Christ into his life. Clarissa didn't work so hard on me, she said, because she respected my different culture.

I didn't ask her how Harry knew.

Pinny Hong, surrounded by a bunch of men, was laughing and sticking out her tongue at them. Her tongue looked seductive. She pushed out her chest, and her breasts under the tight yellow and green tee-shirt stuck out like her tongue, like yellow and green baby beach balls. I could hear her two tables over, her voice a kind of American GI accent with a heavy Chinese singsong quality.

"Don't you spend time with her. She's a jezebel, a whore!" Clarissa got up violently and left the hall.

I watched as Pinny went off with the tallest man, her long hair rubbing on his chest as they walked out together.

I was surprised when Pinny knocked on my door, saying "I have a party tonight, my birthday. If you're free, wanna come?" She didn't give the beach balls a glance although they were stacked in a delicately balanced pyramid facing the door where she stood with tightly jeaned legs apart and hands on hips.

Of course I was free. I was always free. No one ever came to my room to ask me to join them for a pizza or a movie.

In three months with no roommate in sight, I had decided it was Professor Lopez I was waiting for instead, but although I smiled bravely at him in the classroom, his head was so full of dates and social ideals he didn't notice me.

"The American Revolution," he had said last week, walking quickly up and down before the chalkboard, "is still the most notable experiment in historical movements. That all men are created equal is the boldest of political philosophies; its consequences are still being worked out throughout the world." I waited for his flashing eyes to fall on me, my own eyes brimming with ideas, unspoken words. He was like no one at Peps, a compact tense physical darkness where almost all the teachers sprawled like white floury doughboys. His shoes creaked, new and loud, as he talked, pacing the sentences that he seemed to discover whole and elegant, as if reading from a book.

I thought of Ah Kong while I wrote down Professor Lopez's words. Had Ah Kong known of the American Revolution? Ah Kong seldom read on the weekends he came to us, only the newspaper. But his money was paying for my classes. I felt Professor Lopez talking to Ah Kong through me, fierce bird-headed Ah Kong, his ghost held back, listening to Professor

Lopez. A black Puerto Rican teacher and a Chinese millionaire — created equal. Professor Lopez was breaking new sensations, in my head, and in my chest. I had already signed up for his American Constitution seminar next semester, hoping he would get to know me in a smaller group.

I went to the suite Pinny shared with other Hong Kong students. They were full-fee paying students like me, and they had the latest music set-up, a twenty-eight inch television, a huge electric wok, and a rice cooker. Pinny was the only work-study student there. I had seen her checking in books at the library.

Although it was snowing hard outside, the den and kitchen were packed with sweating bodies. Everyone had brought a birthday gift for Pinny. She kept unlocking her bedroom door, throwing the packages inside, and locking the door again. "Oooh," she squealed as more presents appeared, "nice of you! I ROVE presents!" Drunk, she was dropping her L's. Guys were hauling six-packs of Budweiser, Canadian Ale, Michelob to the kitchen counter.

I recognized some of the students milling about. Most were vague faces I had glimpsed at lectures. In the middle of the den someone lit a marijuana joint, and soon a circle of dopeheads were sitting on the wall-to-wall carpet sucking on joints and passing them reverently around like communion wafers.

Clarissa's Harry came in with a large box wrapped in fancy silver and purple ribbons. Couples were dancing to Bob Marley in the dark, weaving between cross-legged bodies falling asleep over the marijuana, with the light from the kitchen coming through as others opened and shut the kitchen door. No one was paying attention but me as Pinny took Harry's present, unlocked her bedroom door, and disappeared inside the bedroom with Harry. I stopped thinking of Pinny when I saw Professor Lopez standing alone by the window watching the smokers.

When I went up to him, he gave a shrug. "I didn't know there would be so many here. I have an asthma problem and I can't stay."

"I'll go with you," I offered.

"Oh, no, this is an event for young people like you. You mustn't leave."

"How about some Chinese food?" I pointed to the table pushed against one wall where the food was laid out, platters of stringy noodles, bowls of soy-colored fried rice, beef and mushy cabbage, and where the Chemistry and English professors were filling up their plates.

He waved at the air in front of him as if to get rid of pesky flies. "Too much smoke."

I followed him out into the quad, into a sudden enormous wintry silence. The reggae music throbbed faintly out of the closed windows. Snow was falling in big white flakes. Shining incongruously, the moon radiated on the spinning crystals. Looking up I saw giant spokes of cosmic wheels in the January sky. It was so cold my ears buzzed faintly, and I gulped large painful breaths. It was the wrong thing to do; my lungs ached immediately. I pushed my nose into the black muffler, glad for the black parka and its too-large hood, relieved yet sorry Professor Lopez couldn't see my face.

"Well," he said, "you wrote a good paper."

"You know who I am?"

"Swee Wing. 'The Federalist papers and the 1960s civil rights movement in the South.'"

"Actually, my name is Wing Su Swee. My sisters call me Swee."

"Sweet Wing? Swing?"

I was flattered, alarmed he had discovered Yen's childhood name for me so easily.

"You write well for a freshman."

"I want to be a journalist."

"So young and already you know what you want." Professor Lopez's bare head was spotted with melting flakes. "Shall I walk you back to your dorm?"

The path was unlit, unmarked, and slippery with crystallized snow layered over weeks of old tough ice. I had never bought boots and I slid every so often where the snow gave way under my sneakers. The wet was freezing my toes but I didn't dare complain.

Professor Lopez reached out and gripped my hand to steady me. He was gloveless also. His palm, shockingly warm and huge, covered my pain-tingling hand like a deep pocket, a human pocket wordlessly pulsing with the intensity of the wintry universe locked up in my imagination. I didn't want to let it go. I didn't want to go back alone to my mateless suite.

A week later, Pinny knocked on my door again. By this time I had thrown out the balls. Manuel had said they were childish, my sense of humor immature.

"Thank you for the scarf," Pinny said.

I had brought her the red-blue-gold-colored scarf Clarissa had given me for Christmas. Clarissa was trying to break me away from wearing black, and I couldn't tell her the three years were not yet up since Ah Kong had been laid underground. Of course, once I saw Harry with Pinny I was sorry I had also betrayed Clarissa.

"I hear you write for the *Daily Peps*." Wrapped up in a stuffed goosedown jacket, Pinny still managed to look as if it would zip off her easily. Her sleek hair, hanging lushly out of the jacket down to her waist, freshly laundered, was making its statement, "Look at me, look at me!"

I tried to block Pinny's view of the room. Without the crimson apples and the colored rubber spheres, I had set up a shrine to Manuel. The four books for his US Constitution seminar were lined up on my desk and I had taped a photograph of him I had ripped off the college yearbook in the library to the wall.

"I'm sorry, my place's a mess," I mumbled.

"Don't worry. I just came by to say I hope you enjoy my party?" Pinny gave me a slanted look. "I organize lots of them. Many kinds of professors come to them!"

"Sure," I stuttered, "I had a good time."

"I'll invite you for the next one, only I don't know when I

will have it. See, I have a couple of incompletes. One of them is English 3, you know, the long essay. But, you know, if you help me write the paper, maybe we can have another party this Saturday?"

Pinny was very confident, looking past my shoulder toward my desk. "Lots of professors will be there!"

I finished the paper for Pinny an hour before her party started, even though I knew Manuel wouldn't be there. He had promised me over the phone he would knock on my door Tuesday night when he was back from New York City.

The night of Pinny's birthday, I didn't know what it was I couldn't believe. That Professor Lopez, whose words I had been hanging on to for the last three months, was actually kissing me. That Manuel's shoes were sitting neatly lined by my bedside and his prickly hairy legs were thrown over my thighs. That I was letting a strange man do such terrible, wonderful things to my body. But not just any stranger. I held Manuel's body close, closer, wanting to melt into his bones, riding pleasure like riding waves of honey and butter, sloppy, delicious, not wanting the carousel to stop.

Later, buttoning his shirt, Manuel said he couldn't believe it was the first time for me, he hoped I wasn't disappointed, that his asthma had affected his performance, and he was better when it was warmer.

I was afraid to clutch him goodbye, afraid to take liberties with him. He was a black god come down for Christmas. He left, taking the telephone number for the suite, saying he would see me during the break.

Manuel never came to another of Pinny's parties. In early February and March, he called three times altogether, and knocked on my door twice. Each time the waiting was painful, his body and mine as surfeit as I had fantasized. He told me not to phone him, but I did. I rang his office over a dozen times, but he was always away. The telephone trilled and trilled in an empty room. I knew he had an apartment in New York, in the Bronx, and when there were no classes, he came up to campus only occasionally.

I went by his office often, hoping to find him at work. He was in once, a late afternoon, and then we made love on the office floor.

"Manuel Lopez. Manuel Lopez," I said his name over and over again silently and aloud at night in my room. "Man, Man, Man, Man." Was Lopez related to Lupus, to wolf? "Man wolf man wolf man wolf."

Manuel was nervous in my room. He wanted the door locked and the lights off so no one would know I was in.

"No one comes here. I'm in the room of lost roommates," I told him.

"I could lose my position," he frowned, and checked the doorknob before unbuckling his belt.

"Why don't you try to find your community?" he asked me as he was leaving the last time we were together. "Puerto Ricans are a communal people. In New York, I am a Puerto Rican activist. Here at the college I am only a token."

In late March, the snow began melting although the trees remained bare. Manuel had stopped coming to his office altogether. He did not keep office hours, did not answer my telephone messages, missed two seminars in a row, and scheduled quizzes, film showings and in-class exams for other days when he did not appear.

Slowly the mornings were filling with light, a solitary secret activity to which no one but I appeared to pay any attention. I could hear the slushy water flowing downhill behind the dorm building, a constant underground gurgle, like the way I thought about Manuel, sensations flowing down from head to nipples and overflowing those, lapping down through the hidden crevices, a warm despairing trickle where he had made me gush and cry only a little while ago.

I kept going to Pinny's gatherings — the paper I wrote for her got Pinny a B — but after Manuel, all the professors I met there were stupendously ugly: gray, stiff, creaky, like old unopened books.

"Harry says you are going to be a reporter." Pinny had sidled up to my seat in the library reading room.

"A journalist."

"I read your story about the college being the snow campus. I like that a lot."

My essay had won the annual freshman composition award, and the *Daily Peps* had carried it yesterday.

I was suspicious about Pinny's intentions. Did she want me to write another essay for her English class?

" I wish you would tell my story," Pinny said.

"Why should I? I make fun of everything when I write, why would I want to lose your friendship?" I didn't believe myself.

Pinny pouted. "But you are a reporter. I have such an interesting life. It should be written for everyone."

Three months was a long enough time to make us close friends, Pinny said. Time had a different claim in America, and I didn't want to reject that claim, wanting to try out everything American.

"You wouldn't like the story I'd write."

"Of course I will. It's the story of my life, so how can I hate it?"

I thought Pinny rather dull for all that she slept around. Still, I admired her. Unlike me, Pinny was pulling bad grades, but her eye on Peps men and their pockets seemed to give her the ability to like herself and to see the world in a clear light.

"My reports are always about sad or funny things."

"Well, this one won't be. My life is sad," Pinny's face softened in a glow of self-delight, "but it's fascinating. Who would believe the things that have happened to me?"

I felt a story twitching, a little spirit digging in a hollow, like the little woman digging in another hollow just below my neck between the two breasts, the one who hammered at me when I was about to do something stupid, like speak out of turn or dial Manuel's telephone number again.

"All right, I will." Perversity was burrowing in the space above my nose between the eyebrows, although with my plain features and sparse eyebrows, Pinny probably didn't notice anything peculiar. "How shall I name you in the report?"

"I want you to use my true name. I'm proud of my story."

"All right, Hong Nga."

"No, that's my Chinese name. Use my American name, Betty. That's the problem, telling a story from Hong Kong, finding the right name." Pinny ignored the frowning student at the other end of the library table. "They're wrong, Chinese names. No one knows their meanings, making up translations like Peony Happiness or Bright Peacekeeper or whatever name some old person told them."

I gathered my papers, driven away by the disapproving student, and whispered as we walked to the exit, "American names are no better. Why do you choose 'Betty,' when you don't know who Betty Crocker is?"

Pausing at the library doorway, I pointed to another student. "There's Cecilia. Her mother can't get the c right or the l, so what she says is sheshe or zhezhe. My sister's best friend was Elvis Tay Seng Leong, who wanted me to give him special tuition so he could get an English pass and enter university. Then you know that Thai student, Cher, who wears white lacy three-quarter-length-sleeved blouses and attends the Baptist Bible group meetings?"

When Pinny burst out laughing I felt an odd generosity. Maybe I could like Pinny after all, her giggles following me as I left her at the checking counter.

"Whatever can you have in common with Pinny?" Clarissa, no longer attached to Harry, was full of summer plans. She was going to North Carolina to intern with her father at the refugee camp. "I don't know why you don't try to help someone better in your community," she complained, sitting on my desk and kicking her feet. "It's plain selfishness. And you're a straight A student! What can you get out of being with her?"

Clarissa couldn't know anything was better for me than sitting alone in my room, waiting for Manuel's knock on the door.

I was beginning to like Pinny quite a bit. She took my mind off missing Yen and Mama, whose short irregular letters had finally stopped reminding me of my duty to wear only black. Instead, Mama and Ah Chee kept appearing in my dreams, two figures in black garbling in my ears. I thought of them hissing at me even as I was slipping the latch to Manuel's knock. "You want to die! No shame!" But I wanted to live. I wanted Manuel's warm butterscotch body.

After a few visits, when Pinny told me about coming into Hong Kong under cover of night from a village in Guangzhou, brought over by an old man who'd promised her a good job but delivered her to a small business family looking for a concubine for the oldest son, an opium addict they feared would end up with syphilis if he continued picking up prostitutes in Kowloon, she stopped coming around. Pinny had dropped out of college, her roommates explained, lowering their voices, because she hadn't paid tuition and was asked to leave; Clarissa told me she was expelled for blackmailing a chemistry professor who turned her in to the Dean.

Manuel knocked one last time in April, late at night after I had gone to bed. He wouldn't let me turn on the lights. "No," he said. "I haven't told you before. I'm married. My wife is Carmen Lopez."

In the dark, I could still make out his expression, stern, the same look he wore for giving out quizzes and grades.

When I didn't reply, he asked impatiently, "Don't you know who Carmen Lopez is?"

I couldn't answer.

"She's Director of the Women's Health Institute in Washington, DC. Everyone who is anyone knows her, her name had been included last year on the short list for a sub-Cabinet position working directly with the President of the United States." His face glimmered in the room, picking up brown electrical ions from the air.

"I'm not black," he had corrected me once, disapprovingly, "I'm Puerto Rican. You should go out and learn more about America instead of hiding in a small hick college!" His chest was a coffee blend, smooth warm surface buffed to two pink-brown nipples, his face bone-sharp chocolate-sweet, and his hair crinkled like the nub of a black fleece. In bed he smelled like fudge-caramel ice cream, sweet and yielding under my tongue.

"I'm not seeing you again. It's too dangerous."

I couldn't contradict him. I didn't know Carmen Lopez, the woman who was his wife. I couldn't imagine him married.

"We own a house in the Bronx, a renovated brownstone. She's fiery, like all Puerto Ricans. That's how I like women. You are different, quiet, timid. So Asian."

I lay silently under his weight. I knew I could tumble him off the bed if I wanted to.

"She'd kill me if she found out." He moved his smooth muscular body rhythmically, then faster.

Climbing off, he made a sad gesture with his hands. "Please understand, you mustn't contact me again."

I wondered what Carmen looked like. Fat? Tall? Shorter than me? No, a Puerto Rican woman had to be taller. Prettier? Perhaps in bed she lay on top of him.

Later I tracked a Bronx community newspaper, *La Raza Unidas*, in the library and found a photograph of Carmen in a month-old copy. She looked like an ordinary white businesswoman in a skirted suit, a little overweight, curly hair hanging below her ears. The caption read, "Director of Women's Health Institute, Carmen Lopez, addresses PS 42 graduating class." The face was expressionless, nothing to be read into it.

But until I saw her face, gray-blank in newsprint, I could not stop thinking of her. Everyone knew her, Manuel said. He was afraid of her. She was fiery.

Instead of dwelling on Manuel's soapy-smooth amber skin, I wondered about Carmen. Was she also glowing brown like Manuel, honey fleshed? Did she know so much about the American constitution that the President of the United States wanted to give her a job? What was a Puerto Rican, and why did Manuel see me as unlike a Puerto Rican?

I was failing the course on the American Constitution. Professor Lopez came late and left early. I sat right in front of the class, hoping he would speak to me, but he didn't take any questions. He was so nervous he stopped dancing in front of the chalkboard. I hated to see him frightened. I rang his office but hung up when he answered, remembering his plea.

One Friday afternoon I phoned the history department. "'Allo," I said carefully, speaking loudly into the mouthpiece the way I thought Carmen Lopez would speak, "I must speak to Professor Manny Lopez in the Bronx. This is an urgent message from Washington, DC, for his wife, who is Director of the Women's Health Institute. Can you give me their Bronx telephone number?"

The secretary gave me two numbers, one for his Bronx Community Organization office — he was appointed director of the BCO last month, she said — and the second for their home. I took down the home number on a scratch pad, tore off the page, then rolled it like a cigarette and put it in my coin purse, where I could fish it out whenever I wanted to make the long-distance call.

On Tuesday, before the seminar hour, I stood by the bayberry bushes under Manuel's office windows, which were four stories up. The snow had almost melted by now. In four weeks, classes would be over, and Manuel would vanish into the exotic Bronx. I would not be able to feel his energy, like a brown sun radiating above me, shedding dates and laws and famous American names in reams of magisterial knowledge, while, a mere writing tool, I chased after the flow, murmuring, wait, wait, slow down, how do you spell that name, repeat the title of that legislative act, even if his eyes would not look at me, even if he was smiling now at red-haired Kathy Pelan, his research assistant, whom everyone snickered at for spending hours in his office with him. During the seminar hour, I opened my coin purse and rolled the cigarette-address in a kind of ecstasy. I knew Kathy Pelan was not going to get what she wanted.

The late April afternoon was full of white threads of dandelion fluff, like smilt clouding the watery air. Standing under his windows, my feet trembled, struck by envy of Carmen Lopez. Carmen, who held Manuel in her power, who straddled the United States Constitution all the way to the White House, where the President wanted her. I imagined Manuel with his keeper, the unseen figure from the island. Fiery, he had said, a word reminding me of volcanoes, their fire-red magma oozing out of hidden vents, over the high lips, blood-viscous, the ground shaking and rumbling, fissures breaking, breaking in open mouths.

Carmen would not have lain quietly under him, I knew. She would have shaken him, scratched him like a cat with a lizard, lifted him up on her thighs, bitten his tongue till it bled.

I looked up where the panes reflected the low 4 pm sun. He never opened his windows, but even if I could have scaled the brick walls, he would never see me staring in, a morose phantom, the glassy insets dustily glittering, too dirty to see into or out of.

A phone call was very much like the windows — opaquely separating two bodies, even as it placed them close enough to summon each other.

The operator asked for a dollar and eighty cents for the first three minutes. My fingers tumbled the coins carelessly into the pay box.

Someone answered even before the third ring, impatient, abrupt, impolite. "Yes, who is this?"

I thought of hanging up, but it was too much money to waste.

"Carmen Lopez?" I was whispering.

"Yes, speaking."

I could see her frowning, thinking, "It's Manuel's woman."

"I am a woman," I said.

"I don't take calls for the Women's Health Institute in my home," the voice said, cutting me off. "Get me tomorrow at my office."

"Wait," I wanted to cry, "I'm not that kind of woman. I want to know who you are, why Manuel won't see me because he is afraid of you, how come you have power over him."

There was silence at the other end, someone waiting for my answer, a faint irritated breathing.

"I'm sorry," I whispered, "I won't try again."

"No, I don't mean that." It was a loud confident voice, the voice of a television broadcaster, an administrator, queen, someone who could shake a man. "This is my home number, you understand. What do you want? Who are you?"

I hung up and pushed the return lever, but the machine kept my coins.

I left as soon as the final exams were over in mid-May. No roommates except for Manuel had arrived at my suite all year. Peik had sent me a grown-up letter after I had written Mama that I didn't like Peps College and was coming home. "Shake the dust off your sandals," she wrote. I was going home to shake Manuel's golden brown dust off my body. My head a black fog like my clothes, I couldn't write the paper for his US Constitution seminar, but when I received the transcripts in Malacca, Manuel had given me A for the course anyway.

It was the straight string of As that persuaded Mama America had been a good choice and I should return to study. "Yes, yes," Mama repeated when I protested, "you must return to college, only this time you take Yen to America with you. What to do? The eldest must follow the second. Peik will stay here with me, and you your sister keep."

Five

Two months in one-main-street, squiggly alleyway Malacca, and I was ready to return to America. It didn't matter where as long as it was away from Ah Kong's house, from old women and nags and black curtains hung everywhere.

"You are nineteen," Ah Chee said, "and not too young to be marrying."

"*Em zai si*," she said to Mama, pointing her chin at me. "Not afraid to die! Soon, Swee will be an old woman like me, and no one will want her. A good-for-nothing. And no grandchildren for you."

"It's your turn," Yen crowed. "Stay here and save me from Mama's yak-yak."

Mama was too comfortable to scold, but she turned to Ah Chee to consider the important family matters.

"Peik mustn't be encouraged to be like her sisters. Eighteen years is a good age for wedding. If we wait for her sisters to marry first, her lucky day will never come."

Peik had been baptized last year.

"So funny," Yen wrote to me, "she make Mama and me come for her baptism, you know, at the CONGREGATIONAL EVANGELICAL CHURCH" — Yen wrote the name in block letters — "many kinds of people go there. Peik change her name to Pearl. She wear white dress, white veil, white shoes. I think she looks like a dead bride, but Pastor Fung said baptism makes her a bride for Christ. She is only girl that day. Many boys also baptized, maybe 12, 14, or more. Peik got same treatment with boys, stand on same line, say same prayers, same holy water. Sure not so bad to be Christian for Peik. Christians not so old fashion about girls as Kong-Kong. Maybe Christians save women more than men."

Among the parishioners, Peik, like her new name 'Pearl', was a person of high social standing. "I have a new heavenly life," she explained to Mama. "Peik cannot be translated into English because 'White' is not a Christian name. Pearl is better. It means 'precious in the eyes of God.' Pastor Fung chose the name because in Chinese philosophy, 'pearl' also means 'great knowledge.'"

As Pearl, she would have as little as possible to do with Yen, although at home, as Peik, she owed Yen the respect of a youngest sister for the eldest.

I refused to attend the Sunday Youth group with Peik because Yen was not invited.

"I can't have her there!" Peik protested. "She says shameless things to the men. Even the pastor cannot control her."

"That's hypocritical!" I wasn't sure whether I should laugh or pretend to be angry. "Yen is harmless. I think I am more dangerous than her. She likes to flirt, that's all."

"She wants to lead our parishioners into mortal sin. Robert confessed she made improper suggestions to him."

Robert was the pastor's son and Pearl's Bible class leader. After the Sunday Youth meetings, he walked Pearl home still warmly arguing over religious matters, like the propriety of reading the Psalms to the kindergarteners.

"Don't talk to him!" I whispered to Yen as Robert approached us at the door one Sunday. "He doesn't like us."

"Nonsense!" Yen replied loudly, addressing Robert. "He's minister's son, so he must like everyone." Then she took his hand and held it against her chest. "Isn't it true, Robert? Your duty is to like everyone, especially sinners? You like me, yes, Robert?"

Robert's face paled. "I never ..." He stopped, snatched his hand from Yen's grasp, and walked rapidly away without saying goodbye.

Peik had also turned ashy. "You're no good. I can't even pray for you."

She clenched her leather-bound Bible with both hands like a shield against her pink Sunday frock.

"Why? Because Robert like me? It is natural for men to like women. I like men and someday . . ." Yen smirked.

Pierced by memory, I saw Manuel's brown body as it had looked immediately after sex, the skin moist with the gloss of pleasure, and I knew this was the day Yen had in mind.

"It's alright, Robert. Yen doesn't mean any . . ." I spoke loudly to Robert's retreating figure when Peik interrupted, "No, no!" Her voice was almost a screech. "No, Robert doesn't like you. He hates you! He likes me, and he's going to marry me!"

That was how the Wings arrived at our first and only wedding in Malacca. As if to make up for Mama's status as a second wife, for Yen's ill reputation among the parishioners, for my sinful year in New York, the Sodom and Gomorrah of the West, Pearl, as she now insisted on being called at home, wanted the most respectable wedding a Christian woman could boast of. Pastor Fung invited the Bishop to drive down from Kuala Lumpur to officiate, and Pearl had flower girls and pageboys, so Yen and I sat in the front pew with Mama instead of at the altar as Pearl's bridesmaids. Mama wore a Western-style dress of black flowered silk, like the one Pearl had seen in a photograph of Queen Elizabeth on the last royal tour of Australia. Together with the Wedding March, the choir sang 'Rock of Ages.'

Everything was proper except for the speed of the arrangements. She was married in two months. By end of August, Yen and I were alone with Mama and Ah Chee, and the house appeared older and more run-down.

"So, what you want to do?" Mama asked me a week after Pearl had gone to live with Robert and Pastor Fung.

"Today?"

"No, lah! I mean, when are you going back to America to study? Your friends still in school. You cannot shake leg all day in the house. Never meet anyone here. Peik meet Robert only because she is church member. Maybe you can also attend Peik's church and take Yen with you. Or go back to America."

"Yes, take me with you to America!" Yen surprised us, springing across the kitchen door like an overgrown cat. "I want to go, I want to go!"

"But it's not so easy for you to get a visa. You will need to register in a college for a student visa."

"Well, you will find a college for Yen. She cannot stay home forever. Ah Chee complains every time I'm not doing my duty as mother, I must find husbands for you and Yen. Go to America to study if you do not wish to marry. At least you will save face that way!"

I looked at Mama sharply. What would she do with all three daughters gone?

Mama caught my glance and sighed. "Now I pay for my sins. Ah Chee is planning we make pilgrimage to Rangoon to the Swe Dagon Pagoda. We stay in Burma to learn the sutras. Then maybe I also come and visit you in America."

In the months I had been home, I had been collecting information on colleges in the United States. I was never returning to Peps College, where the traces of Manuel's body, his warm spurts, I was sure, were still sifting through the residence suite and classrooms like invisible yet potent particles, to ignite me again with misery. Instead, I was looking for a college as far away from New York State as possible.

I checked out Alaska, but it looked too grim for more than eight months of the year — plunging to minus 40 degree celsius and no sunlight — and all the food had to be brought in from somewhere else. For a week, I considered Hawaii, but the descriptions of plumeria and frangipani reminded me too much of Malacca. I wanted difference, not sameness. Mama was giving Yen over to me, and Yen was enough of home for me to bring over to America. No tropical pineapples and rice. Just Yen.

California was the only state left on the map I had not studied. It looked larger than the Malaysian peninsula, a state larger than a country. I checked out its meaning in *The*

American Heritage Dictionary. Surely the dictionary could explain the heritage of a giant place like California!

California had no existence in *American Heritage*, although it did have three flora and one bird named after it — the California laurel, California nutmeg, California poppy, and California quail — each sounding exquisitely exotic. The California laurel, I read, was "an aromatic evergreen tree of the North American Pacific coast, having clusters of yellowish-green flowers and yellowish-green fleshy fruit."

"Aromatic." The word lingered in my ear like Manuel's breathing, its companions in the Thesaurus spelling his memory. Aromatic, meaning fragrant, perfumed, odorous exhalation, subtle breath, delectable spoor, penetrating, whiffable, musky, spicy. Scenting the air with yellow flowers and yellow fruit, embalmed. I decided to go where the Californian laurel grew wild.

Just one college accepted Yen based on her high school grades — a two-year college in Long Beach. On the map, Long Beach appeared almost right on the North American Pacific coastline. The only information I could find on Long Beach was that it was close to Los Angeles. That was where we would have to fly into, the Buenavista College letter of admission informed us.

I was accepted by the University of California, Los Angeles, whose letter of admission informed me how fortunate I was to be one of the few singled out of hundreds of thousands of applicants. Seven other state colleges also replied to say my transcript from Peps College was impressive enough that I was already on their Dean's list.

"You must come to the same college with me!" Yen pleaded. "Yah, one college just like another. See how easy it will be if we take the same classes and have the same teachers! Swee, please come with me! Only for the first year, until we know our way around, I promise."

Of course, Yen was right. It didn't matter which college I attended. Last month, the accountant in Singapore who had prepared my tax statements, after Ah Kong's lawyers had completed the sharing of his assets, told me if Ah Kong's timber companies, tin mines and business corporations continued to do well, I would never have to work.

What did it mean, never to have to work? Ah Kong, who had been so stingy with Mama's house expenses she had to hide our tins of British toffees and New Year silk frocks from him, had not prepared me for this future.

I had immediately felt a lightness of spirit — to be a free Wing, released from staying indoors every Saturday and Sunday, bound to the duty of gratitude. To be duly grateful for breakfast, lunch and dinner, the clothes I wore and the chairs I sat on. Grateful for daily constrictions in the small space I knew as home.

But I had also felt dread. I feared this freedom, for what would I do if I did not work? Would I ever grow up to become my own Wing, if there was always Ah Kong's money to keep me?

All around me people were toiling. I was taking the Singapore Airlines shuttle back to Malacca that same afternoon after the meeting with the lawyers, oppressed by the rackety city where everyone seemed to be occupied. The accountant, direct and formal, friendly and distant, as if to say, you are only a business to me. The accountant's secretary, the elderly woman with the rag wiping down the marble walls at the lobby, and the Tamil newspaper vendor at the corner of the office building, were deep, lost, at work. Even the white tourists walking through the covered arcades, heads bent over maps and guidebooks, staring into store windows at freshwater pearls, fake Tang horses, and embroidered silks, were laboring on their vacations. The accountant did not tell me what I should do if I did not work.

Standing in the Singapore city furnace, outside the icy glass towers, waiting for a taxi, I realized suddenly the goal of Ah Kong's life, the reason for the pride with which he had thumped his chest, boastful of his body, the body that had given life to us. He had set up so many money-creating apparatuses — legal partners, incorporated companies, firms, timber and mining contracts, transport hubs and industrial factories — during his life that now, with his death, the accumulated capital would make it possible for Mama and their three daughters and for his Singapore family of five children and First Mother never to have to work. What an astonishing feat for one man! To gather and store enough land, buildings, material goods and possessions, and abstract things like shares, stocks, investments, commissions, rents, insurance, dividends, so that his visible and invisible kingdom could feed, clothe, and protect ten dependents for decades to come. Ah Kong must have had taken great pleasure in this vision. Standing in the middle of the great city's whirling busyness, it became clear to me his entire reputation had been staked on this amassing of more and more, until it became his only understanding of family and, so, our only understanding of him.

I knew I would have to use his money to go away again, somewhere where the last images of his furious face, white eyebrows contorted with passion, could not find me. Where no one had heard of Wing Timber Company, Wing Exports, or Wing Mining Consortium. Where I would find some work, even if it was as a student.

All I had found in my first year in the exclusive college in New York was unhappiness. But this second year, I vowed, I would be different, a guardian to Yen. I would be a working student and live on as little as possible of Ah Kong's money, what he had claimed, beating his chest like an ancient Tarzan, was his body. Yen and work would save me from the nightmares of Ah Kong's fierce beak and the empty dorm room I had filled with apples and beach balls last year.

The second flight to America was also different. Yen made the difference, with her moods and frowns and her fascination with airline food.

"Aiyah! The food is so bad," she complained, lifting the slab of chicken breast with a plastic fork. But she devoured it in just a few minutes, and then ate the rest of my pasta.

At Tokyo airport, the plane filled up with Japanese

businessmen and American women attached to noisy children. I watched the mothers fuss over their babies while Yen paid rapturous attention to the movie screen. They were wives of US military men, I decided, returning to the States from Korea, the Philippines, and Okinawa, to visit grandparents for Thanksgiving.

Buenavista College had admitted Yen and me for the second half of the academic year. The letters of welcome, identical in every way, noted if we arrived before December 7, we could register for spring courses with the rest of the students. We had five weeks to settle in before classes started.

"Where we go now, huh?" Yen asked as we stood at the curb of Los Angeles International Airport with the huge suitcases at our feet announcing to America we were new arrivals.

Black, brown, white, maroon, pink, and blue vans pulled up. Hyatt, Marriott, Sheraton, Travelers Lodge, Hilton. Porters jostled us aside to load jumbles of luggage on board the vans.

It was after three in the afternoon, and a cool breeze stirred the palms ahead. Palm trees, I thought with a pang. But this was supposed to be California, not Hawaii!

I had forgotten to check on housing for Buenavista College. "Buenavista? Never heard of it," the black woman at the information desk said when I went back to the baggage claim hall to ask.

"Yen, Yen, stay with the bags!" I yelled, and ran out to stop a porter from moving them.

"Look, you can see me right from here." I took Yen by the hand and stood her by the five red and green plastic molded bags Ah Chee had bought at the Wednesday night bazaar. "From China," she had said triumphantly, "very cheap and sure to last forever."

I wished again I had had the courage to refuse her. "As soon as we find a place to stay, I'll throw them out. They may last forever in America, but not with me," I'd promised Yen.

"Stay here!" I repeated, growling.

"Long Beach? Why didn't you say so? The next bus is in twenty minutes." The black woman had listened to my anxious orders to Yen and was more sympathetic. "Your sister? Say, is she okay? Long Beach is a big city. Where do you want to go?"

The map she gave me was covered with names of motels and car-rental stops. "You want a triple A motel. They won't cheat you, hon."

My eyes prickled. Suddenly I wanted this woman to be my friend, my guide to the mysteries of California. But already two other passengers were pressing behind me with questions.

Walking backwards, I pulled the three largest bags along the sidewalk, across the street and onto the median to the bus stand.

Yen followed, talking all the time. "Aiyah, so big. How to find our way here? No signs. Maybe we go back to Malacca now? Where you taking me? I think this is not a good idea. Maybe we go New York instead. You never tell me so confusing in America."

The Greyhound bus was almost empty when it pulled up. I pointed on the map to the Wayfarer Inn, right off Route 405. It was advertised as triple A, and on an intersection with Seal Beach Avenue. Buenavista College, I remembered just in time, had a Seal Beach Avenue address.

"Can't drop you off there," the driver said laconically. "Better if you rented a car."

"But I can't drive."

"Can't drive?" His voice was astonished, as if I had said I couldn't breathe. "The best I can do is drop you off at the Crossroads Church Mall. That's two blocks from the Wayfarer Inn. If you call the desk, they might send someone to pick you up."

He waited until I bought the tickets at the Ground Transport counter. "Can't handle money. Company rules. You have two minutes."

I had visions of Yen disappearing with the five giant plastic suitcases on the Greyhound into the continental heart of America. But the efficient clerk gave me the exact change for my one hundred dollar bill, and the bus, almost as long as a Malacca alley, swung out of LAX and on to a huge eight-lane highway packed with all kinds of vehicles. Trailers, sport cars, coupes, small Japanese cars, flashy American limousines, sedans, bakery vans, delivery trucks, motorbikes thundering in between, convertibles with single drivers and convertibles jammed with people, taxis with lighted signs, jeeps, and a few long black hearses. Cars pulling boats, snowmobiles, and other cars, cars topped with skis, bicycles, kayaks and containers, closed and open, spilling with fluttering cloths, ropes, and plastic bottles, rusty pick-ups and bright white pickups mounted on tall wheels. I could not stop staring as these machines zipped by our bus window as if in a noisy dream. I had seen nothing like this traffic in upstate New York.

On the map, Long Beach was just an inch or so away from LAX. It became clear that an inch signaled much more in America than it did in Malacca. There seemed to be more people in cars in Los Angeles than there were people in Malacca town.

"Yes," I thought hopefully, "no one in California will care that my father was Tun Wing Pak and my mother a second wife. No one who will need to know I chose Buenavista over UCLA, a university Paul Frazier said whose degree would be a feather in any cap."

"This is the San Diego Freeway," the driver said when I asked. "Goes all the way to Mexico."

"Yes," I resolved, "I will learn to drive in California, where no one cares about what feathers I have in my cap."

"No, we don't pick up our guests, ma'am. We don't have a shuttle service. Taxi? Not sure where you can catch one, ma'am. We're a triple A motel, guests drive here."

He was polite and firm. "No reservations? A room for two? We can do that. A month?" His voice grew friendlier. "Well, for a month we can do a special rate. Hold on, I'll talk to the manager."

He was back in a minute.

"We'll send someone to pick you up. Miss Swee Wing and sister. Wait by the phone booth. I'm sure he'll make you out."

It was the same voice driving the pick-up with WAYFARER in block stencils on the side panels. He had a buzz haircut and he threw the suitcases into the back like he was throwing sacks of potatoes.

"Squeeze in," he ordered, and drove across the huge parking lot almost empty except at one corner where the sign "Discount Mart" stood. "This place is a mess on Sundays," he added, glancing quickly at me. "You're lucky you're here on Wednesday." Then, as he pulled into the driveway of the motel, he said abruptly, "Ask for the special rate. The manager will forget if you don't."

Six

*H*is name was Sandy Weinberger, and he had been out of the military for seven years. Recruited at eighteen, he decided he could do better than being a private in the armed forces and left with an honorable discharge before he was twenty-two. He had studied business at the local state university, had hated the business world, and was now studying welding at Buenavista College. The certificate would help him get a job at the local Boeing maintenance shop — it was what he'd done in the Air Force, worked on aircraft repairs — but he also thought he might become a sculptor, welding the figures he saw in the sparks of the welding blaster. He told us all this gradually over a number of weeks.

He had narrow blue-gray eyes and hair the color of beach sand. "That's how I got the name," he said, "my sergeant gave it to me because that's what he could see in the showers."

Yen thought his hair color was what Americans meant by blonde. It fascinated her for a time. She'd come up and touch it almost with reverence, "So bright, like sunshine!"

Sandy was flattered. "I don't mind," he said, when I apologized for her, "the kids used to do that at Subic Bay. She'll get used to it." In a few weeks, Yen recognized Sandy wasn't a blonde. Compared to the girls in her classes who were bleached a blinding gold, his hair was ordinary, fading to match the beaches he brought us to.

His real name was Adolphus. "Yeah, I know, a weird name, like in Latin." His parents called him Adolph at home. It wasn't a name he could use in school. "The kids really had a good time with my name; you know, like in Adolf Hitler. Mom said I was named after a bishop, but hey, in California, no one knows that! So I changed it to Ace. Mom and Dad never knew until they got my high school certificate in the mail. Dad hollered, but by then I was out of there. I was in the Air Force, man. Not much he could do."

He was uncomfortable talking about his family. "Mom and Dad, they came from Austria when Eisenhower was President."

He was the youngest of four children, all girls except for him, and everyone had expected big things from him. "Being a motel clerk, that's not what I really do. But they give me a free room, it's only five minutes to the college, and I get to take my night classes for free."

Buenavista College and the area businesses had come up with a special program for full-time employees to keep them in the community, there being, in fact, no community anyone could identify. The region was a sprawl of small businesses all feeding off huge corporations that needed thousands of workers; but the entire economy was transient. It had come about as quickly as a dream — "the California Dream," Sandy said ironically when he explained the program to me — and as quickly the dream could disappear. Unless one took hold of something permanent, he said gravely, like an education that would give one a job for life.

The military had trained him well. He had been all over the world — South Carolina, West Germany, Texas, a short spell in South Korea and in the Philippines. But the civilian world didn't trust Uncle Sam. It wanted to see those degrees before it would hire you, he said.

I was surprised at how short Sandy was, about the same height as Robert, Peik's husband, and surely shorter by far than Ah Kong had been.

I had thought all American soldiers would be tall warriors. After all, wouldn't Americans have to be taller, bigger, stronger than other men, especially Asian men like Chinese and Japanese and Koreans, to beat them at war? Sandy was barely a couple of inches taller than I when I wore my platform shoes, and he struck me as more nervous than confident, more suspicious than straightforward. More like how Manuel was by the end of the year at Peps.

The only thing indicating Sandy might have been a soldier was the way he carried himself, shoulders stiff and back straight like he was still standing for inspection. At first he seemed as unbending to us. For the first week it was quick hellos when he gave us our key or made change for us at the desk. But after we asked his advice about registering for classes at Buenavista, he became friendlier.

I liked him because, to begin with, he was as uncomfortable around us as we were around him. He never pretended to feel friendlier toward us than he really was, not like the other Californians we never really got to meet but who said things like, "How're you doing?" "How's your day?" "Have a good day!" Yen continued to be confused by their smiles and words. She wanted to stop and chat even though the checker was already looking behind her at the next customer. "Your aircon too cold!" she'd say, or "Yah, very tiring to find where got bath soap. Why you not put up sign for soap?" The checker's smile would freeze as he pushed her change toward her. "Hmmm, hmmm?" he'd mumble, and she'd repeat her question more loudly, thinking she hadn't been heard above the Muzak, until she'd feel the woman behind nudge her shopping cart behind her knees and I'd scoop up the change and urge her out of the store.

Sandy was different, more straightforward. I trusted his reserve, his coldness, which made his friendship even more genuine when it finally came, first as a smile, then as short exchanges cautiously offered, and much later as chats filled with advice, suggestions, protective gestures easing him further and further into our lives.

On his advice, Yen and I learned to walk carefully on the shoulders of the highway to get to the Natural Café at the Crossroads Church Mall. Our room had a hotplate and small refrigerator, but we had nothing to cook with. So we ate most of our meals at the Café, the hamburger stands on the other side of the freeway, or cold from what we could find in ready-to-eat packages and in the freezer at the Discount Mart. I was planning to find a real place for the two of us before the end of December, and I didn't want to begin buying pots, spatulas, and plates for a kitchen.

"You can't be eating junk like that everyday," Sandy said the third time he saw me carrying bags of cereal boxes and frozen pizzas through the lobby. He knew our trash was full of paper plates and plastic forks and cups.

He was curious about us, but in an off-hand manner, almost as if he wanted to know just so much and no more. Enough to know we were no longer strangers but not much else. That we were sisters from Malaysia looking for an apartment near Buenavista College, that we were registered students. Then, we were simply there, in his life — he had no name for us except Sue and Yen, and in that way we became Californians.

After his first visit to our room, the room for which we had given him a month's rent in advance, I learned not to ask him questions.

"Americans consider you're rude," he said, "if you ask what they call 'personal' questions." But even with this warning, often I couldn't tell the difference between personal and acceptable questions. Personal questions had to do with family and names and someone's past. The past was always personal, off-limits unless volunteered, although one could share the most intimate physical present, like eating or having sex or getting drunk together.

Staying at the Wayfarer's Inn with Yen was different from staying alone in the suite of lost roommates in New York. I was grateful for Yen's continuous chatter, more lively than the speech of beach-balls, but truth be told, I was even more grateful for Sandy's silence. When he came to our room with pizza and soda, even Yen learned to be silent around him, for he became impatient if we got into his personal space and we were never certain where that was.

But he had immense tolerance for our other mistakes. "No," he said patiently to Yen, "you don't leave your purse on the counter of the store while you try the clothes in the dressing room. Someone's going to walk away with it."

"Nothing in my purse, lah, only chewing gum and Kleenex."

"Then you shouldn't be going out without identification and money. What if you got separated from Sue and had to find your way back to the motel? You wouldn't even have change to make a telephone call. What if something happened to you? How's anyone going to identify you?"

"What, you expect me to die, ah? Swee look for me. She sure to find me. I don't worry about identification, I have a sister!"

Still, after that afternoon, I was careful to remind Yen to carry some money with her, and Yen began wearing her purse strapped across her shoulder, "like a postman!" she grinned, proudly.

Just in time before the second month was up, we found an apartment, in a condominium complex in the town of Seal Beach, about a twenty-minute walk from the college. Or we could bicycle on the boardwalk and through a couple of streets to the college. That made the apartment appealing, for I had not yet begun driving lessons.

Yen's English classes started at 10 in the morning. I, Sue Wing — "You'd better change your name to Sue. Just add an e. Makes a lot of difference!" Sandy had told me — had completed all the requirements, and there were not many other classes I could take with Yen. But there was a history class at the same hour, and I signed up for "Race in America" with Mrs Butler, a tall large black woman whose accent, Sandy told me, was from the Deep South.

Mrs Butler's "Race in America" was all about slavery and the history of black relationships with whites. With swelling indignation I read about the treatment of slaves brought from West Africa across the Atlantic to Virginia and the Carolinas; the untold numbers who died in the holds of slave ships and who were thrown overboard like lumber; the children sold from their parents in plantations, and the unrecorded labor that had made the Southern states rich and powerful. Manuel's classes on the American Constitution had not covered this history.

"Some immigrants forget what black people have gone through in this country," Mrs Butler said, when she introduced the section on Jim Crow history, "and they aren't willing to wait their turn. They forget they're in America over the dead bodies of black people."

I looked away guiltily because I was afraid Mrs Butler was talking about me. Mrs Butler asked me in the second week why I was taking her class, especially after my stellar year at the New York college. "Straight As," she said sarcastically. "Buenavista is for working class students who can't get into places like your expensive liberal arts college, not for an A student who wants to be in California." But Mrs Butler couldn't ask me to drop her class. Only fourteen students had registered for African American history, and not one student was black.

On the first day of class, I was surprised to find more Asian than white or brown students — a number of Nguyens, Lins, and names that sounded Thai and Cambodian.

"White kids don't want to hear this shit anymore," Sandy explained when I told him what Mrs Butler had said. "We've been listening to this history since first grade. The Asians, they haven't gotten the message yet. They think they need to learn about race in America. You can't learn anything about race in college. It's all out there, and you just have to deal with it."

But I did think I was learning something about race from Mrs Butler. It was confusing she didn't like me because she seemed to like all the other students. She spent a lot of time in conference with Vu and Tranh, two Vietnamese students who were ESL learners and who had problems reading the textbook; but she bristled when she returned my papers and exams which she'd marked up with red-inked comments and which always received B grades.

"You have no idea of black oppression," she said when I came to pick up my final paper. "Just because you can read and write does not give you an A here. It's all book knowledge with you." She stared at me as if daring me to challenge her grade. Ashamed, I agreed with Mrs Butler. All I knew about race in America is what I had read in her class. Who knew what experiences Mrs Butler must have lived through? Perhaps, like those slave women we read about, she had been raped; she had gone without food, been homeless, walked without shoes, had been forcibly separated from her parents. She had had her intelligence questioned, the color of her skin mocked, her children ripped away from her.

When I shared these thoughts with Sandy, he laughed. "Listen, it's 1982. She's a middle-class American, she drives a Lincoln, and I bet she has credit cards and a bank account. She's no oppressed anybody, she's as free as you or me!"

I knew having money did not mean you were free. I couldn't tell Sandy about Mama who now had Ah Kong's money, who had never had an idea of her own when Ah Kong was alive, and who seemed to have lost the ability to think for herself now he was dead. I couldn't tell Sandy Yen and I had enough money to buy the apartment he had been negotiating for us to rent, more money than he might ever have, but Yen and I might never feel as free as he did. The manager of Wayfarers' Inn would never loan us the motel pick-up to get to the college; and even if we bought our own truck, we would never be able to drive the way Sandy did, dodging eight-wheel trucks and every sort of car, cutting across five lanes of highway to exit at the precise turn-off for the beach to which he was heading.

Mrs Butler had seen something about me that was deficient, not deserving an A grade. Yet she was defensive when she last talked to me.

"I don't want you complaining to the department chairman about my grading. I know you fresh immigrants — you're pushy. You never want to wait in line. I've had to wait in line all my life. You think you can just write some college papers and get to be somebody in America. Well, that isn't so. It's people like Sojourner Truth, Du Bois, Ida Wells, Martin Luther King,

Junior, and Malcolm X who've got you your rights, black people you know nothing about."

She was right. We had only time to read about the Middle Passage, slavery, the Civil War, and the Reconstruction Period. Mrs Butler was going to cover the Civil Rights Movement in her summer course, but I had not signed up for it because it was being offered at the same time as I was to begin selling cosmetics at the corner pharmacy.

Mrs Butler had the class list of students who had registered for the summer course on her desk. "I know you're not taking my course because I didn't give you an A this semester. It shows you're really not interested in black people, you're interested only in yourself, in getting all you can out of this country. The Vietnamese are different from you. They understand about white Americans and genocide; they've had the hell bombed out of them also. They're all staying on with me." Her look was bitter.

"Should I give up my job and take her class instead?" I asked Sandy when he came over to watch the Mash re-run with us that evening. "Mrs Butler's the only teacher who's taken a personal interest in me."

"You Asian women are suckers for punishment," he said, not taking his eyes from the television. Then, as the channel logo came back on for the break, he looked sharply at me. "I know this rent is a lot of money — where're you gonna get the money to pay for this if you give up a job each time someone makes you feel bad about yourself?"

He had offered to help out by sharing the apartment with us, and I had refused. I had a good reason. Sandy had a free room at the motel and was saving for the time when he would begin full-time studies for a degree in something that would cover both science and business. His veteran's benefits would not cover the cost of full-time college, and he needed those savings, particularly as he had just discovered something he'd enjoy doing. Something where he could use his brains and become somebody.

Sandy knew a lot of things. He fixed the TV cables for us and showed us where the switch box was and what to do when the fuse blew like it did throughout the first week because we kept overloading the wires. I liked his confidence, the way he patiently explained how things worked, what to do when the toilet ran and wouldn't stop flowing. He had an intelligence I hadn't seen among the boys in Malacca, a comfort in and understanding of the material world — space, dimension, size, shape, heft, scale, direction and proportion — an exactness that seemed to discriminate carefully yet elegantly and calmed my anxiety about being in a place so new and really so raw, so clearly unfinished as Long Beach. Or perhaps it was Yen and me who were new and raw and needed Sandy to guide us, to polish us through the gates of America.

It was me Sandy liked, he barely put up with Yen. But I wasn't sure I liked him in the same way. He was in between a brother to us and a lover to me. One step either way and I might be caught in something uncomfortable or even dangerous. But it seemed easier to welcome his visits, to greet him like the brother we never had, who cast his masculine eye, like a praetorian guard, on us.

Oddly, I found my first job not through Sandy but through Yen.

"Oh, look, Placement Office!" she trilled as we were walking to classes in our first month at Buenavista. "Maybe it can help us find our own place!"

"Place, place!" Pulling at my arm toward the door, she repeated the word like a mantra. It hurt me to know she was unhappy, cooped up in the little Wayfarer room. We needed to find an apartment soon, even if it wasn't going to be a permanent home, even if it was just for a few months — a short-time place, a make-do, until-we-decide-where-we-were-going-to home.

We were both tired of the crammed room we shared. It faced on to a parking lot, usually empty in the afternoon but full of engine rumbles at dark. Through the night the corridors of the Wayfarer Inn bustled with strangers, loud talk, and explosive noise: breaking bottles, slamming doors, bursts of laughter, percussive thumps that could be music or sounds whose sources I did not want to imagine. In our room there was hardly space to pace between the narrow twin beds. A chest of drawers made of something like plywood separated the beds. Jammed by the window was a card table Sandy had loaned us, on which rested an illegal hot plate. I tried sitting on the toilet seat for some quiet when I could no longer bear the mechanical music and yuk-yuks from the television that Yen had on for all hours of the day, but Yen was insulted by my behavior. "Wah, you like toilet more than me, yah? What, cannot read in same room with me, ah?"

Living so close to each other, Yen claimed me more and more as herself, while I grew desperate to move out of the range of her voice.

We looked for weeks for a place but could not picture a home from the ads in the papers. "Why it is not in English?" Yen asked, as she passed me the real estate pages. "Cannot understand this, just like cannot understand this country."

"4 BDR, 2 B, large yd. cream puff condt. 450 K." "2BDR, handyman's special, needs TLC, close to gd schs, 320 K firm."

The pictures, however, were clear: bungalows, concrete constructions, apartment buildings, empty lots.

"Don't waste your time reading the real estate pages," Sandy advised. "There's no way you can afford to buy a house in LA. I'll ask around for you. That's the best way to do things here. It's who you know." Sandy had moved to Long Beach from his parents' home in Solvang, a town up north, as soon as he could once he had left the Air Force, and from his time as desk clerk at Wayfarer Inn, he'd become friendly with a large number of people passing through who'd eventually settled down in LA.

But he was taking his time finding us an apartment. It would soon be the beginning of our fifth week at the motel. Then I saw a rat in our wastebasket which Yen had stuffed with the remains of the supermarket burrito that had tasted like old paste.

The Placement Office was only a front counter and some flyers. "We want a place," Yen said to the woman who emerged from the inner office when she banged on the counter. "A nice place — no rats, nice big kitchen. Must have two bedrooms, no, three, for when Mama come to stay. A place just for us. . . . ." She began to talk with her hands, shaping the square of the house, the peak of the roof, her fingers beckoning to this future.

The woman didn't wait for her to finish speaking. "The Housing Office is in Hamilton Building." She frowned. "We don't have rats in Long Beach, at least not in Buenavista College. Perhaps where you come from they're common. We're the Placement Office. You'll have to finish your degree here first before we can help you." She disappeared through the door into the inner room.

"Let's go," I said, gripping Yen's hand. "She doesn't want us here. We're in the wrong place."

"Wait, wait, let me read what they have here. Look, it's free." Yen took the flyer on top of the pile. "'Help wanted. Apply Wells' Pharmacy.' See, someone does want us here. 'Help wanted.'" She smiled. She'd found something I hadn't known about.

The pharmacist studied me carefully before saying, "You can't work here. Not until you've completed a semester at Buenavista. We don't hire aliens." I went back end of May once my grades were in, and he was friendlier this time. Looking at my transcript he said, "A in English. Very good! You'll do OK."

The pay was minimum wage, and they needed me only for twenty hours a week, 8 am to noon, Monday to Friday. These were slow hours and I could work alone.

The rest of the time Mrs Hailey took over. She was full-time and worked also on weekends when it was busy. Everyone called Mrs Hailey Faye. "After Faye Dunaway. You mean you don't know who she is?" she asked me incredulously. Mrs Hailey knew everything about cosmetics, the right kind of day or night cream for dry, oily, normal or combination skin, the best shades of lipstick or mascara for brunettes, redheads and blondes, the newest fragrance, the ideal shampoo for frizzy or baby-fine or split-end hair, what deodorant women should use, alcohol-based, talc, or plain baking powder. She could sell anything, and the pharmacist loved her.

She wasn't a morning person, she explained, so Mr Pearson simply had to find a way to deal with it if he wanted to keep her. They had to let the woman who had the position before me go because she wanted to work more hours. "No way she could have my hours," Faye said, glancing at me to make sure I heard her. "Then Mr Pearson found she had a kid and was going on welfare and he told her she had to quit."

She shrugged and tapped a long sharp middle nail on the file she was carrying. "OK. Back to the inventory. This may not look like much," she swept a pencil over the cosmetic area, "but we have one thousand two hundred and sixty-five products, and they all have to move, because we don't carry duds here."

I wondered what Mrs Butler would think about Faye. Mrs Butler never seemed to talk about white people except for what they did to blacks, but Faye seemed oblivious to any but white women.

"Well, we have some Asian women coming in now and again," she had said grudgingly when she'd first met me, "but I don't know how Mr Pearson expects you to sell anything."

She was right. Except for Yen, all the regular customers I met in the months I worked at Wells' Pharmacy were white women. Some left without buying after asking for Faye. Others bought the non-specialized products — baby powder, the super-sized bottles of generic shampoo, cheap brands of face and hand creams, stuff put on sale because they were getting close to their expiration date or their wrapping had crushed; products that sold themselves. Only older women shopped at Cosmetics in the mornings. Even the mothers with strollers, I noticed, would be pulling up into the parking lot around lunchtime, when Faye appeared, freshly lipsticked and perfumed, at the store.

I met Mrs Butler in the corridor one afternoon as I was hurrying for my Advanced Communications class. She looked tired and miserable. I wanted to avert my eyes, it was like accidentally seeing something private and intimate one wasn't supposed to, but Mrs Butler called out, "Wing!" For a moment I thought I could pretend not to have heard and dodge into the classroom ahead, but I still would have to pass by her, and there was something about Mrs Butler's dark stocky body that could not be by-passed.

Silently I stood before her. This was how I had stood before her during every meeting last semester while she lectured me on my ignorance.

Now I could see why Mrs Butler was bitter. People like Faye and Mr Pearson seemed to know nothing about blacks in America nor did their ignorance seem to worry them. The customers who came to Wells' were almost all white. Fair and pink, they looked well-fed, well-groomed, jovial, and completely unaware that just a block away around the corner, Buenavista College's classrooms were filled with Hernandezes and Nguyns, Figaroas and Kims, Guttierizes, Lees, Patels, Vongs and Wings. I dusted merchandise, wiped down counters, checked inventory, and straightened the displays, while Faye sold cosmetics the rest of the day to the white women who came in droves to talk to her about their skin problems, their fading hair color, their broken nails, unsuccessful tans, sagging pouches under eyes, and age spots.

I could understand it. After all, how could these women expect me to know their bodies — flesh reddened by sun, freckled and mottled; noses and cheeks, pulling in different directions, casting different shadows; brows and eyes with different curves and of strange luminosities? I couldn't look at them deeply and knowingly the way Faye did, as if to say, I understand you. We share the same skin, the same color. You don't have to explain your problems to me. We're sisters. You can buy from me.

Black women did not buy cosmetics at Wells' Pharmacy, which did not carry products made for them. Occasionally a company would send samples of liquid foundation, eye shadow, blushers, cover up powder for black women, and Faye would toss them out. "No go," she'd said when I caught her doing this one afternoon as we were swapping shifts. "Black women have their own lines. They'd never buy from a French house." In five months in the neighborhood I had talked to just one black woman, Mrs Butler, and I didn't know if Faye would have counted her as a woman, because Mrs Butler did not wear make-up.

Standing in front of Mrs Butler, I wished I had saved some of the make-up Faye had thrown out for her. Perhaps it would show Mrs Butler how well I thought of her and she wouldn't now be facing me with two straight lines furrowing her forehead.

"I know you went to complain about your grade for my course."

I shivered. I hadn't thought about Mrs Butler's grade since I'd received my transcript.

"Well, what do you have to say?"

Mrs. Butler's lips were flaky and could do with a chapstick. Her dusky cheeks were heavily freckled. Faye was wrong when she said only fair skin was dusted by the sun. I wanted to tell Mrs Butler she had better do something about her skin before it was too late. Skin was skin, and dark skin got wrinkled and beat up just like white.

"I hope you're happy I've been warned about fair grading. I knew you were trouble soon as I saw where you had been to. That college for rich kids." Mrs Butler stepped aside to let me pass.

"It wasn't me. . . ."

"You expect me to believe you? You were the only one who didn't re-register. The dean showed me a copy of your paper and asked how I could have assigned you a B. 'This is superbly written, she's the kind of student we want to keep.' As if I don't know what my rights are. No one can undermine the instructor's right to grade as she thinks fit. As if he knows better than I do what you don't know!" Lips pressed tight, she walked away.

"Yeah, I took your paper to Mr Canby," Sandy said equably when I questioned him later.

He was giving me a ride back on a second-hand Harley he was trying out that had been offered to him last week by a biker who had run out of money to pay for his room at the Inn. All sorts of things came his way from such situations. Luggage, a pair of boots he had admired, a cassette player, tapes and books left behind that the Mexican maids gave to him because they knew he was studying at the college and they didn't read English. The Harley was the best offer so far. The manager had agreed to dock his pay for a few months to make up for the unpaid room. This way the Inn got its money, the biker did not have the cops called on him, and Sandy got the Harley.

"Ha ha," Yen had said gleefully when Sandy rode the bike over last night to show it off, "Harley sound like Hailey comet. All this is very good luck. All matching, same-same, must mean Swee and I are doing OK."

Now we were cruising slowly from the supermarket to the apartment. Sandy was on night shift again and had time to eat supper with us.

"How could you, it's not your business!" I shifted uneasily on the high seat behind him.

When he had told me about the bike, I had seen a sleek low machine disappearing fast down the highway. But Sandy's Harley was a tall, massive machine. More like a cathedral than a chapel, more air-carrier than cruiser, Sandy said grandly, trying to explain to Yen what a Harley actually was. He rode high on the bike, as if sitting on a throne, his trunk straight and stiff like he was standing at the parade ground. If the Harley was a woman, it would be a nine-month-pregnant giantess, its fuel tank an extended shining steel womb. But it was capable of taking us on six hundred mile runs, Sandy said. To me it couldn't be anything but male. It rumbled like a deep bass from a heavy chest, and I gripped it between my thighs, feeling its steady shaking. The wheels spun so fast they formed solid circles carrying us home through dust and clouds of carbon monoxide.

Accepting the ride back on Sandy's bike was like approving what he had done to Mrs Butler. I wanted to get off and walk, but walking on the highway was dangerous and illegal. Besides, Sandy wouldn't understand. Asking to get off right there would be the end to our friendship, and why should I lose his friendship over Mrs Butler who didn't even like me?

"Ever heard of such a thing as justice?" Sandy was shouting, his face turned toward me so the wind would blow his words my way. "Yeah, I read your paper — just for curiosity, you know. That kinda paper is like what gets published in the Sunday magazine. In a book. I was real proud of you, and it killed me she gave you that crappy B, so I gave it to Mr Canby. For a second opinion, you know. . . ."

The bike rounded the bend to the parking lot and I lost the rest of Sandy's words as he swerved it around the cars circling for spaces.

"The A isn't important to me," I began as we were unpacking the groceries.

"They don't call me Ace for nothing," Sandy said, handing me the package of frozen chicken.

"It's my paper, not yours!"

"Hey, you're my friend! Fair is fair. I didn't get her into trouble. Everyone knows she and Canby hate each other's guts. But how would I know Canby would get the dean in on this?"

But his voice was pleased; I knew he was glad it happened. He sounded as if he had won something, or won out, triumphed.

I couldn't understand Sandy's attitude. It was like a hidden birthmark, imperfect pigmentation splotched on a body, coming into view, Sandy's dislike for Mrs Butler.

I won't raise her name again, I vowed to myself. We will never have to talk about her again. Buenavista offers hundreds of classes. There are hundreds of teachers, full-time and part-time. We'll drop Mrs Butler out of our lives. There was now the bike to talk about instead.

Seven

Sandy's skin was like washed silk except where bristles of hair grew on his chest, his legs and arms, and even the bristles were soft and curly. The first time he was naked with me I was surprised to see how different his body was from Manuel's. It was off white and pink, and when I put my face right up to his chest, I saw his skin was sprinkled with tiny red spots, like specks on the strawberries Yen loved, buying six or more baskets of fat bright red berries at a time and eating them straight off the baskets before they could be brought home.

I had refused him for months when he pressed his body against me, kissing me gently as he left for his night shift. But the Harley made it easy for him to come by in the summer mornings to pick me up for work, when Yen was still asleep.

Yen stayed up late watching the talk shows and didn't wake up till eleven to get to her first class at 1 pm. She slept while I was at the pharmacy. Although she had managed to pass every course in the first semester without being in the same class with me, she still refused to be at Buenavista College for her summer classes unless I was also somewhere in the building.

Because Sandy helped us fix up the apartment — getting the TV connected, the jammed window sash unstuck and oiled, the unreliable electrical circuit safely rewired — we trusted him with a key to the apartment. He let himself in quietly and made a fresh cup of coffee before waking me for the ride to work. The third week he walked into my bedroom with a cup of coffee for me, he smelled of stale smoke because a stranger had sat up all night in the lobby talking to him and smoking cigarette after cigarette. "He was bummed, his wife had just thrown him out," he said, sitting on my bed. Half-awake, I was reluctant to stir and turned my cheek instead against the smooth nub of his kaki pants. He'd set the cup of filtered European coffee on top of the stack of books I'd piled on the side table covered with pages from an assignment I was writing for an American literature class.

What a mess Sandy's life is, I thought sleepily, the smoky aura on his shirt confusing me. I put my arms around his waist comfortingly, and as he held me tight and then more tightly, it suddenly seemed right to have him in bed with me.

Unlike Manuel he wasn't in a hurry; he was deliberate about giving me pleasure, saying into my ear, "You're safe, you're safe!" I wasn't certain what he meant, if I was safe with him or he with me. But I did feel safer. About taking my time, about coming.

Sandy never thought of locking the bedroom-door. He wasn't afraid to be seen with me. Placing my face against his back as we sped to the pharmacy later that morning, I wondered at his difference, at why I had been so struck by Manuel, if there had been a secret part of me that understood Manuel's fear, had welcomed and wanted it. Sandy's body had made me forget Manuel's, or at least they seemed to merge as one desire: their ridged thighs, the masculine tufts of hair on their chests, the smoothness of their entries and the pleasure that filled me seemed to dislodge Ah Kong's image from mind. I was safe in their sex.

Sandy wasn't around most nights, working the night shift, but it didn't matter, my bad dreams were gone. In the mornings, he was always careful to wear a condom. "You don't want any babies, do you?" he whispered as he slipped out of bed to find the package in his wallet. But he didn't want any babies either. Marriage was never anything he talked about.

Later he asked his manager for the day shift because the advanced welding class he wanted to take in July was offered only on Tuesday and Thursday nights. The college rented space in a machinist shop a few miles away, and the class was taught by a couple of guys who had once been supervisors in a company that made parts for military aircraft but that had been forced to close down when the inspectors found it had been using non-spec steel.

"You gotta like them — they lost their pensions, paychecks, everything. But they're managing. They're not down the tubes. They've got this spirit."

He had learned about the class through a group of men he had met at a veterans' meeting. "There are these groups, see, like the Elks, the Lions' Club, the Shriners, the Masonic Lodge of Brothers, the Knights of Columbus. There's a bunch of them, more than you can count, and they try to get the vets to join them. But with some, it's like you need to be a businessman and wear a suit to get in. And some of the meetings are filled with blacks and Mexicans. I'm not saying anything about your people, Sue, but I don't like those sharp-dealing Japanese and Koreans. I don't know where they get the money they're flashing, buying up malls and houses all over LA. The other groups don't let these people in, but lots of them are full of fathers who're only interested in coaching junior baseball league or soccer for their daughters. George and Keith understand what's happening in America. They don't let the government pull the wool over their eyes."

I didn't argue with him. Sandy knew the kinds of Americans I never met. He was reporting from a world I couldn't even glimpse. I was meeting only students, many of them, like me, newcomers to the United States, outsiders who didn't understand what was happening in this country that never saw itself as peculiar, who didn't read the newspapers because nothing in the pages related to anything they knew. We foreign students were like pupae in our tattered cocoons, borne by intercontinental winds from familiar fields and trees, and fallen on fertile land, but not the land of our ancestors. We were struggling to emerge, but to a world none of our instincts understood.

Sandy went off with George and Keith and other students from the welding class to drink at a camp up in the Angeles National Forest. They rode big bikes — that was how he got interested in that particular class to begin with — the vet who approached him had noticed he had come for the meeting on the Harley. It was a long ride — sixty miles from Long Beach and sixty miles back — but the hours on the road were good for him, he said.

"There's nothing like air hitting in your face and the black road spinning under the wheels!" he explained. "It's what freedom is about. Sitting in a car doesn't begin to compare. You're really open — just you and the road, and anytime something could hit you, blow you away. But you have your hands on those handles and the engine in between your knees and the guys riding with you. It's like you own the road. No one gets in the way when we're tight together."

One Friday I found him asleep on the sofa. He'd let himself in so late after riding back from a camp meeting that neither Yen nor I heard him.

"You can't keep doing this," I said as he sat up unshaven and smelling of beer and smoke. "You'll lose your job. This is supposed to be a class, not a party for bikers."

"Aw, man! I don't remember what happened. . . ."

"You rode back drunk?"

"No, no. I mean so much happened last night, I sort of lost sight of some things." He massaged his hair with nervous hands. "It's not what you think. It's not like a party. It's more like the Elks, you know, a brotherhood."

"But what about welding?"

"Who the fuck wants to be a welder?"

I was astonished at the violence in his voice.

"I'm sorry, I'm sorry," he mumbled, and reached out to hold me. "Why don't you let me move in? I wouldn't hang out so much with these guys."

I couldn't answer and after a few minutes he got up to make coffee.

"You can take a shower here," I said. "You should. Your boss won't like it if you go to work without cleaning up."

The manager had asked Sandy to park the Harley near the trash containers at the back of the building where it wasn't visible from the road. He said it might make some people uncomfortable. "Like it's a sign of Satan!" Sandy added. "It's just a bike. I don't know why he's afraid of a bike." But he was smiling as he said this. He liked it the manager was showing him more respect because he now rode a Harley. Later, when Sandy asked for the change in shift, the manager had said yes immediately, no arguments.

But Sandy wasn't pressing his luck. He enjoyed his work — it wasn't demanding, and he was managing with the Mexican janitors and maids. He had learned some Spanish through the years. "Besides, I'm going to get the welding certificate easy, and I'll check out for a real job with Boeing. The vet office got the company to agree to give first preference to vets. That's the problem with George and Keith. They got no record any place. That's why when their company folded they were left with nothing. Nada, nought, zipperdoo, zero, nil, null, blank, empty, nichts."

Then, as I blinked with surprise, he added, "Yeah, I speak some German. That's what my folks spoke at home. You know, Austrians speak German. There's no such thing as an Austrian language, although everyone expects a country should have its own language. I don't know why. Here we are in America and we speak English, although my mom and dad spoke German at home." He stopped, uncomfortable. I knew it was one of those personal question moments.

He decided not to make overtime and to spend the next Sunday with me instead, to make up for scaring me on Friday morning. But there wasn't much for us to do alone. Yen would be up soon and we'd have to find something to do that would include her.

"Tell me what happens when you and your friends ride to the National Forest," I asked, moving away from his discomfort.

"Forest" sounded different from "woods," which was what had been around Peps College. The woods were pretty. Yellow and red and brown in September when I had first walked through them, gray and black trunks, gnarled branches and hatch-crossed twigs in winter. They were shades of green mottled in sunlight in the spring when I was leaving. The woods made for good walks, Clarissa and me walking through them as a way to leave our assignments behind, to feel our age — young, young! — and not old like the books we were reading.

"The Forest" was a mystery to me. I'd seen jungle in Malaysia when my high school class had taken a field trip to Tanah Merah. I couldn't imagine what "forest" was. Somewhere between jungle and woods, between wild and tame?

But this was also the wrong question.

"What do you want to know?" He was evasive.

"Well, could you show me someday?"

He shrugged and turned on the television. "I might."

Instead he took Yen and me in the pick-up truck to Malibu Beach, Venice, Santa Monica, and as far north as Santa Barbara, but nothing there was close to what I imagined "forest" to be.

Those places were more like what I'd first expected of Buenavista College in Long Beach — long miles of sandy dunes and blue, green and white ocean tumbling in lifts of surf as it came up to shore.

On our first day at the college, Yen and I were confused to find Buenavista College was made up of a number of cream- and rose-colored low buildings and what looked like mobile homes on a busy avenue blocks away from the ocean front. We walked from the Wayfarer's Inn across a few abandoned factory lots and through streets of residential apartments with small concrete and grass front-yards. Some students biked on the boardwalk, but even after we moved into our apartment, Yen couldn't manage the changing terrain. She panicked and braked at the wrong moments, and after she had gone flying off the bike on her second trial run, I met her at the pharmacy every day after my morning shift, and we walked to and back from Buenavista. The view from Buenavista College was industrial and temporary;

dull, depressing, looking out eye-level and straight ahead on to parking lots alternately too full or empty. It didn't even possess those palm trees that seemed to stick out of nowhere in the oddest places in Southern California. But it did have a flagpole — its most prominent landmark — and the US flag was always flapping from it, like a tethered red, white and blue kite we trained our eyes on as we walked in the morning, to calculate how much closer we were to approaching our classrooms

    On the real beaches, however, one could look at California and think of it as the state between sand and salt water, the horizon and sky stretching beyond promising a kind of nirvana where memories got washed away, turned into pure sunny sensation. "This is where America ends," Sandy said, with pride in his voice, as if he was showing us the edge of his own vast property. "We're between the Atlantic and the Pacific. This is where the pioneers stop, where we draw the line." But there was no line where he was waving to, only waves erasing the last tidal mark and bluffs eroding from the last winter storms.

    "So where is Solvang?" Yen asked, toes immersed in the Pacific. She was looking out at the islands, low-banking cloudy land materializing like darker mist on the channel where Sandy said gray whales and dolphins could sometimes be seen.

    "It's inland, farther up north." His answer was short, dismissive.

    Yen stood on the edge of the water because, she said, Malacca was somewhere over the horizon, with Mama and Ah Chee.

    "We go see your high school? Where you were a little boy?" she asked, enthusiastic. She enjoyed finding places that had personal meaning for someone. Everything else passed her by like calculus problems, impossible to decipher and putting her into despair.

    "Maybe some day. None of my friends are back home. They're all gone."

    I pulled Yen away as a large wave rumbled up and we scrambled toward dry land pursued by a swath of water. "Look, Yen," I pointed, "there are oranges on this beach!" Oranges and lemons floated gently as the water ebbed. Pebbles like used soap bars glistened wetly on the tideland, and as I pointed to individual green, peach, yellow and gray-blue stones, Yen picked enough to fill both our pockets.

Sandy was reluctant to bring us to meet his family, I thought. Besides, family wasn't important to him.

But I also didn't want him to meet Mama and Ah Chee and the other Wings in Malacca and Singapore. What would they have to say to him? They might look down on Sandy, unlike Weena's American boyfriend, an ex-air force maintenance man, a motel desk clerk, someone training to be a welder in a factory. Perhaps Sandy was as afraid to have us meet his family as I was to have him meet the Wings.

I stood still as the waves pushed up against my legs, up to my thighs. Water and dry land could only meet so far, even on a shoreline that accommodated both. I didn't trust how long Sandy and I would be together.

Eight

Swee was afraid something bad might happen to me. She was always afraid of something horrible with me. I saw this in her eyes, the way she tried to smile at me, grouchy. It was a pity because she was supposed to be carefree, not glum, and I was sorry she frowned so often because of me.

Without me she might have been a happy and pretty girl. Like Mama when Ah Kong was alive and before we grew up.

I was only daughter to remember Mama like that, smiling and beautiful because of Ah Kong. We were her fingers and toes. She'd stretch us out for Ah Kong to see. Happy fingers, pretty toes! She liked to say Ah Kong believed it was very good fortune to have three daughters — like an Emperor — even though Chinese men usually wanted only sons. Ah Kong had enough sons already in Singapore, Mama said, and they fought to take over his business.

When we were good, Ah Chee praised us for being Ah Kong's amulets, his omi-tu-fu, what Buddha's name had written down for his fate. And Mama was his favorite, his Number One Daughter.

Ah Kong meant "Grandfather." We should have called him "Baba," father, instead. I didn't remember why he became Ah Kong to us. Maybe because "Baba" didn't express enough respect. It was only one generation difference. "Grandfather" was two generations away.

Ah Kong was proud of his age — each year made him more powerful, more like God. Mama told us God was the oldest man in the universe.

What was funny was Ah Kong liked Mama because she was

so young. "Young flesh for an old man," Ah Chee said when she was cooking sharks fin and oyster soup for Ah Kong, but she refused to explain her words.

Swee would never be like Mama, and part of the reason was me. Mama never wanted to take care of me. "So much trouble, lah!" she said. "Nuisance! Why you cannot be like Swee and Peik?" Mama asked. "Get good marks, keep your clothes and hair clean, your mouth shut? Why so bony and brown?"

I was Swee's responsibility. She worried about me. She didn't want me to get a job. "OK, lah. Going to class every day harder work than selling make-up," I told her.

I didn't tell her California scared me. I couldn't understand it. Like how to get from somewhere to somewhere. Where anything was. What direction to go. What point I was at.

Once, Wayne took me to South Coast Mall. He was going to a veterans' reunion, he said. He pick me up where he dropped me off, in three hours. But the mall was closed, not open till 10, and it was only 9.30 am.

I was frightened. Everywhere was dark although the sun was shining outside. All the stores were closed. They had iron gates and steel doors. Stores with display windows empty — they had taken away pearls, diamonds, gold and whatnot, left only fake satin cases. Not a single person inside or outside in parking lot! I wanted to spend the morning with Swee at the pharmacy but her boss didn't like me to be in the store with her. And then Wayne found he had this emergency meeting, and I had to be alone with empty, empty shops for the morning.

I walked and walked, and I found a large sign. "You are here," the red arrow pointed, but where was here? My head ached, I couldn't think. I thought I better stand by the sign. At least it knew where I was, so I couldn't be lost.

I stood there until my feet hurt. I saw men and women coming to work. No one stopped to ask why I was standing by the sign. Maybe they thought I was waiting for a friend. Maybe I was a tourist waiting for my guide. I saw gates pull up like window shades, steel doors clang open. Lights went on. Women wheeling bunches of clothes out to storefronts. The dresses looked like skinny women dangling on racks.

    I walked to the open stores. It was too early and no one wanted to talk to me. In Malacca the first customer of the day was the princess. The salesgirl tried to sell her something — a bangle, sandals, blouse, even a hairpin — anything, so long as she paid up. Her purse opened up the day for the shop. If the first customer did not buy, then everything was set back, meaning bad sales all day.

    It was hard to be a Chinese in California. I was out of step. I was the first customer no one would serve, just like Swee complained she was the salesgirl no customer would buy from, no matter how hard she tried to sell.

    That made Wayne a good customer, or a good salesman. Wayne said he loved me. "I'll buy anything from you, babe," he said, and Swee frowned at me to say, "Don't believe him. He's putting you on."

    But of course I had to believe. I couldn't believe anything I learned in Malacca. Where I was when I stepped out of the house, what direction to get me home, shop girls serving me first thing in the morning — nothing made same sense here.

    Soon the mall was crowded. Women with shining white hairdos, angels' heads, but with wrinkled faces and snaky green-veined hands. Girls with smooth pale cheeks, just like their bellies showing below their tops, and eyes shadowed green like those old hands. Fat people whose stomachs jiggled, bigger than cows. Children running and mothers yelling, "Come back here, you hear me!" Children pulling at arms. "I want it, I want it!" I thought I was in a circus. Players walking back and forth, all knowing their parts, except me. It was bright now in the mall, brighter than outside where the sun shining on hundreds of cars come from nowhere, and I felt low and humble. I knew nothing of any importance to this place.

    I bought a coke, medium-sized, from a stand suddenly

appeared in middle of courtyard. The coke container was as large as a watering can. I sat at a table while a brown man mopped floor around my feet. I couldn't find my way home. Swee would never find me here. I tried not to cry sticky tears. It was too much coke for me to drink.

The floor had long ago dried before it was time for me to get up, and when I found Wayne, I held his arm like Peik said she held onto Jesus Christ. "I place myself in the arms of the Lord," she prayed. "Say grace before we eat!" she insisted at dinner table, although Ah Chee grumbled grace was not Buddhist. Say. Grace. I told Wayne I said grace when he came and got me, and he laughed.

Now I knew my way to classes. Next year my second and last year at Buenavista College. "Not fair!" I said to Swee. "Just when I know where the buildings are, I'll be finished here."

I didn't ask Swee where we go next.

Sarit, the girl from Thailand, told me I was lucky, I didn't have to work. She and her mother and sisters did sewing in a factory, making gowns for a big-name fashion designer. "See," she said, bringing Vogue magazine to our class, and pointing to some pictures, "this is the dresses we make!" "These are the dresses we make," Mr Lucas said, but Sarit didn't understand difference between is and are. "Sharing our stories," Mr Lucas said about that assignment. Sarit was so proud and excited to share her story, but no one was interested except me.

"My mother and sisters, she work 9 to 1 and 2 to 6 everyday. They give me money to study Buenavista College. I work three days to study hard my English," she read aloud. She waved her fingers at me in the washroom. They were full of holes, like pincushions where needles had gone through them. "I careless worker, that why I am daughter go to college." Sarit asked me to correct her grammar and spelling. Even Swee said my English was getting better.

Wayne liked my broken English. Make him laugh, he said.

His name was Wayne Patrick Stanhope, and he got real blonde hair, not like Sandy. Bright yellow, like the monks' robes. Or turmeric powder. "It's Swede, on my grandfather's side," he said. "Not turmeric."

"Cannot be real," I said, and he laughed some more.

"It's real alright," he answered, "not like those actresses in their bikinis!" He said they peroxide their hair, "a bunch of fakes looking for the producers to get them into the movies."

Wayne and Sandy both veterans, but Wayne was older. Sandy said he was still in elementary school when Wayne was in Air Force.

Swee was not happy with Sandy for setting up a blind date for me. They argued back and forth for a long time. "But he's an old man," she said, "a Vietnam vet!"

Sandy got mad. "That makes him a leper? He's an American patriot, a gentleman. Look, if you're going to be my girlfriend, you've got to accept my friends. He's like me, only older. He has a good job at the airport, and he hangs out with bikers like I do. We're brothers."

Sandy said I was weird. "You laugh funny."

"What?" I talked back. "Just because you never laugh, you think I'm stranger than you? I think you strange. Always serious. Always frowning. You make Swee frown, just like you."

"Sue, her name is Sue."

"She's my sister. I know what her name is!" I called her Sue also sometimes, but I liked to argue with Sandy. Sometimes I said Swee, and he got hot and bothered, like I reminded him she was not American like him.

First time we met, I wasn't sure I liked Wayne back. "Wayne's more weird than me," I told Sandy. He had many rings on his hands. I counted seven, four on right hand, three on left. Silver rings, some with blue stones — turquoise, he said, bought from an Indian powwow with his last girlfriend — and two with crosses and skulls. I thought he was too old to wear rings like a young girl, but this time I knew to keep my mouth shut. Swee said with Americans, better I zip up my lips.

Wayne said he liked me from day one. "You remind me of Vietnamese women, bones so thin the rain drops can fall and miss you. I got used to small women. I wouldn't describe them or you as skinny. Look!" He took my wrist in between his thumb and middle finger. "This is what I call refined!"

One Sunday we took a trip to the Angeles National Forest. Swee suggested the ride. Our summer school over, August, she was bored with beaches.

"Some cool park. No more sand. Trees!" she said.

Sandy wasn't happy, but Wayne said, "Sure, I'll take my lady anywhere," and winked at me, and I didn't even know him well then!

I could see Swee was jealous of me, Wayne was so easy-going, and Sandy could see that also. So we went.

That was my first time on a long bike ride. Sandy never offered me a ride — he told Swee I was too unpredictable, it was better I got other transportation.

My heart went boom, boom, boom, like the motorbike when Wayne kicked the starter and turned on the engine, vroom-vroom, vroom-vroom! I climbed behind Wayne. I felt five feet from the ground, but when we passed the cars, the trucks, and buses, I knew we were closer to the road than I thought. I could not look into the cabs of the trailer trucks. I saw only the big wheels turning and turning as Wayne raced them. "Whee!" he screamed into the wind whenever we passed a trailer truck.

We stopped and waited at the park entrance for Sandy and Swee. It was quiet there, no cars, only trash cans with lids fallen off, stuffed with garbage, beer bottles on the ground, and the parking sign was full of holes. "Target shooting," Wayne said. "Must be teenagers."

I took off the helmet and lay on the picnic bench — rough wood and splinters like people kicked against it — and looked up at the trees. Their leaves were clean green and dancing like my blood still dancing in my head from the ride. Wayne was working on the bike, polishing black and steel chrome, when Sandy and Swee rode up.

Boy, was Swee angry! She came up and bent down and whispered, "Tell him not to race!" Her face was white. I knew then Swee was afraid to lose me to Wayne.

We walked down a path, following Sandy. The trees suddenly closed up and it became dark, only a little blue between branches, like blue pinpricks. It was cold and the quiet was different, as if someone waiting for me to make a noise, and I thought I must be very quiet because something hunting us. The path disappeared, and we were stepping between bushes and branches and rocks, around trunks and rough grass. I could hear Wayne breathing behind me. He breathed loudly, like the way he talked, shush, shush, as if diving in water. I thought he'd better be quieter or he would attract a shark. But this was a forest, Swee said, so I saw not shark but wolf, bear, lion, even a wilder animal, like in our children's books — Minotaur, Centaur, Cyclop.

Sandy walked in front. Sometimes he stopped and looked carefully at a tree. I watched him checking a pile of rocks and turn right. Then, sunshine hot in clearing. Trees ended and the cars began. I didn't know how they got there. Many were junks, broken windshields, no tires, engines rusting without bodies. They looked like dead people — so long dead I wasn't scared of them. Sandy whistled a tune. He whistled same tune three, four times, and I saw a mobile home between the junk cars. It looked just like another piece of junk, unpainted, steel, and it was shut tight.

The door opened and a man came out. He was wearing a green and black uniform — "camouflage," Wayne said — and he had a long stick in his hand. In only a second I knew it was a rifle. The sun was very hot and I started to sweat.

"Why Sandy bring us here?" I whispered to Swee.

The soldier and Sandy moved away and stood talking for a few minutes. Wayne joined them. His voice was loud and cheerful, but I couldn't hear what he was saying. The soldier was shaking his head, opening his mouth. His teeth looked very long. But he came up with Wayne and Sandy to meet us. His voice was so low it was hard to hear him. He said, "Hello, yeah, uh," and never looked at us.

"This is the terrific teacher I've been telling you about!" Sandy said to Swee, "Keith." He did not tell us his full name, and the soldier did not shake our hands. He was older than Wayne, his hair thinner, brown, not blond. He looked like someone who used to be fat, who exercised a lot and became hard, but his paunch was still hanging out. Lines ran everywhere on his face, and his goatee was almost all gray. He had blue eyes, same as Sandy, and he didn't want to turn them toward us. He didn't want us to come into his mobile home.

Swee had to use bathroom, and he pointed to wooden outhouse with a plank door and metal latch. I couldn't go — I thought of the hole in the outhouse, black and purple, smelly, maybe with snakes, scorpions, and centipedes hiding in the knotholes, and my stomach cramped tight. But I followed Swee and waited by door for her. I saw blurry worn-out red and black swastika painted on the side. The rain and sun had tried to make it disappear.

I didn't have time to show Swee the swastika when she stepped out. Instead we stared at the woman who had come from the steel house. She was like mountain of red flesh and freckles, red hair and green clothes. She said, "Gook girls," and didn't smile. She looked offended although we hadn't called her names. "Sluts," she said. "What d'ya mean bringing your hos here?" I saw she was younger than us. She was only a large girl. The soldier must be her father or grandfather. But she was very serious, very angry, like a grandmother or mother.

Sandy was shrugging and backing away like he was seeing the Minatour — a baby monster he couldn't beat up. Wayne put his arm around me and winked. "We're out of here, babes," he said and we were back in the forest, tramping down brown bushes in the trail between the trees.

Swee borrowed a book from the Buenavista library about the Angeles National Forest. "That's the pinon tree we saw, and here is the other kind, the live oak!" she pointed to the illustrations. "And those crackly bushes, those were manzanita." It was her way of trying to understand what happened. To find the names of things she saw there that Sunday from a picture book.

I didn't tell her about the swastika, so badly drawn, crooked and wrong way pointing. I knew it was a bad sign in America. But I also knew its real name. Buddhists painted *Wan'zi* on Buddha's palms and soles. Sign for right motion, Ah Chee taught us. And on Buddha's chest, sign of enlightenment. The clearing and junk cars, the soldier and his rifle, even bad-tempered red-haired mountain woman may be like a kind of enlightenment for Swee and me.

Nine

Swee and Sandy were quarrelling all the time. "They're not your friends," she said. "How can you think of Keith as a hero? And you say she's his wife? She's younger than me — just a kid."

"They're my kind of people. Not her. Never met her before. She's nuts. But Keith doesn't use that kind of language. You can't blame him for her."

Round and round they chased each other. Soon like I could end their sentences. Like rehearsing for school play, only my literature teacher at Methodist School would never put on this play. She liked Shakespeare. "Merchant of Venice." "Romeo and Juliet." "All's Well That Ends Well." Swee and Sandy were boring. Same-o same-o fight everyday.

"Aiyah, you help!" I told Wayne. "Make them girlfriend boyfriend again."

"No way!" He was taking me on bike ride, "Just for the hell of it," he said, and this time we went slow on Mulholland and stopped to look at traffic on the Freeway. It wasn't dark , 6 pm, but already the cars had lights on. Everything looked dusty, yellow, the sun still fierce but so low I knew its time was up.

Swee hated it when I stayed out with Wayne at night. She told me about condoms and birth control pills like I didn't know already. After all, I was Eldest Sister. Wayne was eight years older than Sandy. He was also Older Brother.

We sat close together, the engine hot between our legs, and I stared where Wayne pointed out Wilshire and Melrose, "the bunch of colored lights out there. But you don't want to be cruising there, it's all yuppies flashing their Mercedes and BMWs."

Wayne wanted to move to Venice. "Remember Pete, the owner of the tavern? He's real sick and at the Veterans' Hospital — but he wants to hang on to his burg — it's rent control — and I can sublet it for just the rental. He told the landlord his brother's moving in to take care of the place till he's ready to leave the hospital. That's me. But the doctors say it may be months before they find what's wrong with him and clear it up."

Sandy and Swee quarreled over me. I heard them in the kitchen when they thought I was watching TV in the next room. I listened with the TV on because my special ears could turn TV sound off and on. I learned the trick at home when Ah Kong, Mama or Ah Chee would go on and on, nag, nag, nag. I clicked off their switch and turned antennae in different direction and listened to leaves brush, brush in the garden or Swee humming in bathroom. Now I left the TV on loud so they felt safe to fight over me, and I turned my head till my ears could follow what they said.

"I'd let her move in with Wayne."

"She's not your sister."

"She's supposed to be independent."

"She is independent!"

"Not so long as she is living with you. She has to learn to live alone."

"That's your definition of independence."

"We could find a place just for us."

I heard the rustle and I knew Sandy had grabbed Swee. He used his body to persuade her. I did not want to imagine what Swee must feel.

Sandy wanted to take my place with Swee. He didn't understand it was impossible. We were Wings, we didn't have to express our feelings for each other the way Americans did. What Swee and I owed each other Sandy could only beg for.

But, still, I felt bad, because I knew Swee was worrying for Mama. "What happens when Mama finds out about Wayne and you?" she asked.

"Wah, she not find out about you and Sandy?" I talked back. But Mama never worried about Swee. Swee was always the smart daughter, sure to do well no matter what. Only I was the nuisance daughter, the oldest one, headache for Ah Kong.

This time I agreed with Sandy. Pete's house in Venice very sweet. "Funky bungalow," Wayne said. It had two small bedrooms, and outside the front room a big porch stacked with different kinds of wood. "He sold driftwood, just picked up these dried-up sticks from the dunes up north, polished and shellacked them and sold them to the tourist shops as beach art." I liked that idea. Working by walking on beach. I could do that also. I didn't know how to tell Swee she was right, but Sandy more right this time.

"Let's ride to Pete's," Wayne said to Sandy. It was Friday and Swee had no work the next morning. Next week was Labor Day. She said she would quit selling make-up after Labor Day so she could finish her degree quick quick and transfer to a university after December. She told me she already learned in three months everything about being ordinary worker. "No one cares. You're just a nobody. This work has no meaning." Now she found something with more meaning.

"My game plan," she said grandly to Sandy when she quarreled with him. "You're smart! You don't have to stay at the Wayfarer Inn as long as you have. The *LA Times* says the aerospace industry is dying in California." She shook the newspapers at him like it was baby rattle and he supposed to reach for it.

"Uh uh!" Sandy said to Wayne.

They shared this special American language. Like the shorthand Mama wanted me to study last year. "See Weena learn shorthand, become ex-e-ku-teev sec-era-ta-ry!" Mama didn't add Weena also Paul's mistress, working in his office. Weena not lose face because Paul was a big shot consular. Sandy and Wayne's shorthand was like Weena's way, a way to reach the top. They kept their thoughts away from us but open to others like them, buddies, brothers, pals, the good guys, regulars, the gang, bikers.

"Friday's the night the 260 rollers eat there." It was like Wayne had given Sandy a secret sign. "Mama-san will be there.'

Sandy got up from the sofa where he was watching news on television and hollered, "Sue-ee, let's go eat!" only his voice was make-believe, playing cowboy and cowgirl.

I didn't know the bar room would be so smoky and dirty. First I thought we were the only women there. So many men in black and blue clothes, blue jeans, denim shirts, black leather jackets, cigarettes and ash dropping off their lips like snot, big mugs of beer on the tables. Even Wayne and Sandy wore black clothes that night. It was like a funeral, except Wayne said it was a party. Then I saw the other women. They dressed just like the men, only they were smaller and hair longer. Red, brown, blond. They looked up when we walked in. The noise went down as if the show about to begin. I felt eyes stab, stab — like the eyes at the mall when I went into the store and no one come to serve me. Swee said I just imagined everything, but here she knew what I saw. Then they turned to each other and started talking again, very loud. Blare, blare, blare. Someone played the jukebox: guitar chords and a woman's voice singing Sandy's favorite music, country music, he told us, the Grand Opry, he listened to in Dusseldorf, Seoul, and Subic Bay. He played the records he'd bought at the PXs all around the world for us.

It was so dark I tripped and Wayne held my elbow until we got to bar counter. The bartender was a woman, a Chinese woman! I was so excited I sat on a stool and I smiled. "Mama-san," Wayne said, but she didn't say hello to me.

"So, that's where you've been!" Mama-san gave Wayne big friendly grin. She wiped her hands on short skirt, filled mug under beer tap, and pushed forward to Wayne.

Her long hair dripped into beer puddle under the tap. Swee sat next to me.

"Mama-san, remember my pal, Sandy?"

Mama-san turned to look at Sandy.

"Pinny!" Swee's voice was funny, like she was choking and squealing at same time.

"You know her?" Sandy sounded not happy.

Mama-san stared at Swee. "Wrong person. No Pinny here."

"Hong Nga. Betty!"

"Betty, that's it!" Wayne laughed. "Where d'you two meet? Not at Buenavista I'll bet."

This time Mama-san didn't smile. She tried to look dignified. "We were classmates in better college than Buenavista. Buenavista is a lousy college."

"Hey, that's my college!" Sandy interrupted.

Swee was quiet all this time.

"A pitcher of draft. . . ." "Mama-san, we're getting thirsty!"

Mama-san had to leave us. I saw she was tall for a Chinese girl but still short compared to the women crowded in the room. Her thighs were white, like those suds sloshing in the pitcher, and she had big breasts, just like headlights jiggling through the black leather jackets.

"Mama-san speaks good English for a Vietnamese woman," Wayne said to Swee while he chomped on salted pretzel sticks. "The place has the cheapest beer in town and the best pho, but the pho doesn't get served till after 11, so if you want to eat it you have to drink first."

"The bar is crawling with Nam vets," Sandy said. "Pete was at Danang in '70. He was willing to go back and beat up the Commies in Saigon. We should have never lost the war." The war was over by the time Sandy signed up, but he talked like he was there.

Wayne grinned. He never talked about the war the way Sandy did. I tried to think of Wayne as a GI in Vietnam. Whenever I asked him, he said, "You were only a baby when we landed. Why talk about it now?"

But I saw now Wayne was still in the war. Everyone knew his story at Pete's. He and Pete were caught in the same fire once although on different patrols, and they were both dragged out and laid up in same field hospital. "I got a piece of shrapnel in my butt — it was our own shrapnel — but Pete caught a bullet through his belly, sort of embarrassing — it hurt us to sit so we walked around the whole damn camp. We were the most ambulatory. Did a lot of r & r, that kind of thing."

Sandy was listening to Wayne like he was in church. They forgot to find a table and we stayed at the counter.

Swee was talking to Mama-san. Who to listen to? They were all talking at the same time, and I wanted to listen to everyone. I kept my special ears on Wayne. It was so noisy he thought I couldn't hear.

"He's back at the veterans' hospital. Diabetes and now gangrene. Nothing to do with the bullet in Nam. They're cutting him up, but the docs are more concerned about his lungs. Cancer." They shook their heads like tonight was a funeral, a future funeral for Pete.

"He doesn't like Keith and George. They tried to run a meeting here, get the guys stirred up about the Mexicans coming in across the border. But we've got brown vets and black vets. That kind of stuff doesn't fly here. Besides, Mama-san is his lady. He doesn't go for the Aryan Pride talk."

I thought this Pete must be the friend with the house in Venice. I looked at Mama-san. Maybe she would not want Wayne to have Pete's house. Or maybe she would stay in the house with Wayne. I tried not to think about this.

Swee and Mama-san were polite to each other. I saw Mama-san make a face trying to smile, "Two years in Long Beach, plenty good times!"

Swee's face was like wood. That was how she looked when she had to lie. She could not have any expression because otherwise she would look ashamed.

"A coincidence," she said, introducing me. "Of course, all roads lead to California. Pinny, I mean Betty, says she's from Saigon. She came out during the time of the evacuation. In fact she swears she saw Wayne flying his helicopter on that day when she was trying to get in through the doors of another helicopter."

"Of course he don't remember!" Mama-san laughed. Her long clunky earrings hit against her cheeks. I saw her black hair caught in the earrings. She shook my hands and I smelt the perfume she left behind on my palms, the strong bitter patchouli the hippie college girls bought from the pharmacy.

"You Swee Wing's sister? I'm also her sister — at that college in New York. Yes, Swee, remember my birthday party? You gave me a nice scarf I still keep. Red and gold, like Vietnamese New Year. You know, Vietnamese have many same festivals like the Chinese. Vietnamese New Year is Tet. Vietnamese and Chinese are like long-time family, share many things together. Many Chinese live for a long time in Saigon. We left Saigon in a hurry because when Americans leave, Communism comes in. We are loyal to democracy. We hate Vietcong, hate Ho Chi Min. . . ."

Mama-san was talking very quickly but Swee had same wooden look on her face.

"You cannot be Swee's sister," I interrupted. "She already has two sisters. If you're her sister, you also my sister, and I'm not sure I want you."

Swee smiled but poked me like she was disapproving. "Betty means it in a metaphorical way."

I didn't understand "metaphorical." I knew Mama would faint if her daughter took a job in a bar. Ah Kong would have killed her. Swee wrote to Mama she was temping at a pharmacy, but she made it sound like medical training. Mama thought Swee was studying to be a doctor.

Mama-san tossed her hair. I saw a horse, a woman horse, a mare tossing its mane. I expected her to gallop off, neigh, neigh, but she filled up more pitchers from the taps, then wiped down the counter, singing with the juke box, "down the road I look and there stands Mareeeee. . . ."

So many people were singing with her it sounded like the Methodist church choir except everyone was holding onto a beer. Soon everyone except Swee and me was singing, "green greeeeen graaaass of hoooome!" I couldn't hear anything but the voices, trying to rise louder than the others. Across the bar room Wayne and Sandy were singing along, their eyes shining. They were in love, I thought, just like everyone in the room, only I didn't know what they were in love with.

"No, I don't want to stay for the pho!" Swee was being prickly. When she was like that I stayed away.

"Bad news," I told Wayne, "better if we leave now."

"Aw, I haven't had Mama-san's pho for a couple of months. Come on, Yen, you'll like it. It's addictive. All that beef and tendon, it puts hair on the chest." He took my hand and rubbed it on his chest and sighed loudly "Aaaahh!"

My stomach rumbled and I laughed.

But Swee gave me a dirty look. It said, "Don't you dare!" It was telling me, "I am counting on you."

I decided I also didn't like Pete's Tavern. I coughed and coughed. "Too much smoke, I cannot eat," I said, waving my hands in front of my face. "You want you can come back and eat pho with Sandy." I knew Wayne was too much a gentleman, he would not leave me for the night.

But Sandy was sullen. He walked quickly out of the door and Swee had to trot after him. I couldn't tell his black leather jacket from the others. Mama-san was slow taking Wayne's money and we hurried after them.

They were still arguing where the bikes were parked. Wah! Must be one hundred or more. Not only Harleys. I saw Japanese names like Suzuki, Kawasaki, and Honda and fancy European names like Ducati. They were new looking, shining bright steel, straight and curved and curled, parked in rows like in grown-up toyshop. I could see why Sandy and Wayne loved their Harleys; Harleys stood out like the biggest presents in shop.

"Swee is not bossy!" I disagreed with Wayne while we waited for them to finish their argument. "She has a strong mind. She has beliefs. Not like me. Swee says I'm like water and wind. I flow where the lowest pressure is, follow path of least resistance. That's why I cry so easy. Water and wind become tears, flow down my face. I cry at nothing. But Swee is like earth and fire.

She is hard. You must dig and dig to follow her thinking. And she is hot, very fierce, can burn you if you're not careful!"

"Uh, uh!" Wayne wrapped his arms around me. "Give me water and wind any day. So soft and nice." He blew into my ear. His breath tickled my neck and face, and I felt myself go wet and easy, like the waves on my legs when we walked on the beach, one wave after another, breaking between my legs until I was impatient and wanted to jump into the surf to feel something big and strong wash over me. Wayne knew what I was feeling. He pressed his big strong body on me as he held me in front of him. I felt like a little doll a big boy was holding and I wanted the boy to do anything he wanted with me.

Then I heard flapping above. Was it bats? I was always afraid of bats, flying squirrels, flying foxes, flying cockroaches, every night flap-flaping wings, things not animal not bird, belonging with vampires. A big furry thing got into my room one night, rush, rushing around the lamp, and Ah Chee had to take a broom to frighten it out the window. I was no use, screaming and screaming. She told Mama I was mad, to be afraid of a bat Chinese knew meant happiness, to scream at happiness.

I looked up and saw it was the American flag, just like the one at Buenavista College, only on short flagstaff. It was blowing in the wind, snapping loud slapping noises against the wood like straining to blow away.

"That's the Santa Ana," Wayne said, letting me go. "Some call it the devil wind, coming from the mountains and heading for the Pacific. It dries everything in its path, sucks up the moisture. Makes good firewood out of Californian timberland."

I remembered our hurry-hurry walk in the wild Angeles Forest last week. "You think that mountain girl in the forest park hate us?"

"D'you mean, what do I think of her? You know you'll never be a slut or a whore to me. You're too good for me, never mind where you're from."

Funny, I wanted to believe him. I wanted to say, "You swear? You swear with the American flag flying above you?"

But Swee was hurrying up to us. "Sandy says we'd better leave now. The wind is kicking up and it won't be safe riding if it gets stronger."

I looked at Wayne who looked at me. But I was not ready to tell Swee anything. I was not ready to leave her.

Ten

I was tired of eavesdropping. Sandy and Swee become such a knotted couple they forgot I was also living in the apartment and could hear them fight.

Sometimes I thought Sandy tired of Swee. He stopped asking to move in with us and spent more and more time with his friends. He received welding certificate, but he also still working at Wayfarer Inn. "There's more security. They've put me on a pension scheme, and I'm going to be promoted to manager when Bob retires to Arizona," he told Swee when she asked about his change in plans.

Keith invited him to teach next welding class with him because his partner George moved to Michigan. "There's a kind of commune out near Ann Arbor. Farmers, truck drivers, university dropouts, you'd be surprised at the kinds of people that show up there. Even some professors come to the meetings. It's not a dope place like those sixties hippie places in San Francisco. Everyone's properly married, does a job. George takes care of the heating system at the university." Sandy said when George phoned Keith, he told stories about how commie the university was. "It's all about race quotas, black rights, women's liberation, bilingual education. Except for those professors in the commune. They bring books and articles, and they give talks on American history. They prove how screwed up America has become from what the Founding Fathers intended."

Sometimes Swee was on best behavior. She kept head down pretending to listen and tried to keep her face clean. "Inscrutable, I hate that!" Sandy muttered. But better that way. No words, no quarrels.

But sometimes she couldn't hold herself in anymore and decided to act for a change. Then I thought it was Swee who was tired of Sandy.

In the beginning of fall classes, she stopped working at the pharmacy, gave one week's notice. "Mr Pearson was disappointed. He said he could always trust me not to steal anything, there weren't many employees he could feel that confident about. Faye didn't care. She said she wondered why I even wanted to work at Cosmetics because I didn't use enough make-up anyway. It was bad for business to have me in sales."

Sandy didn't have to come in morning to take Swee to work, and she asked for apartment key back. "Yen and I'll walk together to Buenavista. It will be good exercise. You can always call before you come."

Sandy was confused, he didn't know whether to be angry or sad. He said, "I'll keep it. You can never tell, you might lose your key. Then you'll be glad you gave me the spare."

"But I don't want you coming without calling first. Especially after your welding night classes!" Swee's voice jumped up. She was telling him she didn't want him if he was going to be with Keith, to become like Keith, only Sandy didn't understand her.

"Don't worry, I'll go to Pete's where I can find something to eat and some people who'll want to talk to me!"

It was like this for weeks. Slam, slam, slam! Doors banging shut day after day. I wondered they still together.

After all, everyone we knew moving away or already moved — to Arizona, Nevada and Michigan, like men in Sandy's group, or from Solvang to Long Beach, like Sandy. Swee and I doing the same thing as everyone else, moving from Malacca to Los Angeles. Long Beach, Wayne said, not Los Angeles, but I didn't care. Everyone in Malacca knew Los Angeles. How to say "Long Beach" to people in Malacca? It was like saying the moon.

Wayne said Americans moved so often they must find new ways home over and over again. "After a couple of times they stop making an effort to know anybody where they live. They're going to move out anyway, or the people next door are going to move away. Keep your energy for the late night show. At least you get entertained there." He never said where he'd moved from, "It's too boring to talk about." He was like Sandy. They didn't want us to know who they were before they met us. Or they didn't want where they were before they met us to know who we were.

Wayne predicted Sandy and Swee break up soon.

Perhaps Wayne and me kept them together. Wayne worked regular hours, not like Sandy. "No more grease monkey," he said, grinning, after he got surprise promotion to flight manager. "I make the decisions on who can go up, who can come down, and when and where. That's what I get for taking those computer programming classes."

"But what has computer programs to do with airplanes flying?" I asked, and Wayne cracked up.

"The world's changing, babe," he tapped finger to forehead. "All the wars are going to take place up here. It's finally going to be like we always knew it to be. Soldiers don't fight wars. Ideas fight wars. Ideas sneaking up like stealth bombers. Ideas like coordinates and heat-seekers, smart bombs and ultra-light vision. America's got the world by the balls because we own these ideas. If there's another war, I can get to be a warrior no matter how old I am, because I have these ideas here," he tapped his head again, his smile as big as the sun.

Swee was still disapproving, but by now she had given up. She couldn't be a good example, and she was smart enough not to be a hypocrite.

Wayne was careful not to insult her. We did it only when Swee was out of the apartment or in his bed where I could make as much noise as I liked. He said I was like steam engine train, I went hoo-hooo-hoooo when I wasn't thinking anymore. "Babe, babe!" he said. He groaned and groaned like an old man, so we were like Jack Spratt and his wife. We were young and old, yin and yang, and we licked the platter clean.

Wayne said I was different from his other girlfriends, I wasn't shy in his bed. But why be shy? "Sex is the reason why there are so many people in the world," I told him. "Must be countless times humans have fucked on earth," I said.

He was shocked. He said I shouldn't use that word, Americans would think I was that other kind of Asian woman. "*Fucked*," he was serious, "real women don't use that word. Men only use it to swear. It's a cuss word. You should understand that better than American women do. You'll lose face, you know, really lose face, big-time!"

Wayne learned about losing face in Vietnam. He had nice Vietnamese girlfriend in village north of Saigon, daughter of rich landlord, just back for holidays from France where she was college student.

The girlfriend was young and pretty like me, but when her father found out, he made a big fuss with Wayne's unit commander. "Loss of face," captain said to Wayne, "these Asians don't want their daughters dating American soldiers, even pilots. It's the race thing. White isn't acceptable." Next thing Wayne knew, the girl was sent back to France. Then he got a letter she married a Vietnamese student also studying in Paris. "I don't know what she thought sex was. It was just hands and mouths. I wasn't allowed in, you know, all the way in."

Poor Wayne, I said, and we stayed in bed longer. But later I thought about his story. He was telling me he wanted me to be like the first girlfriend, keep face, but also to let him in. I didn't know how to do both.

Sometimes we went on double dates with Swee and Sandy on Saturday. Swee was almost finished with her Associate degree. She decided Communications was the best subject for her. "I'll transfer to UCLA. Or to Berkeley," she said. "What do you think of San Francisco, Yen?" She brought home books about Berkeley, San Francisco, the John Muir Redwood Forest. She read about the building of the Golden Gate Bridge, the Temple of Fine Arts, the history of Chinatown. I knew she had decided to go to Berkeley.

She left the books in my bedroom, for me to read, she said,

but so Sandy wouldn't find them. She was keeping secrets from him, but I thought this was her revenge because Sandy began the whole thing about secrecy.

"I can't tell you where," he said to Swee when he went away for a weekend. "It's with Keith and some of the guys. You know I'm not going to mess with a woman."

He thought Swee was jealous, but that was because Sandy didn't understand Swee. She lived in her head. She was not jealous of bodies, only of ideas, if others had ideas she didn't, that she should have.

Swee never explained herself to Sandy. She believed Sandy wouldn't understand. Sometimes I felt sorry for him. Swee treated him like she treated me. She loved us, but because she was cleverer, she tolerated us, and tolerance meant she forgot she really loved us.

"Love is stupid," I told Swee when she asked me what I saw in Wayne.

"His crude jokes! This is the most he will ever be!" and she gave a shudder, like when she saw a spider or cockroach.

"Cockroaches survive longer on earth than humans," I told her, but this time, it was she who didn't understand.

Sandy's secrecy irritated her. It irritated her so much I thought she was frightened.

His promotion also came through, but unlike Wayne, Sandy was disappointed. "It's just more of the same thing. More of the responsibility. More drunks at night, more hysterical women, finding a doctor for a heart attack, throwing out the hookers, chasing deadbeats trying to sneak away at 3 am, keeping the vagrants from stinking up the john." Sandy now manager for nightshift, five nights a week, but he made it sound like being warden in a madhouse.

Swee decided she was going to get many, many As so she could get into Berkeley, and she took classes all day and studied all night. When they met they were tired, one ready for sleep and one just up from sleep.

One time they connected was when she was writing a paper

on code communication. She was doing research on wartime codes, cryptography, she said it slowly for me. Buenavista College library had no books on the topic, so Sandy offered to take her to the Los Angeles County Library to check out the books. They returned on the motorbike laughing like the schoolchildren who stole oranges from Mrs Mendez's yard on the corner, two big shopping bags of books balanced on the bike between them.

They read the books together, Swee showing Sandy parts she liked, and Sandy reading important pages to her. He dug out a lot about espionage, how urgent information gathered and sent to enemy, using homing pigeons, traveling salesmen, newspaper notices, radio broadcasts, and what-not surrounding people everyday but no one had any idea these all carried secret messages. He told Swee about hidden machinery of war and described different kinds of victories, from Greek times to Cold War.

Wah, then I saw what Swee said about Sandy was true. Sandy had good brains, one very smart mind. Only I still could not understand why he was nowhere in life. Just like Ah Kong would think, I wondered why Sandy was not in good job, was not BA, MBA, like our Wing brothers. Swee so smart she could see how brainy Sandy really was, but I told Wayne brains proved nothing if Sandy wasted his life. "Loser," I said, "brainy loser."

Sandy and Swee concentrated on writing about "the evolution of encryption." "How ciphers, codes of communication, have changed in order to remain secret; becoming more and more complicated, devious, disguised, camouflaged, concealed, hidden, obscure, veiled, masked, mysterious, invisible," she wrote in her term paper. Of course she got A for the course.

"We do get along!" she explained. "Sandy can think very well when it is something that interests him. He put in as much into the paper as I did. I just put into words a lot of what we discussed."

She had this aura I had not seen in her for a long time. Not since the first time she left for America. It was confidence, or hope. When Swee came home after first year in America, Ah

Chee said Swee stopped being a girl in New York. "Not good," she complained to Mama, "Swee think like woman now. Husbands always want young girl, but she finish — no more young."

For once Mama talked back to Ah Chee. "Nonsense, Swee is nineteen, she is still young."

But I thought Ah Chee meant Swee had lost belief in future, what Americans called optimism. After New York, she was always expecting not good things to happen. But when Sandy worked with her on the military espionage research, she got some of her aura back. They read, laughed, ate tortilla chips, they got serious, telling each other how America cracked the Japanese code in 1940 and how important the Navajo language was in winning the war.

This was when we were double dating. Swee wanted us to ride to San Francisco, but there was this invisible boundary for Sandy. He wouldn't go further north than Santa Barbara. "I'll take you to Sea World and Gas Town in San Diego," he said. "I don't like San Francisco. We got more bikers down south than north."

He got impatient with Swee in Santa Barbara. She wanted to find the graves of the Chumash Indians at the Mission cemetery. "They must be here," she said, reading the words on the stones in the garden. Perhaps not a garden because there must be more bones than roots in it. "There were thousands of Chumash working at the Mission, and only a few rich Spanish padres and landowners." She looked at the Spanish names, name after name. "They must be buried here, jumbled in a corner, without a stone. Too many for headstones!" She walked around the garden one more time.

She got me to thinking I was breathing dead bodies, Indian bodies, thousands of them tumbled into giant pit somewhere in this small plot. Wayne grabbed my hand and pulled me out of the gate as I was choking.

"Forget the Indians!" Sandy said. He was so loud a couple of other tourists followed us out of the Mission cemetery. "Let's get out of here!" He slammed the gate behind him. Wayne and I pretended not to notice his bad mood. We sat with him on the fountain wall and counted the money in the water: lots of pennies, some dimes, no quarters.

"The tourists here are cheap," I said.

"I'm giving no quarters," Wayne said and threw two pennies in.

"One penny for you, one for me?" I asked.

Suddenly I remembered Ah Kong. Ah Kong would never throw pennies into a fountain, I thought, not even when he was a young man. And if he had to show his money, he made sure to show a lot of it. Thousands of dollars for someone's funeral. Double thousands for association benefits. Wayne was still younger than Ah Kong was when he met Mama, but he would never have Ah Kong's power. For Ah Kong, a penny was too small to give even to beggars, and Wayne just tossed one for me.

Swee came walking slowly. She must have noticed Sandy scowling, even in shade of the trees. She hated this kind of scene. Like Ah Kong, Swee carried a lot of face. In her spirit was Mama's wish to give a son to Ah Kong. She would do anything to show she wasn't weak, even bite her tongue. She would pretend nothing happened, that Sandy behaving nicely. But I saw her dimming although her smile grew brighter. I felt so sad for her. The more she smiled the sadder I became.

"Look, I bought a Saint Christopher for you," she said to Sandy and gave him a medallion. "We can clip it on to the sissy bar."

"You not buy one for Wayne?" I asked. "Why Sandy so special?"

"I've a Virgin Mary one for you and Wayne," she said, giving the metal circle to me.

Wayne laughed. "Virgin Mary? What's the message?"

"I thought you were anti-religion," Sandy said. He looked calmer. They walked to the bike and I didn't want to hear what Swee was saying to Sandy. I could not bear to hear her give up her face to keep him happy.

And that was before Sandy went off on his first trip with Keith. Soon we didn't double date anymore, because Sandy was gone every Sunday. He left before noon and came back late Sunday night, and we got to see him on Saturdays when he came to take Swee riding.

He tried not to tell us what he did on Sundays. "Oh, we ride about. It's like a paper chase. Every road trip we have a new set of directions, we go someplace new. It's a way to see America like most people have never seen it."

"Do you have to go alone? None of the bikers are allowed to have passengers?" Swee was not begging to come along. She was curious and afraid. Her mind was like a tax collector. Ah Kong always said tax collectors in Singapore needed to know everything because they worked for the government, and the government would fire them if they didn't find who was lying and who telling the truth. Swee didn't know Sandy's secret, what the truth was, and she was afraid something else bigger was in picture, something pushing her out of Sandy's life.

"I told you there's a brotherhood of silence we have to observe. A brotherhood, get it? We don't have women on these rides."

"But who makes up the paper chase?" she asked. "Do you know the paper chase began as a horse and hound chase? Fox hunting, to provide riding thrills for the aristocracy in Britain?" — I saw Sandy already stopped listening — " They'd go chasing a little red fox with packs of baying dogs, whipping their horses with riding crops, till the fox gets tired out and the harriers tear the poor animal to bits of fur. Then they return to their mansions to eat huge suppers and feed their hounds large bones as reward for a good day's work!"

"Guns are legal here, Sue, and we don't need hounds and horses to do our hunting for us." Sandy quickly drank his coffee, trying to make nice because he liked to have a quiet Sunday breakfast.

He enjoyed making breakfast for himself in our apartment. That's what he missed most about his free room at Wayfarer Inn, not having a kitchen. He made a big drip pot of coffee, the

Austrian way he said, with fresh cream, "No half-and-half", and fresh-baked pastries he got from the bakery at the Crossroads Chapel Mall. "They're not as good as my mother's. Her strudels were the best thing about the weekends." He said this almost every time he took the apple fritters and raisin buns out of the white paper bag.

Swee and I didn't eat much breakfast. Besides, sweet things are bad for you first thing in the day. You need salt, hot water, rice — chok, buns, fried noodles, even leftovers. Swee forced herself to eat sugary food with Sandy. As long as she did this, I knew she still holding on to some hope for herself and Sandy.

This morning she didn't eat the fritter. The caramel frosting cracking over it like brown plaster, and she crumbled it with her fingers.

"Guns? Do you ride with guns? Riding shot-gun?"

Sandy looked annoyed. "I was speaking abstractly." He returned to her comments. "This paper chase, if you change it to a hunt, you have to know who you are, whether you're the hound or the fox. You shouldn't assume anything. Depending on whether you're dog or fox, you'll have to have a different strategy to find a foxhole. The military trained us to think like foxes. We don't like those hound-dogs!"

"So, are all the bikers vets like you?" Swee drank Sandy's Austrian coffee. She was studying for finals next week. She rinsed her insides with coffee every hour. I warned her she'd turn into a rusty coffeepot, but she said I fussed with her because I didn't want to study for my exams and write my papers.

"I told you Keith never signed up. He was married by the time Nam came along, four kids to raise."

"That girl his daughter?" I asked.

Sandy got up to wash his cup. Being manager of a motel made him tidy. "I have to fill the bike with gas." He looked at Swee as if he was waiting at a traffic light. "D'you want me to come by tonight?"

She looked back at him and I knew she was seeing that soldier with same blue eyes as Sandy's. She saw Sandy — her good friend, her boyfriend — and she saw the soldier. "I don't know," she said, but he thought this was her answer and his face got tight.

"I'll call you when we get back." For the first time he didn't give her a hug.

She went to the window, I thought to watch him walk to the bike, but she pulled down the glass. She didn't want to hear the spark plugs gun up as he pumped the bike full of gas.

Eleven

At first I didn't know when to tell my sisters we were in South LA, only miles from their last address in Long Beach. After so much time, I was still angry with Yen for her lascivious words, shaming me before Robert. Yes, I was relieved when Swee took Yen away to America, but I had suffered — again! — because she had chosen Yen before me. I could still hear Swee that morning when she spoke out, defending Yen, her face shades pinker than Yen's, as if her mind, which Mama warned was bound to get her into trouble, was also a rosy power. Swee's mind always sharpened her eyes. It curled her lips and made her head crooked with unnecessary talk.

Although not two years younger than Swee, I had been born too late for my sisters to take me into their lives. Their time together before I was born was like preset concrete, fused into a foundation, and my birth was an accident, not essential to either.

Until that Sunday I'd believed I was more like Swee than Yen was. We even looked more like sisters, unlike Yen who with her lean lanky haunches, gangly arms and long thin torso looked exactly like an unhealthy, voracious appetite. Swee and I were shorter, but we were well proportioned and we shared Mama's crescent lips and earnest eyes. True, Swee was more vigorous. She seemed to enjoy everything more than I could — school, books, swings, arguing, eating. My name reminded everyone I was a pale white to Swee's rose color.

My grievance from as long ago as I could remember lay in Yen. Swee could choose to look ahead or behind, to be with Yen or with me. But she had wanted to grow up faster, to be taller, stronger, bolder. She looked to the horizon and couldn't see me trailing behind her. She went with Yen wherever trouble was to be found, Yen whom Ah Kong disliked because she couldn't control herself, whose mouth outraged modesty and virtue.

My resentments troubled me, but when I spoke to Pastor Fung about these sins, he said I would know to reconcile with my sisters when the time was right. It was the Lord's plan we were doing our work in the same Promised Land where Yen and Swee were studying. Besides, for the first few weeks in Los Angeles I was so busy and tired running the church care groups I took the excuse not to call the number Mama had given me.

After marrying Robert, I began easily to call Pastor Fung "Father," as he requested, and only to speak of him as "Pastor Fung" when I was addressing him publicly or speaking to the Auxiliary League of Church Women. After all, Robert called him "Father," and I followed Robert in most things, great and small. Like me, Robert was quiet and observant. Father called him God's handyman, although from the moment I met them when I was sixteen it was clear to me Robert served as son and mother to the pastor. That was what opened my heart to him. We were both forsaken children, he without mother, brothers and sisters, and I left alone, forgotten, by mine. But the Church gave us more brothers and sisters than we could hope to embrace. True brothers and sisters in life everlasting, not in this life that passes for earthly existence. We'd embraced each other, Robert and I, when I was baptized, and I knew no loneliness after that.

Father said I was Robert's helpmate and a great assistance to both of them. "Who can find a virtuous wife? For her worth is above rubies," he read to me, from Proverbs 31. "She seeks wool and flax, and willingly works with her hands. She is like the merchant ships, she brings her food from afar." He meant this kindly, as praise for the many good deeds we had achieved with the Auxiliary League, but I was uncomfortable with his words. "Mate" had a certain unclean association. Perhaps it was unusual for Robert and me to be cautious in the ways we came together. That first night, Robert was very quiet, so quiet I fell asleep afterwards without asking the questions I should have asked. Which would have been what? Was he happy? Had I been helpful? "She does him good and not evil all the days of her life," the Proverbs instruct us, and I wanted very much to be good for Robert.

Some of the church teachings used the word "helpmeet" instead, a mellifluous word. And so, reading the Scriptures closely, I was able to help Robert meet his pastoral duties, the most important now in this new church being to support Father in his ministry.

The invitation to preach to the Mission of Eternal Light on Vermont and Western Avenues came from Bishop Stonehill, who was visiting the evangelical churches that had been established in Hong Kong, Taiwan, Korea and Malaysia. He told Father the Archbishop had sent him on a search for a minister from the East for the Los Angeles mission because the evangelicals had been particularly active and successful in the Far East. In the Los Angeles mission, the congregation had increased enormously from under 200 to over 2,000 in just five years, and after some consulting, the mother church in New York decided it needed a different kind of pastor, someone who would be closer to the new parishioners than the old pastor who was retiring.

Moving to Sun City, the Bishop said, in just three months. I had a vision of Christ coming down and carrying the pastor clinging to His purple cloak up to heaven. "Our faith in America is now more multicultural than ever," Bishop Stonehill explained as I listened, dazed by the image of the old pastor's fiery ascent, "and the Los Angeles Mission is especially so. You are the person to lead the flock."

Sun City, he later explained, was in Arizona, and the pastor, who had taken to golf as physical therapy when two of his vertebrae had fused, would minister to the retirees in Sun City. He had never been comfortable with the Los Angeles community, and Bishop Stonehill couldn't find another minister in America who was enthusiastic about taking over this ministry.

Later, when I began asking who Father's congregation would be, we discovered that among them they spoke at least twenty-three languages. Over sixty percent of them were, to describe them kindly, the Bishop added, recent immigrants, and about eighty percent of that group in need of all kinds of services — legal, financial, spiritual. They needed help in dealing with landlords, teachers, the police, their employers, banks, their husbands and children — more than seventy percent were women and a majority of them had more than one child.

And of course they all wanted to hear the word of God. That's what brought them to the Mission Sunday after Sunday, clapping their hands to the music, crying their amens, and joining in the hymns the choir hollered, with accents flying off in different directions, returning to the four corners of the globe from which they had come. That was what also brought me to them.

The church building was presently undergoing seismic retrofitting, Bishop Stonehill had told Father at the meeting in Malacca. Father looked puzzled at this, and the Bishop explained California was a land of restless troughs and mountains, where God was called upon to do more work than in most other places. The building, he warned, might be condemned altogether, and the congregation was meeting at a temporary site until they could raise the money for a new building. While Bishop Stonehill spoke to Father, Robert and I listened hungrily, although we remained silent.

It was Father's sanctity, we knew, that had drawn the Bishop to Malacca, just like the scent of the white *bunga tanjong* drew the dusky moths at late evening to the tree's tall foliage. Not Robert or me, young, plain, and green even in God's eyes.

What riches lay on the other side, we said with our expressionless faces to each other. Two thousand parishioners and languages as thick and noisy as in Malaysia! We could help Father, who was too old to learn a new language. We would gladly walk among two thousand worshippers, visit them in their homes, while Father stayed in the Mission, preaching his gentle sermons and occasionally going on his arthritic knees in submission to the One whose spirit he could evoke, whose wings folded over all who stopped to listen to Father preach.

I had found this so. I had heard many testify to Father's genius with words. Let Father speak, we said to each other that day, and we would do for him, actions being weaker than the Word but also necessary.

When I first saw the temporary building, I knew why the Bishop had gone to Asia to find a minister. It was nothing but a storefront. Although the name had been painted out in whitewash, anyone could still read "FELDMAN'S DISCOUNTED FURNITURE BARGAIN PRICES!" on the long signboard above the steel-gated doors.

Father stood silently for a long time in front of the Mission. I could see he was praying. It was hard for me to think about his disappointment. "The new Promised Land!" he had exulted as we were waiting for the flight from Kuala Lumpur to Los Angeles. When Father closed his eyes in prayer after the bishop's invitation, we knew immediately he was going to accept the call. He prayed over every decision, but it was always clear to us how he would decide. His prayers were permission forms sent to God for His signature. Father had a decisive mind, which was why he was so downcast when he discovered the Los Angeles church was not what had been promised him.

Yes, no doubt it was a large church. The number of worshippers, especially after Father's arrival, was rising every month. Parishioners brought their relatives, elderly neighbors, friends, office workers, colleagues. Many had arrived recently from San Salvador, Belize, Guam, the West Indies, the Philippines, Hong Kong, Malaysia, Vietnam, Thailand, and especially Korea. There were even Tamils and Sri Lankans by way of Southeast Asia. Many were women from countries like Mexico, Honduras, and Guatemala, coming without husbands but somehow appearing with children and grown sons, brothers, and brothers-in-law. So many were babies just baptized. So many poor, sick and feeble or simply old and worn. But the Mission also attracted middle class and professionals — Filipino nurses, Korean storekeepers, grocers, and beauticians, Vietnamese video-store managers and restaurant owners, Hmong car-park owners, Mexican plasterers and gardeners, even college students who came from the cheap rental apartment buildings in South LA.

Father said although he sometimes wondered why so many different nations and tongues were coming to the services at the Mission of Eternal Light, the miracle was they each understood how Jesus died to save all souls, brown, black and yellow. There was no color in Heaven, he added, all are dressed in radiant raiment, all are glorious and gorgeous. In Los Angeles, Father's sermons, which had always been in the most interesting English, became even more pronounced. They came out of his mouth like a gush of clear warm water from a spring so unexpected that everyone who listened was moved at the sounds from this small Asian man with white hair and sallow unadorned features. He could open his lips and speak words that went straight to where your feelings had been stored. Like sugar kept away from ants. Suddenly you were weeping and opening up those stores, giving them to the neighbor next to you whose name you did not know, to the son who had not called you in a year, the man who had raped you last Christmas, the woman who was your best friend whom you had found in bed with your husband, your boss who criticized and threatened to write you a bad evaluation even after you'd brought in a big sale or stayed late three Fridays in a row completing his project, the gangbanger who had killed your nephew. Suddenly, all you had stored in bitter thrift, being a steward of your feelings, all came out of you like the wings of the Holy Spirit stirring up a wind and scattering the good and the bad feelings, until you felt cleansed, clean, swept and watered and mopped up good, and you knew now it was not sugar after all, simply the dirt of old things moldering, ashes strewn and in the clean place, a fresh sweet beginning. His sermons did that to his listeners. No one knew how he did this magic except it must be God who spoke through him.

Father had not noticed he had left out white souls among his list of the saved, because there were so few white worshippers at Eternal Light, among which were a handful of drunks trying to sober up on Sunday morning and staying for the social hour. They came for the food the parishioners prepared: tortillas, chili, chicken mole, sapodillas, quesidillas, carnes, eggrolls, lumpia, adobe, shrimp toast, rice sticks, char kway teow, roti, curries, dal, stringhoppers, poi, tapioca, fried and mashed plantains, conch fritters, nasi goreng, roast duck and crackling pig, braised tofu, kimchi, bulgogi and mandu; the desserts of flan, cinnamon-dusted rolls, pumpkin cakes, almond jelly; and fragrant rainbow-colored fruits — mangos, bananas, oranges, papayas, pineapples, guavas, avocados, and cherimoyas. The women were proud of what they provided for the weekly communion meal. No matter how little each had, they brought enough to share. "Feed my flock," Father reminded us when some complained about the drunks who showed up empty-handed every Sunday, and shamed, they brought even more food to the next communion lunch.

"From each, according to his abilities; to each, according to his needs," Father preached, only he should have used the pronoun "her," for it was the women who kept the church going.

And they came to me when they wanted to say something to Father. Mrs Munoz needed a crib and baby towels for her daughter's baby. Bessie's husband had been arrested in an illegal gambling deal — he was a numbers runner and not a congregation member — but she still wanted Father to stand for the bail. Josefina was afraid her three sons had joined a gang, and the youngest boy was only eleven. Sunyit's mother in Pattaya had written to request her return to Thailand, but she had finally found a good job taking care of Mrs Tan's children. And the many, many women with purple and blue flesh where the fists of fathers, brothers, and husbands had landed, red puckered scars where a glass or knife had cut, and deep darkness in eyes in which fears for their babies and themselves crept in to hide.

I seldom went to Father with their problems. He didn't understand women's needs. Their tears and wants made him uncomfortable. I had seen his eyes shift like birds desperate to escape when the women pressed on him after service. To escape from their large bosoms and meaty arms, exposed faces with pouting lips and flushed round cheeks. The church got so hot on Sunday afternoons Father could not ask the women to cover themselves up completely, but I knew he disapproved of the way the young girls dressed in short skirts and tight tops, even of the open-necked embroidered blouses his Guatemalan parishioners wore, revealing coffee-colored flesh gleaming with sweat.

I saw little of Robert in the first year. The men were supposed to go to Robert for advice, and we didn't discuss the different needs between men and women unless we were mediating between a couple having problems. The scriptures we read did not teach much about what husbands and wives should do when they were alone together. Father was our model, and he had been widowed for all the time Robert had been his son, for she — his wife and Robert's mother — had died at childbirth.

Because of his family history, Robert did not want to make me big with child, and we carefully followed the rhythm method. He wrote a record of the days I bled in a small journal he kept in his back pocket, counted the days till the egg was safely dropped from my body, and took the temperature of my aperture to discover when we should be as man and wife. All this discussion had to be carried out in the softest whispers, for Father's bedroom was directly across from ours, and he was a light sleeper.

Such maneuvers meant, of course, we were modest with each other, perhaps especially when we were alone together. Much of our time was spent thinking about how to help Father with his ministry. In this mission, we were truly brother and sister, dividing the pastoral work between us.

Unlike the women worshippers, the men Robert worked with were more exclusive in their fellowship. The San Salvadorans did not usually talk to the Koreans, the Tamils to the Colombians, or even the Taiwanese to the Chinese from the Mainland, although Father treated them all equally when it came time to elect the church elders. He consulted with as many men as he could. When he preached, "You are all heads of your households, and like God our Father, the rule of our church is in your hands," and appealed to the men to volunteer for the Council of Elders, the parishioners nodded their heads, even the women.

Robert said women were easier to mould than men, for we were more agreeable and mixed easily. So many activities brought us together. Sweeping up after the service. Picking up the playground and nursery even as the children continued to clamber over swings and turnabouts. Laundering donated clothes in the two commercial washing machines in the church annex. As the women took out the warm clean sheets, two pairs of hands needed for shaking, squaring, and folding, it was easy to share talk about children, food, sickness, weddings, births, and then the shameful things, the blows, screams, empty larders, the men leaving one after the other.

Thrift pulled them together, thrift and sharing. The women who now had businesses — hairdressing salons, pedicure centers, counter restaurants, convenience stores — remembered when they were poor. They no longer wanted their old things from those days of discounted clothes and furniture, and they gave them away, thanking the Lord for blessing them with prosperity. And other women gladly took their charity. When Father preached, "Blessed are those who give and those who take," the women's "Amens!" were always enthusiastic.

I was Father's girl Friday, and he joked Robert was his man Thursday. With two of us on his team, he was able to compose his sermons on Saturdays and preach well on Sundays. The other days were for active healing. Robert chauffeured him to visit the sick in the hospitals and the shut-ins and elderly at home; sometimes, to pray with a church member in the penitentiary, who'd fallen on the wrong side of the law; and more and more often, to talk to children and teachers in the public schools about spirituality and multiculturalism.

Father worked very hard on the school talks because he was never sure what ages the children would be. Once, he spoke to a third grade class in South Central Los Angeles. He came back in time for tea but so upset he asked for warm cocoa instead. It wasn't the classrooms' crowded conditions that agitated him, for there were only about twenty children in the room. But, as he indignantly described it, about five of the children, drooling, appeared medicated, their heads laid down on their desks. The Central American children had bright eyes, like pieces of fired-up coal he said, but they were shy when he asked them questions. He found they spoke only Spanish, and one mute child, the teacher said, was not really mute but understood only an Indian language from a mountain region and so would not speak. The Hmong student, a pretty girl, gave the best response to his simple request they write on a dream they remembered, but she too had laid her head on her desk, as if she had learned to melt with her drugged classmates into the crazy silence of their classroom. The other half of the children, refusing to give in to muteness, jumped up and down constantly. One asked if she could touch Father's clerical collar. Another ran to and fro, between the desks, until the teacher made him stand on his chair. The teachers whom Father ate lunch with said they deserved combat pay for teaching in the district. Their voices were hoarse from yelling, their bodies exhausted from herding the children from classroom to classroom, and they kept looking at their watches as if waiting for the heavenly gates to open and let them in, away from the school.

Father said he had always thought he could teach little children. After all, Jesus had said, "Let the little children come to me." But after this experience, he asked to be invited just for the upper grades. By the time they were fourteen and fifteen, the children had learned some restraint, or perhaps, as a high school teacher told him, those who didn't were in reformatory schools, in jail, or in a cemetery.

Father had quickly become recognized as an expert on multiculturalism. He could talk about how the different colors met as equals in church, how community was the answer to the world's ills, how we have to understand Paul's words, "Unless ye have charity, ye shall be like sounding brass." He was careful never to criticize Americans. "After all, we are guests here. It is only polite to respect their customs," he repeated, as if afraid Robert and I would break that code of behavior, and in his talks he always included a list of the many virtues he found in the American people. The generosity, warmth, and tolerance exhibited by the greatest Christian nation on earth.

The school children who had driven Father distracted were not the children of Father's parishioners. We met these children every Sunday, lots and lots of them. Sleeping in their mothers' arms and in strollers that passed from one mother to another like used cars. Solemn, sucking on fists and lollipops during worship. Running happily around the nursery area I had filled with playground swings, tricycles, see-saws, turnabouts, and indoor sand-boxes.

This indoor playground was the first thing I spent my money on in LA, for I saw if Father was to succeed, he would need the women's support, and the way to get their support was give them time away from the children. The playground was expensive, taking up almost half the space in the old furniture store, which itself filled a whole city lot. But it was worth my money, for the women came in droves to church, where they could leave their children to play without looking out for used needles, molesters, gangbangers, cars driving too fast, wild dogs, cat piss, human and animal poop. Everything they could not get away from in their neighborhoods.

But, then, I noticed church attendance was standing still. Some of the congregation said they found it hard to follow Father's sermons on multiculturalism. At first I thought it was because they had given up trying to understand God's words through his strong Malaysian accent. Their English language skills were minimal to begin with, and his accent and habit of using elevated words, they had first complained, had made it difficult to understand him. But it was only when he began preaching the same talk he gave at high schools and to the city council that the men began to fall asleep. Or worse, they stood up mid-way through the sermon to go to the men's room and then they'd stay outside the church smoking till the women came out.

Even the women were not much interested in hearing Father speak about the glorious mosaic of races, how God had ordained America to be the beacon of multicultural brotherhood in the world, that we must repent of the sin of racism and become like little children to enter the kingdom of heaven, for children are the purest of all races in possessing none except the mark of the Divine Father, innocence. As Father preached, a mother would smack a restless child and hiss, "Silencio!" as if to break the rhythm of his words.

This Sunday, Donna placed her thirteen-year-old-hand on her belly and made a face. I knew the baby was kicking inside and hurting her. "I think my baby grow up a gangbanger," she joked last week, "see, how he kicks here!" Women like Donna didn't disagree with Father about the innocence of children, but they didn't believe it either. The women talked about mortal sin as they arranged their dishes on the long tables for the communion meal. Shreekhar described a drive-by shooting a block away. Pena had been beat up so bad by her boyfriend she had to have her jaw re-attached by steel pins. Theru told of a neighbor's daughter dying of some unknown wasting disease, and Jednna interrupted to berate her father who had run off who knows where, leaving her mother and six younger children still living at home, and who knows now how they were to have a home? Sometimes, Mrs Alvarez said, you couldn't tell whose mortal sin it was. Was it Mario's for abandoning the familias, or was it this cruel country that wouldn't give him a job when he broke his good right arm and couldn't do any more plastering after fifteen years of hard work so he grew ashamed and ran away?

"Shhhh!" someone said, glancing at where I was stacking the paper plates beside the large platter of fried bee hoon the new Thai family had brought. We always placed plates and forks next to the starches and far away from the meat so people would fill their plates first with what was plentiful. We had no miracles of loaves and fishes, only a system.

Smiling, I went up to Mrs Alvarez and took her hand in mine. There was no physical barrier between the women. We hugged, held each other's faces between our palms, kissed cheeks and necks and hands, walked with arms around each other's waists. We were like each other's mother and sister, affectionate with each other's body, free to touch lovingly because the men felt no jealousy when it was a child or another woman whose hand we were holding.

    I turned Mrs Alvarez's palm up and looked at it. "This is a good hand," I said, while the other women laughed. "It cooks well, it works well, it comforts. It knows more than it can tell. You have no reason to be silent."

    "That's not fortune telling," Mrs Kim broke in. She was wearing her green apron, the same kind as the one she wore at her pedicure shop. "I say the same thing to customers in my shop!"

    "You tell mine!" "Tell mine!" "Me, tell my fortune!" Suddenly the women grew excited, thrusting their hands, palms up, at me. I looked around at the circle of palms, many reddened and callused. Mrs Manley's brown palm with its pink worn lines. Kumari's dark cups with a stump for a ring finger where a mugger in a Bombay slum had cut it off to get the ring — and it not even a diamond, she had told everyone, just big glass. Huyn's pale palm that hardly saw sunshine because her father needed her to do the cash register during the day when it was safer for a woman. Even Mrs Kim held her palm out, too soft and white, like the belly of a fish on ice for too long, from hours soaking other women's cuticles in softening liquid.

    "Pearl, is the meal ready?" Father's gentle voice scattered the women, sent us back to gather the children from the swing sets and sand-boxes, to call the men from the meeting room where they were discussing what to do about raising church attendance, and to yell for the other men standing outside smoking or sharing whatever they shared about day jobs and corner pick-ups for the next week.

    It was while everyone was sitting on gray metal fold-up

chairs and on mats, eating from paper plates full of tortillas, rice, noodles, carne, and stir-fried beef, that the idea for my real mission came to me. Father drew women to the Mission because it had the best playground and nursery my money could buy. But men would come to the Mission only if there was something also to attract them. The blanked-out sign in front, its stripy whitewash barely covering over the giant block letters of Mr Feldman's store, like a transparent sheet revealing rather than concealing an ugly body — that was not drawing them to church. Since Father began his services here in April, we had only a small note, "The Church Mission of Eternal Light," hand-painted on a stick-in board Mr Leong had taken from his real estate office. It wasn't the impressive call a church with over two thousand worshippers deserved. Standing behind the table, mechanically serving a scoop of fried rice to each paper plate presented before me, I heard something, perhaps not like an angel whisper but my own voice, saying, "We need a real sign!" Something even larger than FELDMAN'S DISCOUNTED FURNITURE BARGAIN PRICES!

My head expanded, grew light. Robert, of course, must lead the men in the congregation on the project. Putting up a real sign, the biggest possible, a cross, visible from miles away, that would draw worshippers from the many neighborhoods of LA. A cross so large The Church Mission of Eternal Light would be entered into Ripley's *Believe It or Not*. It would be a cross so tall and bright no one could miss it in South Central LA, not even when speeding over the Freeway. You would have to see it to believe it, to believe when you see. It would be lit at night, brighter than those neon lights in the bars and whorehouses on Vermont Avenue, a cross of light outshining the stars the way Jesus outshone the Pharisees and Romans. Then, men would come to listen to Father preach. They would come to hear anyone who preached with such a cross before him.

Already I knew the cross would have two thousand electric bulbs; better still, three thousand. Six hundred down three times, a tall, solid axis like the heavy trunk that bore Jesus on Calvary. Four hundred across thrice, the axle forming the crossbar, lighting up the axle tree to beckon and save. The men would have to figure out how to electrify the cross, where to lay the cable lines, for the power for such a cross could only be carried on thick insulated wires. The elders would work with Father to convince the city to license the project. It would be a cross to draw the men together into a brotherhood of light, the incandescent glow of three thousand 100 watt bulbs burning as one everlasting light, perhaps visible, like the Great Wall of China, even to the cameras of the satellites circling the earth.

This was what Ah Kong's money was intended for — a Christian memorial to him. I saw then it was time to call Swee. I would need her help to write up the proposal for Father and the elders. I had the vision, but she had the gift of writing to persuade. Between us, Ah Kong would some day be risen with Christ in Los Angeles.

Twelve

"*H*a, Ha!" Yen shrieked, "Mama always say I'm the crazy sister, but now we know it's really Peik!"

Yen licked the stamps she had laid out on the kitchen table, one cent stamps, five cent stamps, ten and twenty cent stamps and a few dollar and two dollar stamps. She remembered Ah Chee's collecting mania and talked of how much pleasure the stamps would bring her. With Ah Chee nine thousand miles away, Yen adored her memory and mailed her stuff no one needed.

Now she was packing a large box, picked up from outside the Korean liquor store three blocks away, with smaller boxes and containers: pretty pastille tins, some still containing a few purple and green sugar drops, pale glass bottles emptied of their bath salts or face lotion, and not one but three different chocolate boxes. Empty boxes embossed with fancy gold hearts and crimson roses, fat naked cupid babies bearing bows and arrows, and stately looking women from another century. They held brown and silver paper cups, smelling of butter creams, truffles, parfaits, chews, cherry cordial and mint.

Whenever Yen opened a new box, she would call out the names of each chocolate piece printed on the packaging, as she eyed them greedily, before choosing one to nibble. Then she chewed silently with eyes closed, the smile on her face almost as ecstatic as when she was listening to Wayne on the phone. America made her ecstatic, its sweets and colors, sensations and excesses. It seemed everything Ah Kong had detested about her — her impulsiveness, greed, noisiness — America would love her for.

I stopped checking to see what Yen considered irresistible for Ah Chee and watched instead as she carefully pasted the stamps onto the big liquor box, our address printed in large letters on two sides, to mail tomorrow, home to Malacca.

So much lunacy everywhere! A box of trash costing twenty-two dollars to airmail to Malacca and a one-hundred-fifty foot cross of blazing copper filament advertising a church in a storefront. I could not persuade Yen against flying boxes home, but I tried very hard to dissuade Peik against her scheme. "Why not use your money to rent a better building in a nicer neighborhood?" That seemed so rational.

"This is where Father's ministry is, we like the location. Father says this is the center of the new Promised Land, the place of multicultural America." Peik's voice over the phone, that is, Pearl's voice, for she now used only her Christian name to make it easier for the congregation, was familiar. It still sounded proper and obedient. But I heard a different timbre of obedience, to something new. Her voice was strong with faith where in Malacca it had been merely faithfully prim. She wanted me to write a proposal for Robert to bring before the Council of Elders and that would finally be presented to the mayor and City Council.

"Well, as a civic venture, it will be more visible than the Hollywood sign," I thought aloud, "but I'm not sure how the mayor will feel about it."

"That's a good point to make in your proposal. He can't criticize its size, otherwise we Christians can say he is more supportive of Hollywood."

"Pearl, America is a secular state, the city cannot support a religious symbol!"

"But this will be a private sign, for a church. We won't be asking the city for funds, we'll do our own fund-raising, and if the mayor cooperates, we'll invite him to the launch ceremony." She was, as I remembered her, stubborn and sure about what she wanted.

"Launch ceremony?"

"Yes, like when the Queen Mary was launched. We'll have the Ripley's people there to document the lighting ceremony, and the church women will prepare a communion buffet for the communicants and the press."

Who cared about communion buffets, I wondered, and where did Pearl learn about such things?

"It's Father. He's been interviewed by so many reporters, for newspapers, for local cable television, about his ideas on multicultural affairs. I've been serving as his appointments secretary. It's been quite exciting." Her voice was smug.

For the first time in my life, I was jealous of Peik now that she was Pearl. The professor who had taught Communications and Public Life had lectured on the importance celebrities placed on working with the press. Fame was what reporters said it was, although reporters themselves remained commonplace, a dime a dozen, he said. I had put down 'reporter, press secretary' as two jobs I was interested in when I signed up for the Communications major, and there Peik was, ahead of me, and without even having to go to college.

"If you're so good at this, you don't need me to help."

"But I do! I can have these ideas and contacts, but if I don't have a good proposal on paper, nothing can happen."

"If your church has a thousand worshippers, find someone among them to write it. After all, this is church business."

"I can't! It's personal business. My ideas, your language — I can trust that. Besides, many of Father's congregation members aren't very good with English. They're new to America. And it's over two thousand parishioners," she added, even more smugly.

Personal. It was hard for me to resist that appeal. With Sandy, 'personal' was forbidden. He wouldn't talk to me about his family, his history in the Air Force, or his life before we met. "Nothing, there's nothing interesting about any of it," he'd say; and now I couldn't ask him about his weekends, about Keith and his biker buddies, what he felt and thought. He wanted us to be a couple but without my entering this other life. As if we could form a life together, while he kept his personal life separate from me.

What was it about Sandy forbidden to me? Or in which I was forbidden? Men going off to the Angeles National Forest to drink, curse at the government and their bad luck, blow off steam? Or was it his parents? Perhaps he could not see them, Austrian Americans, fair skinned and fair-haired, in the same room with me, with my black hair, my Chinese face and eyes?

True, I also saw Sandy could never be like Yen and Pearl to me. My sisters were blood of my blood. Still, after so many months together, Sandy and I formed our own story. Without either's father and mother, even without Yen. We had our own code, unknown to his buddies or my sisters. Confidence in our touches, our bodies swinging from bike to bed. Like the paper we had worked on together, we had mastered an evasive system of signs that saw us riding fast and low, passing in and out and between monstrous machines and coming through safe, safe from nightmares of dying and into each other's arms. Such swinging was enough to keep me with Sandy, despite our quarrels.

I kept Pearl a secret from Sandy. It was easy to do. He was gone every Sunday now.

I went to Pearl's church to work on the proposal and came home after the Sunday buffet lunch, what she called the communal meal. She was relieved Yen hadn't come with me, and packed generous leftovers for me to take home.

Yen and Wayne must have spent the time watching Sunday movies on television and messing around, as Wayne put it so indelicately. I could smell their sex when I came through the front door, bitter semen, female marigold juices, tangy sweat, the harsh chemicals under armpits and groins. "Ouf!" I said, and sprayed the living room with natural fir scent, the only chemicals that could overpower their weekend of sex.

"Aiyah, your spray stinks!" Yen came out of her bedroom, hair tangled and eyes gooey with sleep.

"It's 3 o'clock. Aren't you and Wayne dressed yet?"

"Dressed for what? Sunday lah. No work, you know. Also, Wayne is tired. Monday to Friday 8 am to 5 pm work."

I thought fast. Writing the proposal I needed some language on electrification of the cross. I needed some cost accounting — the kind of technical and budgetary information I didn't have and I knew Sandy didn't either. I had never thought of Wayne as smart, but suddenly it seemed to me he probably knew a lot more about that kind of world than I did. He'd worked with his hands, he worked with machines every day, and he was constantly boasting about how the machines were actually in his head, not just steel and plastic stuff.

"Listen, Yen, if I make satay tonight, will Wayne help me with the proposal for Pearl's church?"

"Satay?" Yen gave me her suspicious stare. "The kind with real peanuts, not peanut butter?"

"Yes, Ah Chee's recipe, I swear!"

"Okay, I ask him."

I knew Wayne would say yes. Satay was his favorite Malaysian food. He could eat twenty sticks and more, and all I needed were numbers. He could find the numbers and I had the words.

Thirteen

"Nah, it isn't crazy. So she wants a tall cross with lots of lights. No one will give her a hard time so long she's got the money and doesn't expect the city to pay for it. It doesn't make sense right now, but that's different from being crazy. Sense is what's in your head, and once that cross gets into people's heads, no one's going to question it."

Wayne talked to Swee like he was the one who had idea of cross in first place. We were drinking beer and eating satay, like a family, three of us. Not like Ah Kong and Mama at home, but like American family, like I see on television. My favorite foamy cold beer — sweet and bitter at same time — and it made me light, like my body not set in place. Not gone away somewhere else, but not solid present. I closed my eyes. Even after so many months this was how America tasted to me — sweet and bitter. The beer pushed my body like a kite swinging in sky. Still tied to a string, still present, but not on two feet. Not in place.

"Big question. Where's she getting the money for the construction and electrification?"

I could hear Swee's quick breathing. Talking money, even thinking about money, made her nervous. She did not want anyone to know we had it, lots of it. "It's better everyone thinks we're middle-class," she told me before we left Malacca. "Americans are weird about money. It makes them treat you different — not better or worse, but weird. Like you've got an extra arm others don't have. It's already tough to be ordinary when you're yellow in America," she said, not hearing my yelp. Yellow! What a word to describe us! Untrue! "But being yellow and rich, I think most Americans will have a hard time with that." "Ordinary" was one of Swee's favorite words. "Better to be just like everyone else!" she repeated, but she never explained better for what. We never talked money to our boyfriends.

"Umm, I think the Mission has an anonymous donor. The same person who paid for the playground and church nursery."

"Takes all kinds. Christian nuts rule everywhere."

"But you just say it not crazy to build the cross," I interrupted.

"Yen, you should give up talking bad English, Malaysian English, even if it's just to Wayne and me. Break the habit! That's why you're doing so badly in college."

Swee was always preaching to me. I wanted to yell at her to cut it out, but Wayne handed me a stick of satay, winking, "You talk any way you want to, babe. We understand each other plenty good."

It was maybe time to ask Swee about my moving with Wayne to Venice, tell her how Wayne was shifting his things to Pete's house so we could be together when Pete went to veterans' hospital.

How hard was it to separate from Swee? When she left for America I waited for her to come home and get me. A whole year! Every day I talked about what Swee was doing to Mama and Ah Chee. "Now Swee is getting up and walking to class." "It is six o'clock in New York and Swee is taking her shower." "She's studying now — Swee always likes to study at night."

"Stop!" Mama said. "You're driving me crazy!" But more often she listened and nodded head as if I had a television line attached to Swee in New York and could see what she was doing. Sometimes Mama encouraged me. "What's Swee doing now?" she asked, and I tell her.

But Wayne was breaking this line, snapping the sister feelings tying me to Swee, cutting them one by one like he clipped copper strands on that electrical line when he was fixing our television. Each time I fell back in bed giddy and surprised and tired from Wayne, some of Swee's spirit left me. Instead, Wayne's face shining brighter in front of my eyes, like sun and moon and stars and electric lights and television colors all over America. I did not know it would be so easy to separate from my sister, to become American.

Suddenly someone was knocking at the door. It was Sandy. Swee looked confused, like she caught doing something behind his back, and when he came into the kitchen where we were eating, he did not look happy to see us.

"Yo, what's up?" Wayne's voice blurry, too much peanut sauce.

Sandy stared at Wayne like he was panhandler. "Whatcha'll doing?" His voice was not nice. It said, "Get out of my way!"

But Wayne too full of satay goodness — fresh roasted ground peanuts, brown coconut sugar boiled with turmeric, jintan, cinnamon and what else that Swee so good buying in bulk from Vietnamese stores in Long Beach — to give Sandy any kind of attention.

Wayne licked his lips, brown sauce shaped like impression of cup around them. He was checking out the plates. Three sticks of satay left. He went for one and waved to the others. "Want some?"

"Wazzat?" Sandy already tried Malaysian cooking with us, but he didn't like spice. He said spice made curry chicken and pork rib soup smell like flowers or candy and made him sick. He thought Malaysian food had rotting ingredients because he found a tourist description about belachan. "Tiny fish mixed with salt and left to rot for months till it becomes a brown fermented paste," he read to Swee. "Eeuuw! Your people still eat this stuff? I can see when you were starving, but now, in the twentieth century, with capitalism and western influence!" He picked up the smell of tumeric and jintan from Wayne's satay stick. "Aach! You can finish it."

Swee was smiling like she had not heard Sandy. "We just finished dinner. You want some coffee? There're sweet buns I can heat up."

I pulled Wayne from two satay sticks to the next room, and we snuggled on couch watching a show on airplanes. "That's the

US Navy, babe, the one that saved your parents' pants in World War Two," he said, grinning, holding my hand in his sticky hand. Like a big bear with yellow hair and hot breath in love with me. Wayne was more yellow than Swee or me — yellow and pink body, happy girl colors, I sighed, my face almost pained from smiling.

From the kitchen I picked up Sandy's talk. "So, how about that? Soon you'll be a year in the States. Red. You'll look terrific, red."

I heard Swee giggle — it wasn't a true giggle. More like little nervous burp. Good idea for me to go to the kitchen now. Not often I heard Swee nervous.

But Wayne kept his hot sweaty paw on me. "Don't get up," he muttered, snuffling into my hair. He was getting excited again — it must be the chilies in the sauce — Malays said chilies made people all hot and sexy.

"No, I don't think dying my hair is something I need to do. I like it the way it is."

"But, Sue, you'd be something else with red hair! No, copper is the word for it. Everyone colors their hair now. It's not like you'll be going blue or purple or green."

"Ughs!"

"For me, OK? It'll wash out if you really hate it. Black — that's boring. Every Cambodian in Long Beach has black hair. Don't you want to be different?"

I wanted to say to Sandy, "What, you think Swee not different enough? Different for what? What's wrong with black hair? Mama's hair still black, and she almost forty years old. Swee's just twenty — at least twenty years more got total black hair. Black like very black night sky — you think you see dark blue and shiny sparks, her hair is so pretty. Stupid Sandy!"

But I stayed next to Wayne and pretended to hear only his rushing breathing and groans.

"Well, I don't know. . . . "

"Hey, you said you learned some neat stuff about cosmetics from Faye. Didn't she do hair stuff, y'know, coloring and all that?" There was a sound of a scramble and something breaking. It stopped Wayne who seemed to wake up. "Aw, shit!" he moaned.

"OK, OK. Look, you'd better get the dustpan and I'll pick up the pieces. Watch out — your boots will make more splinters! Yen and I go barefoot, you know!"

Later, Swee told me Sandy left his bikers' group early just to pick up a bottle of Clear Color Crème for her. "He had his brilliant idea right in the middle of some assembly speech and wanted to make it work immediately. He's crazy over me, see, but there's only one thing that bothers him, and he couldn't figure what it was. Then he figured out he didn't like black hair. He loves everything about me but the color of my hair!"

When Swee told me this story, about Sandy rushing off to Long Beach to find a store selling hair color open on Sunday evening, and how he walked up and down the aisles of women's hair products, big boots creaking and leaving trail-bike dirt behind, stopping to read labels and descriptions on boxes, to find exactly what he wanted Swee to do, what color he was dreaming for her hair, she was very funny. She imitated being there with Sandy, watching him sweat in his leather jacket, shifting his plastic helmet one arm to another, and all the time the counter clerk pretending not to see him while checking out his actions in the mirror up in the ceiling. "They don't often see men shopping in that section of the store. They must have thought he was a transvestite."

What's that, I asked, and Swee told me. She made me laugh and laugh.

Wayne didn't think it was funny. "I like long black hair. You stay as Asian as you are," he said, smoothing my hair.

"I'm not Asian, I Malaysian."

"Whatever. Don't change nothing."

But Swee was changing for Sandy. First her hair. Black and red didn't make red, only reddish brown. It was color of rubber tree leaves when trees got sick, but artificial brown made Swee look different pretty, not sick. Then she cut her hair way short. Sandy took her to a hairdresser in LA — "he specializes in punk rockers," he boasted — and she came back with bottles of gummy stuff like glue and her hair standing up in many little pinkies. She did this for Sandy because he promised he would take her riding more often once she changed her hairstyle.

Swee was jealous of me because Wayne took me everywhere on his bike. "Freedom," she said one evening after Wayne brought me back. She always waited for me worrying something bad happened until I came through the door.

"What you worry for?" I asked.

"Freedom," she replied. "You are too free. Freedom has responsibilities, and right now you have none. Wayne is like your ticket to freedom — he takes you everywhere. You don't even know how to get from one place to another without him. Everything you see of America is on Wayne's bike. It's a free ride for you. But how are you going to learn to take care of yourself if you don't learn your own directions? What if Wayne disappeared? Lost interest? How are you ever going to find your way around?"

"You're just jealous," I smiled. "Sandy never take you anywhere except to Buenavista. You must take the bus to go shopping, walk around LA. But it's no fun. I know. You try to take me with you, but what for I go? Walk, walk, so hot. Wayne takes me shopping anytime! Anyway, Wayne says I am perfect lady passenger, he forget I'm on bitch seat."

"Forgets," Swee said, "he forgets. You must speak good English if you're going to live in America."

"I'm more good American than you," I pinched Swee gently. "Wayne say he's going to marry me. He's not going to disappear."

Swee just shrugged. She never believed Wayne.

But that was when she began to be nicer to Sandy. After she cut her hair, they went shopping for clothes for Swee — a black leather jacket with a big patch Swee stenciled Sandy's name for her in big red capital letters. SUE. Black corduroy pants. Black boots. Black and silver head gear. Even goggles like black mask, hiding her eyes and nose. Swee disappeared into black motorbike clothes.

"Wah, stylish," I told her, "like one actress!" Only a bit of her face showed, her mouth, shut whenever she rode behind Sandy. But usually even her mouth covered with black cloth because of grit and bugs flying in wind.

Now Sandy more cheerful when he came to pick Swee. She let him stay some nights in her room, although she still didn't want him to move in. Or Wayne. "Well, you can see Sandy doesn't get along with Wayne," she explained, but I was sure it was me Sandy didn't like.

It was strange Swee and I hardly ever rode together. Sometimes there were group runs, one hundred, two hundred motorbikes. I looked out for Swee because I knew she was looking out for me.

We packed together. She always made me pack a rain poncho and toilet paper. "You gotta go when you gotta go, that's what Sandy says," she said when I asked why toilet paper. "No beer, Wayne shouldn't drink when you're riding," she warned as we stuffed soda and sardine sandwiches wrapped in brown paper into plastics we jammed into saddlebags — and I never told her Wayne bought beer at the stores when we stopped for gas.

We were tight almost like twins, until she climbed on Sandy's bike. Then, vroom-vroom! Swee became Sue, and she and Sandy got lost in crowd although I looked and looked for her. Too many lady bikers, too many little and large women, and too much leather in the back, everyone sitting up high with legs raised and bent like black spiders so you couldn't see tiny seats under their backsides. It was like a show, and Sue just fitted in. She and Sandy got lost in the middle of the parade.

Wayne's motorbike had a big low seat for me and we always went faster or slower than other bikers. Wayne didn't like riding with the packs. He didn't like to wait until order came from somewhere to start moving and the whole lot of bikes went off, like noisy conga line, growling and buzzing to same freeway exit and running through same middle lanes on highways. Wayne impatient to be where no dirty fuel smells came into his face — like a giant fart, he complained. He liked clean air. He exchanged his old bike for a new Harley. He used his promotion bonus money to pay for the Electra Glide Sport — very poetic name! — and he hated the grease and black smoke from older bikes whenever we caught up with a group run.

    When fast moving pack passed us, shiny chrome, smoking thunder, he'd shout, "They're kids," words flying off his mouth, as if it was worst insult he could give! He'd slow down, so I get to see the bent and gray green trees whiz beside us. I knew them from when Swee pointed to their pictures in her Audubon Guide when we came back from the Angeles National Forest that night, her voice brimming like she recognized some friends, "California oaks! Olive trees!" — and I wondered where Wayne would stop for us to hike from road and drink a beer and do it, slow and quick under the leaves, our clothes like magic suddenly half off exactly where we liked them.

Fourteen

I worried how Pearl would respond to my new look. At home, she had sniffed at my spending money on women's magazines, lipsticks, and pancake foundation I hid from Ah Kong. I worried she would be more judgmental now she was officially a Church Warden — the youngest woman warden in the history of the Church, she'd told me on the phone. But when we met for the first time in months to talk about how my proposal for the cross was coming along, I was amazed she didn't blink an eye! She was too eager to discuss the proposal to notice my new appearance.

Something about LA had changed Pearl. Not just her name but the way she looked at the world. In Malacca she paid close attention to certain details about people. A short skirt or a neckline offering a swelling of breasts was enough to get her going on about sinfulness. And forget about falling asleep during Sunday services! Above all, no fooling around. No hanky-panky. I didn't know where she'd learned this word. She used it all the time in place of the three-letter word, sex. But I found her choice of words much more obscene. Hanky-panky. What people did behind cover of a handkerchief, hands panking away. I laughed when I thought how horrified my little sister would be if she knew the lascivious images her prim language roused in me.

Living in America had turned Pearl blind to those defects that used to fill her with fury. The second time I attended the Communion lunch with her congregation, the entire enormous area was overflowing not only with food — smells of onion, garlic, simmering chicken, cinnamon, ghee, a dense world of pungent aromas, overwhelmed me even before I stepped into the building — but with human flesh. Children were everywhere, running between adult legs like a separate species. It could have been a schoolyard, only with less shrieking and more eating. Or an aquarium, with brilliant little shapes flickering in between the giant fish. Except these were humans, not fish. I was impressed Pearl slipped as confidently as the children in between and among the bulky bodies. She was slight, only nineteen, and looked even younger, someone who could have been easily overlooked among the hundreds of differently formed, broad and bony, short and tall, noisy, munching people.

The congregation came in all shades of color. Chiefly brown, from sun-tinged to glowing, milk chocolate, warm brown black, with yellow tints, from pale sallow to robust ochre. And white. All shades of white also, some tanned from outdoor work, but many more parchment-paper white from working long office hours and eating cheap fast foods. The Mission Sunday service was popular, and the communion meal, Pearl was right to boast, drew so many that even the cavernous floor space of the old mega furniture store was too small for all of the big eaters and snackers eager to enter.

The Mission of Eternal Light was now asking for donations from those who arrived without a potluck dish. The number of people thronging through the door, pressing five dollar bills on the young women by the entrance, whose job was also to direct families bearing heavy steaming aluminum trays to their tables, was scary. Who'd imagine so many humans would come to church for a communion meal? And humans who appeared already well fed, with arms as large as shoulders of beef the supermarket featured on special sales, stomachs extended and bulging against tee-shirts, pants that had no where to go but fall below bellies, and triple chins and jowls like daisy chains looped around hidden jawbones.

"Yes, they come for the food," Pearl said. "The dishes are very good. Where for five dollars can you eat your fill around the world? Korean, Vietnamese, Chinese, Indian, Mexican, Honduran, Italian, some Greek, Malaysian and Singaporean, and of course all-American hot dogs and burgers and French fries and Belgian waffles and mom's apple pies. But more important to the Mission, everything here is donated by families. Families eat each other's cooking. In eating there are no strangers. That's why we call it a communion. No one here is only stuffing his face. Here the spirit is fed."

I stared at her sharply to see if she believed her own language. Around us flesh was spilling out of blouses and pants — globular bosoms heaving and sweaty; bellies and butts, as round as the beach balls I had kept in my college room, pushing out of shirts that were getting untucked as people elbowed against them. Flesh with black and auburn and gray and white hairs, stiff, curly, sparse and plentiful. Flesh spotted with acne and black moles, age spots and blobs and birthmarks. Flesh as in red wet lips and cheeks still raw from a razor or sprinkled with shiny powder. More and more people shuffled along, waiting on line at their favorite tables for green chili burrito or a paper plate of chicken rice. Many more stood in the middle of everything else, slopping beans and bits of meat, pastry puffs flaking crumbs onto the floor, fat noodles, into their mouths, chewing and talking, to someone doing the same thing, complimenting the women. Others, perhaps church members, were balancing three and four overflowing paper plates, carrying starches and meats and sweets mashed on plates, to children waiting at the corners and sides of the old selling floor, an open echoing space crammed with human flesh, families and strangers. Now, there was no way Pearl was going to convince me the church was feeding the hungry. All that frantic gluttony seemed pretty sinful to me.

Yet there was something sincere about Pearl's smile, about the way she hugged the women serving generous scoops of menudo and rice and beans. "Kim Yong!" she exclaimed, half-introducing one perspiring woman twice as large as her — and not stopping to see if I had processed the name before moving on to the next table and hugging another woman. "Maria Padillo," she chirped, and so on, until my head was simply a mechanical echo chamber, repeating, "Hello, hello, hello, nice to meet you."

Not for a minute did I feel anything I saw was nice. What

was nice about women doing all the serving, large mouths going at it like tractors mowing down fields of grain, and the unsettling roar of incomprehensible languages — Spanish, Korean, Vietnamese, Thai, how many different dialects of Chinese, and what else? "The children in California speak eighty-six different languages!" Pearl had exclaimed, as if that fact was a Mission achievement. A school superintendent had told her father-in-law this anxiously, she said, but Pastor Fung used that information in his sermons as part of his thanks to God for creating America in His image — omnipotence even in languages.

Had Pearl and I been switched when we crossed over to America? I was beginning to sweat. All the high nasal tones, the rolling r's and swishing ch's addressed in loud voices made me dizzy. I couldn't understand a word. I was supposed to be the smart sister. Instead, here I was, frowning at Pearl as she grabbed teenagers and kissed them, ignoring their crude eye shadow, metal studs in their eyebrows, and rings clipped on their lips. She listened patiently to the men who stopped her to ask in broken English about how to fill forms for drivers' licenses, rental agreements, permits to sell hair notions and shampoo in the Saturday flea market the next town over.

I couldn't see anything spiritual in anyone. Everyone seemed to be looking out for himself, getting his plate filled, looking out for how to survive in a hard place and time. "Freeloaders, hangers-on. America's letting them in by the gazillions!" Sandy complained each time the television news carried reports of illegal immigrants caught crossing the border.

Here, brown men, many unwashed, rank-smelling, pressed on Pearl. She had given up her childish frown. What had taken its place was optimism. "Yes, yes, yes, Pastor Fung will take care of it. Yes, tomorrow. Yes, come back next week. Yes, we'll contact your probation officer." Pearl was no longer "Thou shalt not." She had become, "Yes, we will."

We'd talked about my draft proposal in the annex, during the service. "That's the best time, everyone's quiet and in the service hall." I was anxious because Pearl trusted everything I wrote.

"Aren't you going to comment or suggest revisions?" But, no, the new Pearl smiled, "You'll get it right when the time comes."

The communion lunch was her way to show me how important it was for the Mission to have that cross, but it only persuaded me Pearl had become more like Yen in America, hopelessly irrational. I couldn't eat and began pulling at her arm to leave.

She was too absorbed, holding on to everyone close enough to be touched. She's become obsessed with flesh, I thought, feeling myself shrink from the strangers she was embracing, muttering to her, "Come on, come on, I have to go."

"Well, in that case, here's Mr Leong. He can drive you back to Long Beach. Will you, Mr Leong?" Pearl held on to his arm, looked at him meaningfully, a message communicated between them.

Mr Leong didn't look like a Mister Leong. He was fair, tall, with receding gray brown hair and green blue eyes. A church elder, he had been told about my work for the Mission, still confidential, shared only with a few senior advisors, Pearl said, introducing us. Mr Leong looked like any dignified white senior citizen, stooped, with a brisk professional air even in the middle of a place gone crazy with children and people who should know better cramming their mouths.

He announced he had to find his daughter. She was somewhere in the masses of people standing and eating or stepping in each other's way.

"My father also was much older than us," I said to little Melody, as he backed out of the parking lot. I wanted to show I wasn't scandalized. Mr Leong looked almost seventy. "And how old are you?"

"I don't know." Melody fidgeted in the back seat, sulking because her father had taken her away from the play set where it had been her turn to sit on the wheel for a spin.

"She isn't being rude," Mr Leong laughed, turning to give Melody an encouraging smile. "When my wife and I went to get her from the orphanage in Nanjing, they gave us her birth certificate, said her birthday is February 29, 1975. But there's no February 29th that year. We were told Melody was a year old. We think she might have been older — maybe two or even three."

"You see, I have no birthday," Melody added. "Mommy says I'm ageless."

"Forever young."

"A magic baby, Mommy says."

"A fairy girl."

They had a family story they'd agreed on, that they had told in tandem over and over again. Melody began to hum tunelessly, soothed by the story's retelling.

"My wife's in charge of the cleaning up," Mr Leong volunteered. "I'm the church driver, I know my way all around Southern California, better than a cab driver. Selling real estate, you learn how to get everywhere. There's no place someone isn't trying to sell or to buy in this part of the state."

"So what do you think about the cross for the church?"

"Wonderful idea. Sure to raise property values in the neighborhood. The furniture store was an eye sore. No matter what the city said, it was an abandoned building. Pastor Fung's a miracle worker. In a year the property prices on that street have gone up thirty percent!"

He drove the van expertly through an underpass I had not even noticed, swerved by some garbage cans set up in the middle of a street, around what seemed like a dead-end road to a freeway exit that appeared out of nowhere.

"Only the truckers and I know about this exit," he chuckled. "Selling real estate. That's when you learn secrets. Secret directions. Secret destinations. Hidden canyons, hideaway cabins, concealed rooms. Skeletons in closets. Oh, I know a lot about Californians, more than they want me to know, probably. What they wear when there's no one to see them, whether they color their hair." He glanced quickly at my brown head.

"You know, I have to write a paper on California for my communications class. Could I talk to you about selling real estate?" I knew he wouldn't refuse me. I was Pearl's big sister and a Chinese student. Mr Leong was from Hong Kong, his father a Cantonese, his mother Welsh and Irish, but to him I was still a Chinese like him. It was hard to refuse any kind of Chinese when you were yourself a kind of Chinese in California.

I was excited about interviewing Mr Leong. Meeting up with Pinny again had reminded me how I had wanted to be a journalist at Peps. That and my fall semester's communications course, which was the best class Buenavista had to offer.

I had taken writing classes before. This one was different, more challenging. The professor, Mr Mather, had given me straight As but he didn't even know my name. There were over forty students in the class. It had been over-registered and although he had tried to scare some away it was now almost the middle of the semester and no one had dropped out. He was a temporary teacher, straight out of a big-city university and waiting for a full-time job in a better college to appear. He wanted us to intern somewhere, write real stories for a real newspaper, like Long Beach was a real city and we could just knock on the door of the *Daily Globe* like Clark Kent and get a job.

At first I had worked very hard on my studies; I wanted to get away from Long Beach. I daydreamed over the catalogs from Berkeley, determined I'd get there by next September. But when Yen found Wayne I seemed to have lost that dream. Now the bad Sue was more and more present. It was like I was right back where I was as a girl at home.

The good Swee still studied hard and wrote good papers, only this time I no longer had Yen to take care of. Wayne had taken my place. I couldn't begrudge her that. Yen was happy. No other word for her condition. She was happy when she woke up in the late morning, hungry and smiling. Happy when she fell asleep after Wayne left, sometimes in front of the television, the cushion under one elbow, her legs sprawled as if finally freed from Mama's and Ah Chee's controlling eyes.

Sister Swing

Unsettled, I envied Yen. She and Wayne were like twins reincarnated as horny lovers. Wayne talked about the homes for homeless veterans run by the Federal Government and sometimes, if they were lucky, there were other kinds of homes for the same men if they didn't want to be where they couldn't drink and smoke. There were corners on busy streets where veterans could find each other, some brushed and clean, the military edges and creases still ironed into them, and others blurry and fuzzed by prescription pills and cheap wine. Yen, he said, was finally going to make his entry back into civilian life complete, more than thirteen years after he had come home from the war.

I stared at bad Sue's image in the mirror as I dressed for the thunder rolls, which is what Sandy called the Saturday group runs. Hair bright with bottled color, clothes the color of deep mourning. Black as in mourning for Ah Kong, but this time black for Sandy, because that's the color he chose for me.

"Hey, that's cool," he said, when we went shopping and he picked the black jacket, smelling of warm buffed skin that made me remember Manuel and Peps nights. "Color-coordinated, it's the way to go," he said, nodding toward the biker chicks perched like purple-black beetles behind their guys.

Susie, another biker chick. Sandy wanted me to look like every single one of them, and I felt an overwhelming deep body thrill in costuming to look like them. Thrills charged our time together, as if I were surrendering my uncomfortable sense of self, opening my thighs and entrances, a reckless stranger, to a stranger.

And why shouldn't I change, like Yen? When I was with Sandy I no longer had to be the responsible one. We stopped riding with Wayne and Yen. We were with a pack, one of many machines rushing in the middle of a whirlwind, a wind ourselves, created out of air and returning to air. If we had died right then, I would have not known to mind.

Such moments I stopped thinking and became simply a part of Sandy's energy, magnified by the dozens, sometimes hundreds of other bikes — rushing toward nowhere. Together with them, I was Sue, and I knew we were bad. We would go to Pete's Tavern after an afternoon of riding and no one ever stopped to stare at me. Clothed in black leather and with my brown hair standing straight up, I was just another cunt, Sandy's lady, a chick in black at back, as American as everyone else there.

I told Mr Mather I wanted to write about motorbikes, but he looked at me like I was asking to write about Mars. "Why don't you write about something you know?" he asked. "Like Asians in California. That's a gap waiting to be filled."

It took me a few minutes to understand where he got the impression I knew about Asians in California. It was my name, Swee Wing. If he had met me in my Sue clothes, he might have let me write about being a biker lady. But because I didn't reply immediately, that's what he wrote down in his record book for my assignment. "Asians in California."

"You won't have to do that much research. There's more human interest in getting your community to talk."

That was only last Tuesday. Mr Mather would probably have also disapproved of stories on the Mission of Eternal Light, but Mr Leong, the Asian real estate dealer in California, was a subject I was sure he would find appropriate for Swee Wing.

And it was through Mr Leong I got introduced to the publisher of *Asian Time*, a small weekly newspaper, distribution 5,000, that paid its bills mostly from carrying real estate ads, some of them from Mr Leong's company.

Fifteen

"You know why I named it *Asian Time*? First, *Asian Times* has already been copyrighted. 'Times' is a word every newspaper likes to use; everyone wants to copy the *New York Times*. But I am not like everyone. I don't want to copy. I think it is time for Asians to become rich in America. It is now Asian time for us. First we make the money, then we become President."

Bun Jon waved my copy, still unread, in the air. He spoke perfect English but with an accent I couldn't place. I couldn't tell if he was Vietnamese or Filipino or Thai or Burmese or even if he was from China. He didn't have a colonial British clip, so I knew he wasn't from Hong Kong or Singapore or Malaysia. Later I found he also spoke Cantonese, Thai, Mandarin, Tagalog, some Vietnamese and French. He was multilingual, and he used all his languages to persuade businesses to advertise in the *Asian Time*.

I'd come to his office to turn in my third copy. The first afternoon he had just taken it with a grunt. Mr Leong apparently had called him to run it. The second time he looked at me and asked, "You the person who wrote that Leong article?"

The office was only a room between a Vietnamese grocery and a flight of stairs leading to other offices. Bun Jon sat behind a metal desk that looked as if it had been bought in a second-hand store many years ago. There wasn't even a typewriter in the room, only a copying machine and large plastic stacks on the desk in which papers were arranged. Plastic bucket seats whose cream paint had crackled were arranged in a row against the wall by the door, as if ready for a meeting. But Bun Jon was always alone.

When I told Mr Mather about publishing the first article in *Asian Time*, I didn't tell him what I had described as a newspaper was in fact a type of advertising flyer. After my article came out, third page on the right hand corner, I'd gone around to the liquor stores where free copies of *Asian Time* had been dropped off and picked up multiple copies. I kept opening to the page on which my name, SWEE WING, appeared. I had capped it for the by-line.

Mr Mather hadn't read my copy. He wanted our articles in the final portfolio and wouldn't read them sooner, but he did say, "Perhaps there's some hope for Buenavista with a student like you."

I'll never forget these words, I choked, a hot sensation flooding my chest. It was the same sensation I felt when I saw the *Asian Time* with my name in print for the first time.

"I'm going to be writing regularly for the newspaper," I'd said, foolishly, wanting to impress Mr Mather further.

"You mean you will have a column?"

"Yes." A column, not an essay, not an article. A column.

"What kind? Editorial? Commentary? Not humor, I hope."

"Umm, human interest."

"Human interest," he sounded disappointed. "Good beginning for a woman reporter. You need an angle." His voice rose.

"An angle?"

"Yeah, every columnist needs to have a brand name. Swee Wing isn't going to cut it."

I scrambled for an answer. Manuel had told me I needed to find a community, and Mr Mather assumed I had one in California. I remembered Manuel's lecture on the Constitution. "I'll be interviewing different people. Maybe, something like, 'The People Speak.'"

"'The People? Whadya mean, 'the,' 'people'? That's pretentious." He separated the words as if there was a question mark after each of them. "'The,' 'People' isn't who you're reporting on. They're Asians, right? That's your brand identity. More like, 'The Asians Speak.'"

"But they don't call themselves 'Asians.' Taiwanese, Thai, Hmong, Cambodian. . . ."

"Whatever. You've got to find your brand name. How about 'Yellow'?"

I remembered Yen complaining, "Who's yellow? Wayne's more yellow than me!"

"You'll think of something," Mr Mather said, pointing to the door to indicate the line of students still waiting to talk to him. More than half of the students signed up for his Communications course was from Asia, and no one except me could write good English.

"Yellow. Yellow." The word clicked like a row of prayer beads as I was riding with Sandy that Saturday. I hadn't told Sandy about my writing, the Mission, my plans, now stirred up again by Mr Mather, to go to Berkeley. Saturday was for a couple of hours blinking through dust, sitting up bundled against the wind, propped up by the silly bar behind me, a steel rod that left me every Saturday afternoon with hot pain shooting down my calves, feeling like I had been branded with a long straight iron on my back. It was for sitting in Pete's Tavern, drinking a beer, slowly getting a buzz, easing up on muscle cramps, listening to Sandy and the biker men talk politics and machines, and always silent. I didn't want to speak in case the men, or worse, the women bunched around them, figured out I was alien. Better silence than my clip-clopping sentences that couldn't be lightened into American vowels.

Sundays I was always alone, a condition I had first resented, then more and more grew to prefer. Sandy now had Sunday classes on welding he was teaching with Keith somewhere in LA. He was tired and dirty after class and never came by after work. Yen and Wayne took off, usually to the little bungalow in Venice Beach. The tavern was still being managed by Pinny, but Pete was finally at the veterans' hospital. He had had to wait months before there was a bed for him, and by then he was doing badly. The doctors had stopped the radiation treatments and they had him through some experimental bone marrow transfer and new drugs. Wayne was taking care of Pete's collection of cacti and his cats, all of them adopted after he came out of Nam with the perforated stomach. "Someone's rifle going off when it shouldn't," Wayne had said.

Some Sundays, Mr Leong and his wife, with Melody, came to drive me to the Mission where Robert and Pearl talked to me about what else was needed to get permission from the city council for putting up the cross.

"Yell-O," I thought, in the middle of one Communion lunch, "like Jello. Noisy, talking, mushed together."

But no. Then Mr Leong asked, "You want to meet more of our fellows before you complete the proposal?" Except he said "fellas."

"Yellas Speak!"

"What?"

It was a wonder Mr Leong could hear me in the communal babble, among the grinding and gnashing of teeth. I shook my head and pointed, like Mr Mather had, to a line of people pushing each other by the entrance to the Mission. "It's time to leave."

Sunday afternoons after my meetings at the Mission began to feel inviting, a time when I was hopeful I may yet be happy in America. Alone, sitting with my yellow writing pad, writing with my yellow number two pencil, grateful to Mr Mather and Mr Leong for the title to my column.

The second story I wrote for *Asian Time* was about Melody and the thousands of little Chinese girl babies adopted in America. Everyone knew about white families adopting throwaway babies in poor countries where babies were made too quickly and too often. But I figured most had not heard of Chinese families adopting Chinese babies. Chinese were supposed to kill little baby girls or at least drop them off in orphanages for rich white Americans to love. Melody was the Leongs' fifth Chinese child — two brothers and two sisters had already grown up and become a CEO, two corporate lawyers, and an electrical engineer, everyone too busy to have children. They were trying to raise her without spoiling her, an impossible goal, for she was the last child, and so, seemingly by universal acclaim, deserving of everything. The work at the Mission was supposed to help keep her spiritual, more like the undernourished toddler who'd clutched at a soft terry puppy and wouldn't let go of it for the week it took them to get her from Nanjing into California. Now they had no idea what happened to the terry puppy. "Too many toys," Mrs Leong moaned, "one whole room just for her toys! And her brothers and sisters give her more every week."

My title for Melody's story was "A Fairy Girl, from China to Chinatown." It was unfortunate for the sentiment I was trying to get into the story that Mr Leong was a well-to-do parishioner. He'd found his way to the Mission after a Cantonese plasterer — "maybe the only one in California!" he'd laughed — working on a home remodeling project for a client had converted him. "The real-estate business has been kind to me," he gestured modestly when he drove me past his home, pink stucco partly hidden behind full-grown Canary Island palms and a fancy remote-control gate. Melody hadn't come to an exotic Chinatown, and I worried Mr Mather wouldn't have been satisfied with Mr Leong's Bel Air neighborhood, it wasn't Asian enough, and who'd believe a rich Chinese would consider an abandoned female for a princess? However, for my article, I imagined the whole of California as Chinatown, a place where Chinese gold miners, railroad men, rice farmers, abalone fishermen, peddlers, gamblers and real estate agents came and had never been driven out, had stayed and made the whole state home. A place crowded with cemeteries filled with their iron wood coffins and restaurants serving delicious Chinese food and tea drunk everywhere. That way I didn't have to exactly lie about where Melody landed. Brand recognition, Mr Mather had talked about such things in his lectures.

Maybe Bun Jon did read the second column, because after it appeared, he always had something to say to me when I came by each week to deliver my copy. "Good, good," he'd say, taking the copy, not glancing at the title, "everything's good. Not enough English writing in *Asian Time*."

Asian Time, it seemed, accepted every article sent to it by the local businesses and stores, articles about openings of new branches, special sales, a new manager, competitions and prizes won by employees, annual company dances, dinners and holidays. It had just begun carrying black and white photographs of smiling faces at store openings and events. The bigger national companies were beginning to send news written by their public relations people. My column was the only feature not related to an advertiser.

"Everyone writes only nice things about his business, never care about others. But people here, even Asians, want to read about other people, not always about business. California's a strange place." He said California as KALEEFONEEAA, making it sound even stranger. He wanted me to write longer copy. "Don't worry how many words. I give you center page."

That's when I began writing about other people I'd met through Pearl, my Buenavista classmates being boring as textbooks. Active at the Mission of Eternal Light was Goodwill Chang. His parents escaped from Mainland China to Hong Kong and then to Mexico City and by some unexplained manner managed to enter California. For years they had bought their entire household furnishings from the Goodwill Thrift Store on the avenue two blocks away, down to dustpans, underwear, socks, and Chang's baby layaways when he was born. Thirty years later, Goodwill bought his clothes new, although on sale, from well-known department stores, but he carefully saved everything and gave them away to the Goodwill store before anything was worn out. "What's in a Name?" I headlined that story. Someone mailed the local Goodwill's a clipping of the article and the manager sent me a thank you letter. Bun Jon was impressed. "So, so, *Asian Time* making big time in Long Beach," he said, filing the letter in one of his plastic stacking bins.

I was running out of Asians willing or able to talk to me or to whom I could talk. Malay, Hokkien and English didn't take me far with the majority of parishioners at the Mission. Wrong languages, understood by only a small minority. Of course, the church elders spoke English. At the Mission with its Spanish and Korean and Mandarin, English was the language of conversion. Everyone understood *Hallelujah* and *Amen* and *Praise the Lord*.

I needed a couple more stories before the end of the semester for Mr Mather's portfolio. Besides, meeting strangers and turning them into copy on my yellow sheets every Sunday was becoming addictive. It didn't matter as much anymore that both Yen and Sandy seemed to be moving further and further away from me with the end of each week. Every Monday I could see in Yen's eyes she was calculating when Wayne would return. Her Sundays without me had become her real world and I only a passerby sister. Every Saturday it was harder and harder for Sandy to talk to me. He had become preoccupied, tired, the Sunday work was exhausting, he said impatiently when I tried to get his attention, yet it was clear he was eager for Sundays to come.

Only my work for the Mission, my writing for Mr Mather and the *Asian Time*, were going well for me. The proposal for the construction of the cross, secreted among a number of other requests, was passed by the city council. Dozens of specs for lighting projects came by the city's agencies every month. No one paid any attention to a church wanting to light up a cross. Pearl didn't ask me, but I thought I'd do her a favor and write a column about the Mission and its appeal for its electrification project. A donor was picking up the cost of the materials, and the congregation, many of them unemployed or day laborers, had voted to tithe their hours for the construction, which would include expert steel work, riveting, and welding, besides the laying of extensive electrical lines. "Another LIGHT for LA!" my headline ran, right under the general heading, "YELLAS SPEAK!"

Bun Jon never revised my copy. He probably never read my stories before running them, and until Mr Mather criticized it, no one seemed to be offended by my frequent use of exclamation marks. Exclamation points, capital letters, big print, words in bold type caught the attention of *Asian Time*'s readers. Its ads were full of multiple exclamation points, whole words capitalized. Mine were abstemious in comparison.

Asian Time came out on Wednesdays, and was distributed mostly to liquor stores and Asian grocery stores, hairdresser saloons, and restaurants. Pete's Tavern was not a place where I worried the paper would be dropped, and no biker I knew would pick up a copy if he saw a stack of it when he went to a liquor store to buy his six-pack beer or Jack Daniels.

Having two names was another happy accident for me. As Sue, I never worried about writing for *Asian Time*. Instead I-Sue drank Miller Light and waited for the beer to soak through to my aches, sleepily taking in the flow of cussing, mass singing, and loud banter Sandy basked in.

I-Sue hardly thought of Mama and Ah Chee, although once when I-Sue had drunk too much and knelt on the dirty toilet floor vomiting a stream of warm sour alcohol mash, I heard Mama's voice again, "And when she was bad she was horrid!" My head spun and to steady it I had to lay it on the toilet bowl crusted with dried piss and flecks of shit, a place that would have horrified Ah Chee and would have horrified good Swee too if she were around.

Sandy and I-Sue were as relaxed here as we were ever to be. At the bar Sandy didn't have to manage maids and janitors, pick up after someone's garbage, keep an accounting of receipts, check out strangers for hidden weapons, answer the same old questions, take complaints on cold and hot running water, roaches, and lumpy mattresses, and tell prostitutes to do their business quietly. Going day shift he had to give up the night manager's extra pay, but he didn't mind. "Nights are scary," he confessed, "you begin seeing people different. No one looks safe. It's like the vampire movies have gotten into your head. Night duty at a twenty-four-hour open motel is a perfect stage set for vampires." The Sunday classes were good for him, he insisted, only men were allowed there. Welding was a man's job, and there were unions to make sure no illegals were hired for the work.

I'd seen him once in the Buenavista College shop, sparks flying like angry bees on fire, stripped bare-chest, a primitive astronaut in his goggled mask, gripping a fiery blowtorch and attacking a rusty mound of iron. That was how I imagined him each Sunday, in hand-to-hand combat with a cold gray mass from the factories of America, a Vulcan razing iron and making art. But Saturdays for Sandy were for softer stuff, going for a run with the Harley grumbling like a young volcano, drinking beer, and talking bike trash talk with his arm around his woman.

That Saturday, coming through the tavern door, I recognized Keith immediately, his tense, once stocky, body and those eyes, visibly blue even in the dim smoky air. Behind him at the table was the same young girl who had yelled names at us. Sandy looked unhappy, but we joined them when Keith waved to him. The jukebox music was blasting, you had to yell for introductions, and gratefully all Sandy could manage in the crashing surf of steel strings and drums was, "THIS IS SUE!"

I heard something shockingly soft, like, "My wife," and tried not to stare at her, because she stood out among the women, not in leather, not in black, but in what looked like army fatigues, the kaki green-olive camouflage patches of the big shirt and pants showing vividly in the packed room. She could have passed for a teenager playing soldier, only, when I made what I hoped was a friendly smile, she stared at me like a queen looking at a kitchen slave, proud, contemptuous, confident, preening, dismissive.

I sat down and tried disappearing among the biker chicks milling around. Such bright red hair, still braided like I remembered when she had screamed at Yen and me a couple of months ago — surely it was natural, born red, not like the synthetics I shook out of a bottle and finger-combed into my hair.

I couldn't understand why a baby-fat girl, married to a man

old enough to be her father, should intimidate me. She didn't look like she'd even graduated with a high school degree. She must have bought her uniform from a second hand army and navy store. The pocket flap on her shirt was clearly marked "ROTC." I felt like a nasty insect scrambling to crawl back under a stone she'd turned over. I couldn't pay attention to Sandy and Keith talking, something about patriots and MPs and Western chapters. Something about their Sunday classes.

Perhaps my look of discomfort encouraged Pinny to come to the table instead of sending the help with the beers like she usually did.

"Hey, Swee," she said, loud enough for Sandy and Keith to hear, setting the beers down with a smack, her eyes not taking in the word "SUE" across my leather jacket, "I see you're writing for *Asian Time*."

Sandy's arm across my shoulder, a warm familiar weight, withdrew.

"Why are you interested? Do you want me to write about your Hong Kong days, Hong Nga?" I was furious. As Mama-san, Pinny joked with everyone but me. I'd watched her stash tips in the cash drawer like she had stashed her birthday presents in her room at Peps, and I'd not ever mentioned the old Pinny again. Bikers and veterans liked Mama-san. She was someone they thought they recognized from a past for which they yearned, a figure that reassured. I didn't want to fight with Keith's baby wife but Pinny was fair game.

"Ha, I don't know what you say! I'm not one of the people you write about in 'Yellas Speak.' What did you write? The men working on the church for no money. But everyone knows illegals go to that Mission church."

Even with Bruce Springstein's guitar twanging the air, I knew I had lost the fight.

The masses of sleek female black seemed to collapse back from me, the red braids had swiveled away, and Sandy was pushing the tankard of beer backward and forward on the wet table, staring at his hands.

I got up to go to the dingy toilet the tavern had posted as the Chicks' Room and Sandy followed me.

It was time to leave Pete's.

Sixteen

*T*he television was laughing and we were also, at Lucy and Ricky shouting at each other, because she is trying to hide from him in her clown costume, and he is angry she has followed him to this town because she is jealous he is traveling with his band without her. She is pretending to be a circus clown and he is only pretending to be angry because they will end up kissing each other. "Oh Ricky!" Lucy will say, Ricky will smile, "Oh Lucy!" then they will kiss and make-up.

But this time, when Sandy and Swee came in, I saw the dirty look on Sandy's face, and I said to Wayne, "Oh oh, look out, Sandy very mad!"

Wayne turned off the television and the laughing stopped. "You wanna go to Venice?"

"No, this time I better stay, take care of Swee."

"You want me to stay?"

"Better you leave. I tell Sandy he leave with you, so Swee and I can go sleep early."

Already Sandy's loud voice was banging in the kitchen. "Why didn't you tell me? I thought you'd changed. Didn't you say you were dropping that stupid name? This is America — you're supposed to use English names!"

I waited to hear how Swee would fight back. In Malacca, Swee was like a kung-fu samurai general, very fierce. She kicked and bit back when we fought. And she was never afraid to talk back to Mama and Ah Chee, cheeky like anything. Her school essays were like that, strategic, she said, clever at fighting. But I heard nothing.

"Yellows speak? What kind of game are you playing behind

157

my back? You're doing it to make fun of me, right? All this time I've been telling the guys you . . . ."

Sandy stopped.

Silence, and Wayne coughed, kuff, kuff, to let them know they could hear him, we could also hear them. "Alright, Yen, I should beat it and let you go off to sleepy time." Wayne was so fake I almost laughed.

But Swee must have been pretty mad because she didn't care we could hear them. "Telling which guys? You've been talking about me to guys? You mean the biker boys? Have you been telling them . . . ."

"No, it's not like that. I don't do locker-room talk. It's because you look different. I had to explain you're not like those yellows coming in to California. You're a college girl, good, smart. And now, it's not going to work. I can't swing it!" Sandy's voice became very loud, like someone letting go off a rope, shouting, angry and frightened.

I heard Swee crying and I ran, ran to the kitchen. Sandy was shaking her, his hands on her shoulders, shake, shake, and her head flopping back, flopping front, flopping back again. My head was hot, like a fire in my brain, burning, roaring. I saw Sandy's hands like in movie close-up, huge, thick, monster hands grabbing my Swee and she whimpering, uh uh uh uh, and Sandy still in the motorbike jacket not able to stop, breathing loud, shaking, shaking her like a thief trying to shake ripe mango from a tree. The fire burned my eyes so I was blind for a minute; I didn't see myself jump on Sandy's back, his black leather animal skin not feeling my fingers scratching him. But I heard my voice, "Eeeeeeee!" like Wayne's bike engine when some part not working, gear engaged wrong, "eeeeeeee!" engine getting hotter and hotter but bike not moving. I was trying to pull Sandy's arms from Swee, but his arms felt like iron, stiff and hard. I could feel inside the black skin his muscles sticking out in lumps.

Then Wayne pushed me from Sandy. "Yo, man, give it up." Voice not too loud, not too soft, must have been just right because

Sandy dropped his arms. His smile aimed for Wayne only, a sick boy smile. He looked at Swee strange, half sorry, half confused as if he just saw he broke something, but it was an accident, it wasn't his fault.

I wanted to hit him, bite his hands, except they were too big and hard to bite. Swee was rubbing her neck with her arms crossed in front of her chest, blinking so her tears won't show.

Wayne put his hand on Sandy's shoulder, walked him to the television room, and I hear them open the door and leave the apartment.

I held Swee's hand, cold, trembling, like the puppy's nose, and took her to her room. "Never mind," I said, "never mind, Sandy go crazy. Wayne talk to him, get him straight."

The bikes went vroom-vroom, noises blasting like bombs outside. Vroom-vroom vroom-vroom, for a long time, until I was afraid Wayne and Sandy just warming up the engines and coming back to apartment. I ran to the front door and locked up and double-bolted, then sat in front of the television, listening to the bike sounds moving down the street, and I followed them further and further, two, three, four streets, until they disappeared and became echoes in my ears.

Swee was still sitting on her bed, massaging her shoulders. She took her black shirt off, made a face where her fingers touched the red-purple spots, bad spots like where a fruit is dropped or squeezed too hard.

"Lucky you're not a mango, otherwise must throw you out," I touched where Sandy had hurt her.

She laughed. "I'm going to Berkeley. Is Wayne really going to marry you?" Then her tears came down, heavy, heavy, and I sat down next to her, my poor little sister Swee, and we hugged and cried together.

Seventeen

Sandy and I were finished. It was finished, whatever it had been. My head felt stuffed with cotton wool, white fluff suffocating all the oxygen I was trying to pump into it. I tried not to hyperventilate, worrying about Yen, not wanting to frighten her, but hard as I breathed I couldn't get the cotton wool out of me. Then the blanketing, dull airlessness turned into water and came out of my eyes, my nose, my mouth in sobs and gulps, like I was crying for losing Sandy and Manuel, for Yen and me, and, at last, for Ah Kong.

I had thought I had not thought about Ah Kong for months. But who else did I think about each time I put on my jacket that said SUE? It was to hide me from Ah Kong. He had always known that was what Yen and I would become, bad women with barbaric western lovers, giving away for free what men in Malaysia paid for. In the land of the free, free women. If Ah Kong hadn't died when he did, he would definitely have had a heart attack to learn about us here in the United States.

I could explain Yen and Wayne. They were like each other, although one was Malaysian and woman and the other American and man. They were proof some people are the same, underneath different skins, different bodies, different languages. Like twins, separated at birth, born seventeen years apart, thousands of miles from each other. The different families and countries simply an accident, superficial, a temporary bump in reality. When they found each other, they rushed into each other's arms, filling the vacuum, completing the human. No longer the sound of one hand clapping, lucky people, when they found their pair, finally held water in their palms and could drink from their hands. But I could never explain myself to Ah Kong. I wouldn't even try.

I couldn't see myself returning to Mama and Ah Chee, with Sandy's finger marks stamped on my body, the smell of beer, cigarette smoke, motorbike oil, and peroxide in my hair. Ah Chee would immediately sniff out my disorderliness, but she wouldn't be able to dust me clean, scrub the bad Sue away.

I didn't have to wait weeks like I did with Manuel to understand I wouldn't see Sandy again. When he called, I refused to take the phone from Yen. He came to the apartment, but Yen wouldn't open the door, and I stayed in the bathroom, locked in. Ah Kong would have approved of it, locking myself in away from barbarian men. Only on Sunday did I feel safe, when I knew he was away with Keith and the welding students. I wondered if these were the guys he'd talked about, with whom he had shared news about me.

Who would have thought I'd ever be at a moment when I'd be grateful to Pearl and her church? When Mr Leong came by to take me to the Mission on Sunday, I felt like a refugee looking for asylum. Sanctuary, that's the technical term for it. In church territory, no one was supposed to pursue you, no tyrant could call you out, no soldiers shoot, no harm befall you. In the Mission, I didn't worry about listening for motorbikes, didn't chase around in my head for why I had allowed Sandy into my life, into my bed and body. I couldn't understand him, and he couldn't understand me. He didn't know what was in my head, didn't like what I said. Was I indifferent to his thoughts, had I disliked his words?

No, I liked Sandy. I liked his body — we had that in common, liking each other's bodies. But that wasn't all. I liked Sandy as freedom. That strange pleasure and fear all in one when I mounted the Harley. The queer relief when we bent low together and wove past speeding cars and trailer-trucks, my body at that moment most vulnerable, ready to be crushed under thundering wheels — pain, suffering, breakage, death, just a few inches away. I first learned that thrill from Yen, but for me, that rush toward danger became better than sex.

And admit it! I admired Sandy, admired his American know-how, from the day he drove the Wayfarer Inn van to pick us up, two lost sisters, and told us what to say to the manager. He seemed to know every short cut, every exit, every parking lot; he never got lost anywhere. Everywhere was his home territory, all of America belonged to him, and I wanted to learn that confidence from him.

Like Yen, Pearl didn't need me anymore. The permits for the Mission's Cross cleared and soon the skeletal structure was visible, at first a tracery of rods glinting off the sunshine, and then the axle, glimmering fine steel in the distance. It would be months before it would grow more substantial, taking on mass, although, as Pearl discovered, it would not overtake other crosses that had come up in California, in San Diego and elsewhere, for sheer height and weight. I had not seen Pearl so delighted, almost transcendent in her pleasure. The construction of the cross was to be her success, despite Robert's role as speaker to the community on its progress, and Pastor Fung's increasing eminence.

I didn't write any more stories about the Mission of Eternal Light, and the stories I wrote, now Mr Mather's course was almost over, were lighter in tone. Perhaps, after Sandy's fit of shaking, I became lighter. No more black leather. I packed the biker clothes, fitting the jacket, pants, shirts, fringed vests, bandanas, around the swollen black and steel helmet in one large box, taped it tight shut and sent it to the Goodwill store whose manager had written to me.

I took driving lessons given by a driving school next to a post office, cars and US mail seeming to satisfy some faintly discernible common social need as well as sharing common parking lots. The teacher was accustomed to Asian immigrant students. We were the only ones over the age of sixteen to be taking driving lessons. "The worst drivers," he expounded. "You Asians are too timid — going slowly causes more accidents than going too fast." Then he had to warn me to slow down because I was driving like the car was a Harley, careening on curves and cutting ahead, scooting between. "Watch out, lady!" he yelled. "This is a freeway but there are still traffic rules you have to obey!"

I wrote a check for a brand new zippy American car, bright red like a stoplight, with only space for Yen next to me. Yen was making her way through more required courses but she was pulling Cs and Ds. It was her third semester and soon it was going to be a new year, and time for the blessing of the first stage of construction of the Cross. The first Sunday I drove myself to the Mission, Melody and her parents no longer a necessity, the cross stood, all wires, tangled and draped like vines from the uncompleted structure.

Pearl had asked me to draft a public statement about the blessing ceremony. "Journalists are like lazy students," she told me over the phone. "They want to get copy they can simply use for their reports. No one wants to write their own stories when they can use one we send them."

"About two pages," she specified, "nice sentences, some details — number of light bulbs, how much total wattage, costs, the purpose. Something to catch their attention. PR stuff."

By this time, I was not so easily impressed by Pearl's familiarity with the world of newspapers and publicity. Public relations, Mr Mather lectured, was just a fancy term for manipulation of public opinion, another sales tactic, like branding. Workaday reporters accepted what public relations officers offered, but journalists were careful not to let PR officers do their work for them.

That Sunday night in late December, Yen was with Wayne as usual, out in Venice. I was trying to write the church statement when Pearl called way past midnight. "An explosion . . . not sure what kind of damage. Lots of fire engines, police cars. Do you think it's my fault, trying to do too much? Pride goes before . . ."

Pearl was not coherent, sobbing, a mix of biblical phrases and garbled descriptions pouring out of the yellow princess-line telephone Wayne had installed for Yen next to the sofa. I turned on the local television. The sitcom was interrupted by live interviews with Robert and Pastor Fung. A line of reporters, detectives and fire marshals was waiting to talk to them when those interviews were over. Pearl, hysterical, had been forgotten. Roused from bed and brought to the Mission with Pastor Fung and Robert, she had been left, abandoned to herself, in the annex, and called me.

I parked my little red coupe two streets down, away from the flashing red tops of the police cruisers and the sleek red fire trucks, black and yellow hoses unwound like messy giant chicken guts and the air smoky yet cool at 1 am on Monday morning. There were no gawkers, the church being in a commercial district that was just beginning to improve. No rubber-neckers, although plenty of television vans and groups of men and women under glaring spotlights, illuminating the twisted steel and clutter of shattered glass that lay like bright sparkly snow-glass everywhere around the Mission. I went behind the building, tapped on the annex window, and Pearl unlocked the back exit door and pulled me in.

"I was listening to the police officer. He said something about a bomb, some incendiary device. It wasn't an electrical failure." Pearl's face in the white industrial illumination from the long faintly hissing lights lived up to her English name. She had always been the fairest complexioned of us, "Peik." I was only a year old when Mama had her, so how could I remember Mama holding her, touching her cheek with her finger and saying "So fair. We'll call her 'Peik' — white. Pure."

I must have made that up, or Yen must have told me that story. We had made fun of Peik, so fair she couldn't play out in the sun with us. So pure Ah Kong doted on her. Here she was, ashen, pasty gray and yellow glimmering in the white pigmentation.

"They want to know everything. The funds for the construction, who worked on it, the names of all the men. I can't give them the information. So many of our parishioners don't have papers. I simply wrote checks from my account. They want to know about the Mission's accounts. As if we are guilty for the explosion!"

Even after all these years I could not hug Pearl. She had always been too transcendental, a spirit sister whose body defied physical affection, whereas Yen and I could piss and shit comfortably together.

"I'm not going to tell them anything!" Pearl reached out and grasped my hand convulsively. It was a cold little hand. She had never grown well. Way under five feet, she reminded me of Melody, as slight as an adopted daughter from a Chinese orphanage, her purity stunting her body.

"Of course not." I gripped her hand in response. "No one can force you to say anything you don't want to. The Mission is a sanctuary. There's a law concerning these matters. You'll need a lawyer. I'm sure Mr Leong knows lots of lawyers, they're part of real estate in California. Besides, you have the Mission lawyer who worked on those permissions."

Her hand relaxed, turned passive as I squeezed it. "I asked to use the bathroom and left Robert and Father to answer the questions. Father's accustomed to appearing on camera. The cross is quite destroyed. Do you think we should . . ."

Even in the annex with windows and door shut, a roar, revving and ramming, followed by a high pitched whine, broke through her question. I recognized it immediately. Or I thought I did. It was a few streets away but in the pre-morning quiet of the vacant avenue it flared like another explosion, breaking the world outside into staccatoes of noise retreating swiftly, leaving echoes that might have been imaginary. I had listened for this music of the machine each time Sandy was coming to get me for a ride. He had learned to work the steel and gears so the rumble and drone of the engine would be at their deepest engagement. The harsh grinding of the clutch together with the full-bellied voluptuous outpouring of noise from the V-engine always brought an ache to my body. Hearing the motorbike approach from streets away, my body would both stiffen and soften, as if instinctively preparing itself for hours of buffeting wind and stinging grit, inner thighs clamped around steel trunk, sensations of contact that made muscles tense and quiver with effort and pleasure. Such roar and whine were sufficient to tune my thighs and legs for embracing. Surely this was the exact eruption of sounds detonating then disappearing over South LA.

"You look faint! I'm sorry to call you so late. You must be sick, your face is all pale!" Pearl tugged at my hand, which seemed to have turned to water on me. She tugged again. "You can't drive back to your apartment alone. Stay with us for the night. Robert will take us home."

I was tempted. Pearl as housekeeper for Pastor Fung must keep a clean and austere place. The ruins of Yen's and Wayne's dinner, fragments of chicken bones and sauces spilled on table and floor, soiled dishcloths flung over chairs, dirty dishes and cups and pans slopping in rancid pools of water in the sink, all these smells and sights rose inside me like sour bile.

I pushed the window open. Outside the murmur of voices — police? reporters? The pastor's? — was faint, nothing like that audacious roar and scream of the machine. Did no one notice it?

I remembered Pastor Fung always spoke as if he were preaching. His every sentence could be a prayer. He was a walking bible, Yen joked, if bibles had soft stomachs and wore lift-up heels. I remembered how I hated listening to him talk, like a petty bureaucrat with puffed-up importance because the governor had given him a small-time office, full of words and phrases he had memorized from the governor's edicts. It was his language I hated, not the man, but Yen called him a man made of words — windy words strung together like bad poetry grown old and respectable.

"No, I better sit down for a while, then I'll leave." I looked at Pearl, hesitated to ask her. "Did you hear something strange just now?"

"LA is full of strange noises. I didn't hear any gunshots."

"Is that what you expect to hear? No, it wasn't a gun."

"The freeway is right by the Mission. We can smell truck emissions, not to speak of traffic noise."

The tension left my thighs and legs. I hadn't imagined the Harley, but it was gone — it had never appeared by the Mission together with the explosion that had brought down the cross. I saw Sandy smiling lovingly at me, then his scowl the last time he had shaken me like a cat shaking a mouse or bird it had caught between its paws.

"You should give up the idea of the cross. Insurance won't cover for the damage, especially if you're not going to answer the questions the investigators are asking. Get the mother church to give you a new building somewhere else."

I was good only for leaving. Some things weren't worth fighting for. Ah Kong, Pastor Fung's Mission, Sandy. But Pearl's congregation would follow her no matter where she went. She had faith, and that, more than the playground, the nursery, the Mission's communion lunches, was what drew Mr Leong and Melody and Maria Padillo and Mrs Kim and all the other worshippers to her. Mr Mather had written in my portfolio after the A for the article on the Mission cross construction: "California is Christianity with all the conveniences?" I envied little Peik. Cross or no cross, she was on her way to becoming a Californian.

Eighteen

*A*ahh, Swee couldn't lie to me. Even when her mouth said other stories, I could look into her eyes and watch how her irises rolled to find the truth. The way her eyes shifting told me she was frightened.

My clothes still dirty from yesterday when Wayne took me to Malibu hills to watch the sun coming up. "7 am Sunday, even the RVs are still hooked up. We'll be king and queen of the Pacific Highway!" Wayne promised. We rode out of exit lane, bike racing straight, steady, riding north, waves and big white surf beside, loud rumbles under our bodies, and woosh and sasssh of water guiding us. We climbed and climbed, Wayne yelling out names of canyons, switchbacks, until he stopped at a park, viewing station, he said. I stared down on tumble down land, many big rocks, too many to count, dark and gray green bushes, to blue and white Pacific Ocean far below our feet.

"Just like a giant flowing cloth," I pointed. "And, wah, over there is Malacca!" I jabbed straight ahead, down. "There is Mama and Ah Chee."

"You ever want to go home, Yen?" Wayne's arm strong around me was like cable holding me from falling.

"No. Yes. Sometimes."

"Want me to take you home?"

"No!" I suddenly scared, knowing Mama scold me if I took this *ang moh* to Malacca. Mama just called last week to say she and Ah Chee, finish visiting temples in Burma and Thailand, soon leaving for Japan, to see the Kamakura giant Buddha. Mama was becoming like the Goddess Kuan Yin, so happy. Her life now smooth, she only meditated and did prayer every day to Buddha. But Wayne was surely too hairy and red for pious Buddhist women.

Too late for me to go home. I must stay with Wayne in tumbling-down wild canyon country. Thinking of that made me shiver.

So now I thought Swee maybe frightened like I was. "Why you scared? You see Sandy again?"

Her eyes flickered and blinked yes.

"No, I haven't seen Sandy since that awful fight, and I don't want to. Haven't you been listening to me? It's time for us to leave Long Beach. You're not passing your courses anyway. Buenavista is simply an excuse for you to have fun with Wayne."

"Why now? Soon I finish my degree. In America, I not so stupid. I don't get As, but Cs and Ds also pass, you know!"

Then I told her. I talked for a long time. I told her about Pete's bungalow, about driftwood sculpture in living room and how Pete now back at VA hospital in LA and Wayne caretaker for home. "I not want to tell you, afraid make you sad. Wayne and I are going to live together, I become Mrs Wayne Patrick Stanhope!"

This time Swee was not listening to me. She was drawing with fingers on kitchen table. The kitchen was nice and clean. Wayne and I rushed out Saturday and forgot to wash pots and dishes. Sometimes Swee left our mess and lectured me like she was Ah Chee, but this morning she was still in pajamas and everything was super clean.

"D'you think Wayne knows anything about Keith and his wife, Helen? I've been thinking about what Sandy and Keith do on weekends, what kind of club they have in the Angeles Forest."

"Helen, that fat baby girl? Why you worry? You say you and Sandy all washed up. What will you do when I move to Venice? You come along with me?"

Swee's eyes now signal sorry. I thought she was sad because maybe now we leave each other.

"That place is a rent-control. Once Pete dies, the landlord

isn't going to let Wayne move in. The rent will go up, or he may sell it. The two of you have no practical sense."

"I don't care. I go where Wayne go." I didn't understand "practical sense." Swee always used her big words to win. But all the same I felt a big pain in my chest, right by my left armpit, like my body was being cut. It was my words cutting up my body. I also wanted to go where Swee goes, my sister, my keeper. Even after one year, Wayne was still too new. Sometimes, he rode slowly. Sometimes, he rode fast. Wayne's moods made me laugh, but they also made me scared. I closed my eyes and saw the blue ocean and our Malacca house far away. If Wayne rode fast and left me, where would I be?

Swee's sigh was like a little flute. "We'll manage. If Wayne marries you, he will gain more than he understands now."

I opened my eyes when she hugged me. Her body was bone and knots. I loved Swee, but Wayne's body was flesh and melting heat. It was no competition. Still, when I hugged back, I felt calm, like I had been crying a long time and now felt comforted.

Swee was fiercer with Wayne. She asked him about his job, his finances, his past! "You're not marrying Yen until I'm sure you're free to marry," she repeated even when Wayne just laughed and laughed at her questions.

"Hey, I'm no bigamist! Never married, nothing. Never found someone who laughed as much at my jokes. I'm doing Yen a favor, making a decent American out of her. She won't have to keep going to college to keep up her student visa. She can even end up sponsoring you!"

"I don't need your favors."

"Lighten up. That's supposed to be a joke. See, some people are made for each other. That's the cliché. Yen and I, we're clichés. I'm older, but she's funnier. That makes us even."

But Wayne was not so happy when Swee told him I was an heiress. "That much money? Nah! You girls haven't been straight with me. What would Yen want with a working class fellow like me?" He was hurt. "Were you laughing at me when we were talking about finding a place to stay? Why didn't you speak up?" He didn't like my having that much money. "You'll be independent. You won't need me."

"I give all my money away!" I cried. "I give to Swee."

"If you don't know Yen by now," Swee scolded, "you shouldn't be marrying her."

Wayne took my hand that was rubbing the tears from my eyes. "What do you want?"

"I want to buy Pete's house. I want you to take care of me, not Swee."

Then he laughed and laughed. "It's a bargain. Someone has to live happily ever after, and it might as well be us."

Swee didn't laugh with us. Her eyes were watching Wayne, still suspicious. "Did you ever go with Sandy to those meetings in the National Forest? Remember, that time when we went together and met Keith and that horrible woman, that Helen?"

Wayne was suddenly quiet. "You don't want to know about those people. What you don't know won't hurt you."

"Another cliché? I hope Yen is marrying someone worthy of her."

"You're a strange old-fashioned person, you know that? No one has to earn merit badges to marry. Besides, Sandy is out of your life now. He was getting into trouble there with those militia people."

"Militia people? Like ROTC?"

"Nah, just jerks pretending to be soldiers. We won't have anything to do with them in the military. They're losers. They have to blame somebody, and black folks are the easiest target."

Swee's eyes were moving rapidly as if trying to read a page quickly before it got closed. "It's an anti-black thing?"

"More or less." Wayne was also shifting around uneasy. "The militia on the West Coast are also touchy about Mexicans and Asians. Anyone who's not pure white."

"Like us!" I interrupted.

"Sandy had a hard time with that. He was into white supremacy talk, but Sue was a real problem for him."

"Sue a problem?" I clutched Wayne's hand. "Sandy's the problem, Sandy's the problem!"

"It's over, right? He's gone."

"What d'you mean 'touchy'?"

Wayne shook his head. "It's nothing you can understand. You have to be white folks to understand how white folks feel. Some white folks don't like seeing people who aren't white move into their neighborhood. They don't like their children sitting in the same classroom with black or Mexican or Asian kids. They get uncomfortable when they hear something that isn't English. It sounds un-American. Like Sandy said, it isn't as if it is something personal."

"But what is personal then? Isn't that as personal as you can get?"

"Hell, I don't know. See, Sandy liked you. That's personal. He just didn't like Asians. That's what the militia is about, it's becoming public about what lots of white Americans think but don't say. I've heard some reporters call groups like Sandy's and Keith's neo-nazis, but they aren't German or nothing, just plain ole white Americans."

"That's the swastika! I saw it on the *jamban*!"

"*Jamban?*"

I forgot Wayne could not understand Malay.

"Yen means the outhouse. There was a swastika where we were in the Angeles National Forest?"

Wayne was blinking like we surprised him. "What's the point of this analyzing anyway? It isn't going to help us bring the planes down. Sometimes, someone's machinery gets its wires crossed, then there's all hell to pay. I figured that's what happened to Sandy. He needed the militia to feel good about himself, but he also needed you. Count yourself lucky he's out of your life."

Swee covered her face and put her head down. I thought she was crying. But when she looked up her eyes were dry, only very tired. "I need to be out of his life. I have to leave. You have to take Yen full-time."

"Hey, I'm not a bag, you know! Wayne and I marry, he not take me full-time, I also take him full-time!"

"How about we ask Pastor Fung to marry you? It's time for Pearl to take us all back. And it's time for Wayne to meet us all."

Swee's eyes said to me, "I forgive you for leaving me. Please forgive me for leaving you." They said, "Wayne will never be good enough for you."

For the first time, her lips said, "What do you think, Yen?"

Nineteen

*T*he story was all over the papers the next day, the real newspapers, not *Asian Time*.

Mr Mather had ruled human interest did not include political stories, and so I never wrote about politics. I wrote only from what I knew and saw and I kept my stories light, funny, and easy to read. *Asian Time* carried no coverage on matters related to elections, crime, violence, corruption, state and federal policies, international wars and conflicts, any investigative issues. "*Asian Time* readers cannot understand English that good," Bun Jon explained early in our acquaintance. "You write entertainment. Make them feel good about being Asian, that's enough!"

I was excruciatingly interested in this political story. Pearl didn't know much more than what was in the news. There had been two bodies found under the collapsed steel trusses and wires — bodies with no identification. No driver's licenses, no wallets, only a few dollars in the bloody pockets, and faces broken beyond viewing. "December Church Explosion." The headlines made it into the second page of the California section.

Then the Western Militia of Patriots (WMP) sent a letter to a radio-show boasting it had set off the time bomb at the Mission Church of Eternal Light construction site. The writer noted the timer had been set for a late hour to avoid hurting people, and the deaths of the two men were unintended, an accident that happened only because the Mission had been sheltering illegal border-crossers. The construction was being carried out with undocumented labor, by a foreign organization pretending to be a church whose purpose was to help illegals take over the United States. The KCLP talk-show host's call-in program attracted loudmouth criticism of immigrants, blacks, universities, women with money, women on welfare, men who had sex with men, and generally of everything said to be different. The radio show was always in the news because politicians took their cue from it as a bell-weather indicator of where US populist voters were. But this was the first time it was enjoying a scoop, about violence by one of its audience.

The police, working with the FBI, subpoenaed the letter and through fingerprinting techniques and interrogations of known sympathizers put out an arrest warrant for Keith Rish. A prominent investigative reporter, accompanying the police on their raid of the militia's headquarters in the Angeles National Forest, wrote a gripping account of the mobile home, which had obviously been hurriedly abandoned. The weatherworn swastika sign on the rotting wood wall of the outhouse Yen had talked about appeared in an oddly appealing photograph. It had been technologically transformed to heighten the image, now distributed in sharp black and white, the cracked wood wall, composed against vines and bushes surrounding the outhouse, framed like the black-and-white Walker Evans photographs of Appalachian homes sold as postcards in the art museum at Peps College.

I read and re-read the papers each day to see if Sandy's name would come up. Adolphus Weinberger. A heavy name that would cover quite a bit of newsprint. But the investigators, the television anchormen, and journalists seemed to know of only Keith Rish. According to the same reporter, whose by-line appeared in print as large as the sub-titles of his column, the radio-show listeners were furious Keith's anonymous letter had been subpoenaed. They complained it was unconstitutional, against the American way, of freedom for the press, the talk-show host should have preserved the confidentiality of his source, and, besides, Keith Rish had been protecting the United States from real law-breakers.

No one had come to claim the anonymous men, Mexicans, according to the radio program, who'd been sleeping under the steel trusses, hoping they'd found sanctuary under a cross in California. They were to remain forever nameless. It was impossible to trace where they'd come from, whom they might have been dreaming of at the moment the blast sent the massive rods and beams crashing down. The radio callers did not talk about these men whose faces and bodies had been so crushed, mashed like earthly fruit, even the sensationalist broadcasters wouldn't talk about it, although Pearl did, obsessively repeating what Robert told her he'd glimpsed as the firemen were cutting the steel wreckage to pull the parts out. But Keith's name was recited over and over again by a stream of callers, hailed as a patriot, a leader of patriots, who'd served his country when it needed him, only to lose his job to illegal aliens and to other countries waging economic war against the United States. He was an American hero, and although, like the dead Mexicans, he had disappeared, his name was invoked daily.

"Did you know about their meetings?" I asked Wayne a week after the news of Keith's bombing and the killings broke.

Yen looked confused. "So what? Wayne no longer in military. He now best air flight controller."

Wayne had come straight from work to take Yen to Venice. Pete had not been able to get to his bar for at least six months and the VA hospital was going to send him to a hospice in West Virginia. That was where he had family buried, the only family he had left, and he wanted to be buried in the small town where his relatives' gravestones went back three generations. Wayne had been paying Pete's rent, but the landlord was reluctant to let the bungalow go as a sub-let. Wayne and Yen were meeting with the real-estate agent who dealt with the landlord to see if he would sell it instead, as he was no longer willing to rent it out. Wayne was in a hurry and didn't want to talk.

"But that my sister's church!" Yen clutched at his arm. "You not know mad bombers, right? Tell Swee. We all Wing sisters, one for all and all for one. Bomb one sister, bomb Wing family."

"Brother! I'm not figuring on marrying the whole family." He swung his arm away, thrust his fingers deep into his pants pocket as if to keep them away from Yen. "Besides, I want to stay away from those FBI guys. They're bad news. Once they come around asking questions, my bosses won't be happy, and I don't want to worry about losing a job when we are talking weddings here."

Yen's face puckered as if she was getting ready to let go of one of her wails. I grabbed her waist and pinched her torso. "Wayne is speaking as a matter of speculation. He's not saying he's losing his job."

"Like hell I'm not. If my supervisor thinks I have anything to do with bombing churches, I might as well leave the state."

"I'm not speaking to anyone about you. I'm curious."

"It's Sandy you're curious about. I'm just Yen's guy. Yen and I were having too much fun for me to worry about survival training. All that wilderness stuff, living off the land, wanting to keep the US lily white. That's the kind of world I've been trying to escape."

"But you knew about the militia?"

"Who didn't? All the bikers at Pete's Tavern knew about it. Maybe not the ladies. It's what you read on the walls of the men's toilets. That and phone numbers for blow jobs."

"And Sandy?"

"He was real screwed up. Like I told you, he'd be giving the Hitler salute one afternoon and smooching you the next. He passed you off as white. Asian Aryan, he said. Some of you people came from the Caucasus, he claimed, trading with the real Chinese, the Mongolians. That explained your eyes. No single eye lids, no slant. And your hair. Red. I don't know if anyone believed him, but to tell you the truth, no one at the bar gave a damn about it except Sandy."

"You knew every Sunday he was. . . ."

"Yeah, I didn't see anything wrong if a bunch of grown men want to play soldiers. We've been doing it forever. Some when they were two or three years old. Makes you feel good about being a man. Marching, giving and taking orders. Taking a gun apart, putting it together again. Blowing up rocks and bushes.

That's why Sandy should never have brought you there. Women don't belong in those places. But who'd know they'd target your sister's cross? And who'd expect those two homeless guys to be sleeping under it?"

"That fat baby girl was there!" Yen pushed her hand into the pocket in which Wayne had hidden his. The pocket bulged, wriggled as their hands played together.

"Keith's cousin. She'd followed him from some place in Idaho or wherever, kept house for him, whatever. That's keeping it in the family."

He took Yen's hand out of his pocket and looked at his watch glumly. "That agent might not be there by the time we get to Venice."

"No one's going to ask you any questions about Sandy. No one's asked me, and everyone at Pete's Tavern knew I was his girlfriend."

"Oh, oh, we pretend no one knows Sandy. We don't know Sandy," Yen said.

"Well, Sandy's disappeared also. This murder rap is deep shit serious. No one's talking, but I'd expect all the regular bikers know Sandy and Keith are somewhere together. They were thick, like father and son."

"Talking about bikers, perhaps you and Yen should take my car for this meeting. Real estate agents may be nicer to people with cars."

"We're out of here!" Wayne grabbed the keys from my hand and left Yen to run after him.

I was chilled even though the temperatures had soared unseasonably to the high eighties earlier that day. Yen had only one more semester before she'd get her associate degree and stupidly I had never completed my application to Berkeley. There was nothing at Buenavista to detain me. None of the classes were upper-level. I had gone through the very short list of challenging teachers and had come to a stall, a dead end, spinning my wheels.

Sandy had been California for me, the Saturday bike rides a

dream-drift over the continent, better than the security of sleep, an unreality of speed, followed by the mild languor of alcohol and sex. The sweet life as Sue.

Thinking of Sandy now, I was cold, afraid. He was somewhere out there with Keith. Blowing up the structure, he was telling me I was over also for him. But he could not have known about the two men sleeping under it, homeless, finding shelter in a safe place.

I paced up and down the apartment to keep warm. Sandy and I had shopped together for the sofa, the coffee table, kitchen chairs. Every piece of furniture had passed by his eye. But I had never trusted him to understand what I had brought from home. Ah Kong's money. Mama's smiles. Ah Chee's capable hands. The strong smells and ripe flavors of Malacca. Everything he approved for me was American, white. American and white meant the same to Sandy. I wondered if it was time for me to go home yet again.

Then the phone rang as if to bring me back to Long Beach.

"They caught the man!" For a moment I thought it was Yen speaking. Pearl had lost her quiet tone, and in pitch and accent, she and Yen were suddenly alike.

"Which man?"

"There is only one man. Didn't you read the papers? That Keith Rish. They found him north of Portland. Father got a call and then a visit from the FBI. They wanted to know if Father had ever run into him. How did the militia get to hear about the Mission?"

"What are they going to do to him?"

"Something about trying him for a federal crime because he had crossed state lines. They said the militia had moved from California to Oregon to Washington State. The FBI agent said the bombing of the Mission will become a classic conspiracy case study."

"Conspiracy?"

"Yes, the government is trying to break down these militia movements. There are new anti-conspiracy laws. If they can prove it was also a race-hate crime, and especially if he knew there would be immigrants somewhere near the construction that night, that Keith Rish could be in jail for murder for a very long time."

"Did they mention anyone else?"

"No, they don't talk much, just ask lots of questions. Aren't you glad we are in such a great country? Father says we are blessed to be protected by such law officers. Evil-doers have no chance in the United States."

"Did they say where the militia people moved to?"

"North. They mentioned some towns north, but I wasn't paying attention."

I wanted to reach through the telephone wires and shake the information out of Pearl, who could recite passage after passage from the New Testament, who had swallowed whole the Psalms and Proverbs, memorizing the numbers of chapter and line, but who could not recall where Sandy might be. But the car that would have brought me to her side was in Venice, so I had to be satisfied with studying the *Atlas of North America* and tracing the highways where a bike would have roared through, headed toward a white paradise.

The large North American map was not particularly helpful. There, California was merely a strip like an old curling French fry on the enormous plate of the continent. The state map might be more useful, but thinking of Sandy and how he hated the idea of riding up to San Francisco, I could not see him staying in a region close to the Bay area. I flipped the pages and stopped at the map of the Pacific North-west, green with mountain wilderness, with blue vein-like rivers running down the Cascade mountains into the complex twisty coves and narrow inlets of the North American coast. With my index finger I followed the freeway as it snaked up from Long Beach, past those beach towns he'd loved to stop at: Manhattan Beach, Santa Monica, Malibu, Ventura, Santa Barbara. Further north, after Pismo Beach, Moro Bay and Cambria, following that back-pedaling thread of a road past Monterey, Russian River, across the red state line into Oregon. Even further, passing little clusters of houses making up a town, whose names I was sounding for the first time. Brookings, Coos Bay, Reedsport and Florence, Waldport, Terra del Mar, Tillamook and Warrentown. I could not see Sandy standing on the Oregonian shore of the Pacific Ocean, facing Japan and Korea, and behind them, China, the giant other. The mighty Columbia bled blue like a long incision cutting Oregon and Washington into parts. My finger moved upward tracking Oregon, traversing the open wound of the river, into Washington.

Yes, he would have stopped in Washington, with its thousands of little islands and the huge Puget Sound curved like a blue bowl to catch migrants from the North Pacific islands, that pulled Eastern adventurers like a magnet swooping white filings out of New York and New Jersey, past the great states of Iowa, Ohio, Kansas, the Dakatos, Michigan, Minnesota, Wisconsin. The roll of exotic names flowed under my fingers, drawn to the Pacific, stopping at the San Juan Islands breathless, before launching off toward Asian empires.

The red road wound up past Astoria, Willapa, Aberdeen and Olympia. I studied the large dots of Tacoma and Seattle and followed the artery past Bellingham, Shoreline and Lynnwood, past the deep, deep crevices of waterways. Even more mountains, expanses of dark-green, safe wildernesses for hiding. Here were thousands of inlets, coves and bays, harbors looking not out to water but inland, so gnarled by glaciers one could be by the Pacific and gaze over it into the American mainland. These fingerlings of water and land, twisted like entrails, like trails turning restlessly now out, now inward, reminded me of Sandy the last time we had walked by the Santa Barbara beaches, standing out on the surf, but still gazing in. I was sure if anyone was ever to look for him, he would be found not in California but as far north and west, just short of the Canadian border and the thundering Pacific, as his motorbike could take him.

Twenty

"You knew him better than I figured." Wayne's tone was admiring if grudging. I'd told him months ago, after Keith had been arrested, Sandy had probably left California and gone up to Washington state.

He'd come this morning, earlier than his usual time to pick up Yen, to tell me what he'd heard from a veteran who had come back from West Virginia where he had visited Pete's grave, and who'd heard it from someone visiting a sick veteran, who'd heard it from someone else, all of them men, passing on the story as they traveled across the country and up and down the coast, and who fell into each other's company in the bars they knew about or in the houses in which they were welcomed to stay for a night. Wayne apparently never lost touch with his brothers-in-arms although he was a successful civilian lifer now.

The papers had published the story on the fire, including Sandy's name in full, but it had rated only a short column buried in the middle pages of national news and I had missed it altogether.

"This guy, he knew more than what was reported. Said the FBI had a lock on the coverage. It's still top secret, classified. He'd heard it from the neighbors who didn't want to be identified and wouldn't speak to the reporters but who said the feds were breaking the law here."

My stomach had iced over and my chest felt as if it had been carved up, like I was already a corpse although still sitting up, the expression on my face frozen smooth, interested.

"You were right. He'd gone up north as far as he could go. The owner of the house the feds burned down claimed Sandy had broken in. But the way the neighbors tell it, the owner had given the house keys to this militia organization. The meetings had been going on for over two years — some local people, some outsiders — nothing rowdy but definitely white Aryan groups. There had been flyers sharing their philosophy — to keep the northwest a white-only territory. No blacks, no Mexicans, no Asians. Respectful, straight language, but clear."

I could barely whisper. "And Sandy?"

"Well, he went there to hide out. Thought with Keith caught, the police would come after him next. But he didn't figure on the FBI getting in the picture."

"But why?"

"Fugitive crossing state lines. Funny, huh? The same laws passed for slaves . . ."

I closed my eyes to ease the anguish. I was going to cry, no doubt about it, but I didn't want to cry in front of Wayne.

"You're OK?"

Opening my eyes, I stared at his round moony face, patchy with red, the skin of someone who burned in minutes under the sun.

"How do they know he's. . . ."

"It's that particular location. Trinity Cove. The way this friend of Pete's heard it, it's a steep climb down to the cove, and slippery boulders, huge waves, dangerous currents. You couldn't swim there, even if you wanted to, in the cold water. Instant hypothermia. Besides, the surf would throw you back onto the rocks. The house was like on a ledge with over a hundred foot drop onto the rocks. Sharp slimy granite — broken off in winter storms, not your soft southern Californian beaches. No way he could have gone into that water."

"Trinity Cove? Is it some kind of Catholic name?"

"Nah, don't think so. Don't think Sandy ended there because of his Catholic background. Remember he was running from the police for blowing up your sister's church! And the killing of those men."

"He could have given himself up. I don't think he knew about the homeless men. It was not as if he was a murderer. The pastor would have helped him." I wanted to hang on to the image of Sandy coming in with his morning pastries and doughnuts, smiling, kissing my hair.

"You don't know anything about the law of the land, do you? Or about the US government! For someone so smart, you're like Yen, you know, innocent."

"At least you don't call me 'babe'!" My irritation returned, mingled with the pain.

Wayne looked toward the kitchen door. I knew he was hoping Yen would be out soon so he wouldn't have to talk alone to me. In-laws, we would manage to avoid each other.

"I'm sorry. Is Sandy really. . . ." The word stuck in my head. It was too big, too significant, for me to utter.

"Everyone thinks so. Everyone believes he was in the house that night. It was a hunter's moon night. He would have stayed indoors. Too much moonlight. And out there by the water it would have been spooky. The locals said they hadn't seen it so bright ever. Like lit by a cosmic light bulb. It didn't surprise anyone that was the night the feds came out. They'd had the whole area partitioned off. No one allowed in or out, the roads closed. Although, I guess if a man wanted to, he could trek down the ridges."

Wayne stopped, his eyes brightening as Yen walked in, hair damp from her shower, scents of soap and shampoo, body lotion, face cream, and powder wafting over us like incense promising wishes come true.

"Aiyah! Why so early?" Yen's voice had become softer, its past shrillness tuned down to loving riffs. He got up from the sofa, and she leaned into him, both still drawn together after months of bedding.

"Wayne's telling me about what's happened to Sandy. What he thinks has happened." I could not make my voice fuller. I did not want to see her pleasure.

"Sandy! He still here in Long Beach?"

They were going to be married at the Mission in a few weeks,

and she'd swore she'd complete the coursework for her degree —
it would be easier to do so living full-time with Wayne than being
between Wayne and me. An Easter wedding, a proper ceremony,
Wayne had insisted. No one in his family was going to question
whether he was properly married to Yen. They had given up
on him when he fled the strict Baptist home, enlisted for Nam,
and sent back pictures of himself with pretty bar girls — just
to get back at them, he said. Now he was sorry for this childish
defiance; he wouldn't want his mom and dad to think Yen was
like one of those girls. He wasn't inviting them for the wedding,
but he wanted to send them a pack of wedding photos, with the
white gown and pastor and choir, almost like it would have been
had he stayed home and married the McNeil girl his mother
liked. Yen agreed to everything he wanted. It was strange to see
how marriage meant nothing to her and everything to him.

    This was the first bad news we'd heard since the bombing of
the Mission cross. At least, it was my bad news.

    "Can you finish telling me what happened?"

    "Sorry. I get everything mixed up nowadays. This wedding
stuff is enough to craze me." He rubbed his nose into Yen's hair
to remind himself of his sanity, then stopped at my grimace. "But
that's about it, I guess. No one came out of the house after the
FBI agents issued the warning. They had the place surrounded.
Spotlights, helicopters, agents in flak jackets and camouflage,
night-vision goggles. M-16s and 50-caliber machine guns, M240
weapons, and even AT-4 rockets, one of the neighbors said. It was
like a Hollywood action movie — only slower. They must have
waited a couple of hours, maybe more. Then they began lobbing
smoke bombs, tear gas canisters, all kinds of explosives. All
sorts of new anti-personnel weapons the neighbor never saw in
military action. The feds are really good at this kind of thing."

    "But Sandy?" I wasn't interested in the details of combat.
My face had again masked over. I could not control the freezing
ache, could not warm my cheeks or make my body mobile and
expressive.

    "Yah, yah, what happened to Sandy?" Yen was clutching one

of my hands now, her fingers warm from her shower, rubbing hard to warm it.

"Well, he never came out. And the house burned down."

"Oooooh!" She let go of my hand and held on to me instead. "Ooooh!"

"But how do they know. . . ."

"No one knows anything! At least, the feds may and they're not telling. No one's said anything about finding a body or whatever. But the WMP — you know, the Western Militia of Patriots — are now claiming him as a martyr. He's just gone. The feds don't want him to be known dead because then the WMP have a hero, and the WMP are sure he's dead because the feds are mum on the whole thing."

I was trembling. The morning was cold, so cold. I remembered the monks chanting for Ah Kong. I thought, Everyone deserves a proper burial. Does his family in Solvang know about him? Doesn't he deserve to be mourned, buried with prayers and tears, eulogies for his life spoken?

"Oh, there are lots of events planned around Trinity Cove, this guy told me. Sandy would be surprised at how he's become top gun for the militia."

I must have spoken aloud. Or Wayne was reading my thoughts.

"I'd say he's really gone. You and Yen don't ever have to worry about him again."

I shook Yen's arms off and picked up my purse. The car keys jiggled lightly inside. "I'm going to tell Pearl about this."

But turning the engine over and listening to it rev up then settle into a hum, I thought instead of driving all the way north to Washington, without stopping for either coffee or a bathroom break, fasting, my kidneys clenched tight against peeing, until I would see for myself where Sandy had stopped.

Twenty One

I was going to drive alone up to Trinity Cove. The idea of a house perched on an edge above the cold stormy Pacific intruded insistently on my imagination. Each day, again and again, as I was trying to complete my late application for the journalism degree, I had to put aside the university catalogues, the pages of instructions, multiple forms in white, green, blue, and pink, and take up the shifting shapes of that house — half hidden in the ridges, jutting into air, alone on its ledge, lofty, many-roomed, a black charred mound of wrecked timber and plaster — pushing in from the periphery of my attention. These were fantasy visions demanding I gaze fully on them. The mystery of Sandy's disappearance — I would not admit his death — obsessed me, like a mental rash I needed to scratch at for relief. And the more I scratched what I didn't know, the more painfully it itched.

It was impossible to focus on the applications. The entire process roused my impatience and contempt. Pink! Could one take another two or three years of study seriously if one had to provide the most crucial information for acceptance on pink colored paper? I knew the colors were to help me keep straight all the different categories of information universities required. Past education records. Financial need. Private information on parents' occupations and family earnings. Current address and contact numbers. Lots of numbers requested: social security, business telephone and fax, home telephone and fax, perm address and telephone. It took me a minute to realize perm was not for a hairdresser contact but an abbreviation for "permanent." Could I be admitted to a university without a permanent address? Would I be comfortable at a place where everyone was expected to have permanent addresses and numbers?

I knew my procrastination had something to do with the images of Trinity Cove that flashed into view even as I was reading long descriptions of requirements toward successful completion of a journalism degree. Wayne's retelling of the passing veteran's news — how accurate had it been? What had Wayne left out, with his limited vocabulary composed chiefly of slang and technical language? And the veteran, repeating another veteran's report of what some neighbors, accidental viewers caught on the sideline, had told him weeks after the fire. Had their descriptions been clear? Had the listener heard correctly, not missing a phrase, a sentence that might have changed completely the meaning of the event? I was a reporter who wanted to find the story for myself. I did not trust Wayne, didn't know the veteran who spoke to him, couldn't fathom those neighbors whose anger had started and fuelled the line of telling, until it arrived here in my head, aching with the pressure of recurring pictures, snapshots, now gray tinted, now lurid flames, like cards fanned out by a compulsive croupier. Was there even a Trinity Cove? What could be at stake in this story I couldn't shake off? Had there really been a fire, and where was Sandy caught in these pictures?

It was already late March. Our Chinese New Year dinner last month had been a store-bought cooked turkey that Yen sliced and warmed up in the microwave, all three of us eating sadly. Sadly because I was sad and Yen always felt what I did. Wayne could not wait to finish the meal and take Yen off to Venice Beach, where they were taking Pete's things to storage. Pete had died at the VA hospice in West Virginia, and, as I'd warned, the landlord had ended the lease and refused to consider their bid for the bungalow. Yen and Wayne were looking at other houses, all located in Southern California. She had become accustomed to the cozy bungalow and now resisted leaving our apartment unless it was for a house as familiar, as much as home had come to feel for her in America, as Pete's place.

At first my plans were to bring sodas, packets of chocolate chip cookies, crackers and individual cheese rounds wrapped in thick plastic coats and drive without stopping until I got to Trinity Cove. I studied the AAA map of the West Coast. It would take me about two days of straight driving, I calculated, one day until I got past San Francisco to Eureka, and another day from Northern California up toward the border between Washington and British Columbia, if I drove all day.

I could feel my thighs loosen at this prospect, the urge to pee in anticipation of the drive already on me. Three days. That was the minimum even for a determined driver. Two nights in motel rooms until I got to Trinity Cove. I would find some place to sleep there. There were always motels to be found on the West Coast. I had seen their signs blink by when Sandy was ferrying me clinging to him like a marmoset hanging on to its mother's back. A row of mere rooms, shuttered windows, with doors facing the parking lot. White painted single-storied lodgings lit up with grand names, like Jefferson Suites and The President's Inn. Motels disguised as cottages, motor courts, lodges, cabins, resorts, nooks; advertising themselves as deluxe, farms, houses, inns, getaways. I had gazed at them as they flew up and blew away, mile after mile along the California highways. Somewhere, wherever Trinity Cove was, I would find some motel to take me in on the strength of my credit card.

But finally I could not go alone. It was too scary, the notion of driving for three days north up the coast, with only a radio and cookies to keep me going. What if the coupe broke down? What if the police pulled me over because they had a report of a stolen vehicle matching mine? What if I needed a bathroom break and the only stop was a gas station with a lone surly mechanic holding the key to the toilet? What if it began to rain and the roads flooded and I had to pull over and wait for hours till the water drained? What if I needed to talk and someone who saw me reported me as a crazy foreigner talking to herself in a speeding car and the police. . . .?

"It's only for about six days," I pressed Yen. "Surely Wayne can do without you for a few days."

She was unconvinced.

"Everything will be over in a few months. You'll be married and finished with your degree. Think of it. You'll never have to take another course; and you'll never have to listen to me nag about classes. It will be a kind of holiday, a break, for us."

"But I don't like car rides. They make me sick."

"This will be different. We'll stop whenever you wish."

I was surprised when Yen agreed.

"Our last trip as sisters," she said.

"But we'll still be sisters after the trip!"

"Not the same sisters. When Wayne and I marry, you stay Wing, but I I become Mrs Wayne Patrick Stanhope. No more same family. Next month, I become a different person."

An Easter wedding. It was Pearl's idea.

"Anniversary of the Resurrection," she'd explained to Wayne, who'd asked why they had to wait so long for their church wedding. "You and Yen marry on the day of salvation. It will make up for your sinfulness."

Wayne didn't bother to tell Pearl he and Yen were committed to the sinfulness she was referring to even as the wedding day drew closer.

"Makes it easier to remember our anniversary," he'd shrugged.

We were setting off on our last sisterly adventure, I said to Wayne, just a couple of weeks before the wedding. He would have her for the rest of her life. He could not deny me a few days now. Such a reasonable request, a reasonable exchange. I didn't tell him where we were going or why.

And Yen showed no interest. She had bought herself a tape recorder, a magic machine playing all the music Wayne had introduced her to and which she listened to for hours in ecstatic concentration. She was going to listen to music all the time I was driving, and eat chips and sugared popcorn when she wasn't. That was a break she would enjoy.

We packed quickly. Warm pajamas, a handful of panties and bras, tees and sweaters, jeans. Sisters did not have to dress up for each other. It would be like being home together in Malacca, no male suitors, only we daughters lounging in comfortable, worn clothes, with Ah Chee and Mama keeping a complacent watch. Whom would we meet, cramped in the little machine all day, and checking in from front desk to motel room for the nights?

I remembered to throw our raincoats at the back of the car after Yen had banged down the door to the trunk. Raincoats in Southern California for the occasional winter storm, rain for which we had cannily prepared but which came so rarely that the gabardine coats were as new as the day we had bought them in the South Coast Mall the first time we went shopping there with Sandy.

"I'll miss you." Wayne nuzzled his face into Yen's hair. He intended to stay at our apartment until we returned. I hadn't thought he would be so sentimental. Years older than Yen, he'd become attached. I thought of the old story of the fractured halves of a coin, their jagged edges fitting together perfectly to make the circle whole. Halves broken off, lost, that when recovered and fitted together, regained their magical value, spinning into the blue-black sky, warming a frozen earth, a disk of fire, infinite energy, the currency by which humans live and understand themselves. Perhaps their difference in age was not important. Yen had grown calmer, focusing on those pleasures she saw as Wayne's possessions and soon to be hers.

As soon as I got on the freeway, she had Wayne's favorite tape on.

"Country road, take me home to the place I belong. . . ." She knew the entire song and sang along serious and focused, "Mountain mama, take me home, country road."

"We're taking the freeway all the way," I glanced at her, her mouth wide open in the O of "home."

She didn't seem to have heard me. I tried again, more loudly.

"We'll be driving to Washington."

"Washington?" She stopped singing, sat up with a laugh. "We go to the White House? See the President?"

"No, it's Washington State. We'll get to walk by Puget Sound."

She slumped down again, uninterested, fiddled with the tuner, turning the volume up.

The harsh twang of country music boomed in the coupe's small cabin. A female singer this time, nasal and sassy. I guess if Yen were reincarnated as an American, she would return a honky-tonk woman, living on her nerves, loving a man. From the corner of my eye I watched her impatiently tear open a large bag of cheezwits. The plastic resisted her pull, then suddenly ripped, spilling bright orange balls over her lap and on to the car floor. The sharp bitter smell of synthetic cheese bloomed with the guitar chords. If food reconstituted the cells that consumed it, Yen would have long ago become a full American. I concentrated on pulling on to the middle lane, away from the obese trailer trucks careering up the fast lane. Yen crammed the twisty puffs one at a time in a swift expert flow into her mouth. She licked the salty orange residue from her fingers and glugged the rest of the soda from the can. I felt a tenderness envelope us, as if her very ordinary gluttony were making this trip safer. What was more normal than passengers tearing up bags of snacks and turning the interior of a car into a mess? No police would think us dangerous or weird, surrounded as we were with soda and plastic trash.

The first few hours were easy. We both recognized familiar landmarks — the Malibu beaches, Ventura highway sign, the purple bougainvillea and tall palms of Montecito and Santa Barbara. The tears I hadn't cried for Sandy seemed to stain the sunny, swiftly passing scenes with a bright harsh yellow, a shellac polish my feelings couldn't pierce through, California still an unreality after all this time.

But it was a different sensation driving with my two hands firmly on the wheel from being carried by Sandy on his passenger seat. As if I was learning for myself the freedom I had thought he owned, that he had shown me, what I loved him for. Pushing the coupe to speeds I had to pull back from, I thought about our Saturday thunder-rolls, those days when Sandy had loved me. I was driving north to reclaim some sense of Sandy from the fire, to understand the kind of country he had led me to, that I wanted to be a part of.

I refused Yen's offers of popcorn, cheese balls, candy mints. I did not want to lose the fresh firm feel of the steering wheel, the sensation of wheels rumbling steadily under the flooring. The coupe was a house machine, not at all like Sandy's bike, which always felt like an animal machine. Tented in the cheesy, pepperminty, bubble-gummy, grapey scents of Yen's chewing, I missed the hot highway smells I associated with Sandy. A new car smell lay under the snacks' aromas — fresh plastic, if that wasn't an oxymoron, fresh nylon carpeting, which would soon disappear under the rain of orange cheeritos.

Yen was content to sing along. Wayne had given her his favorite Beach Boy tapes and Mama and Papas. "You'll hear California wherever Sue's driving you," he'd said. "Sun, sun, sun. Surf, surf, surf," the voices harmonized, seeming in rhythm with the variable Pacific we could see rushing and receding to the left. The ocean wildness seemed tame in the morning sunshine, waving and winking, unceasing. Its constancy was making me sleepy. I rolled down my window, yawned, rubbed my eyes, pinched my arms, accepted the caffeinated soda from Yen.

It was hard to keep my eyes on the road, Yen's fidgeting, ripping and crushing of snack bags, and singing and twiddling being so irritating. But I paid respectful attention to the truck in front, refusing to speed up or to pull aside as one, then another and another vehicle reared up in the back view mirror, jammed up close, pulled into the next lane, and passed by in a swelling assembly line of automobiles. Yen's chewing played a counterpoint harmonic to The Mamas and The Papas vocals. I kept the window down. It was warm, not yet noon. It would be dark by the time we got to San Jose.

But I didn't stop for the night till we were way past San Francisco. It was the Vacation Inn sign that persuaded me to pull up, engine running hot, and Yen by this time napping with her sticky fingers clutching a tissue she had used in vain to clean up after the soda spill. I heard Mr Mather's voice, "People look for the security of a brand name," as I pulled into the lot, and a sense of foolishness came down on me as soon as I turned off the engine.

"Lock the doors!" I said to Yen as she sleepily sat up and brushed the sprinkles, crumbs, and wrappers off her jeans. The car was only a few yards from the lobby, but it was very dark at 8 pm. I had been driving for almost ten hours, with just a couple of short breaks. My shoulders felt stitched tight, my thighs ached with the memory of the gas pedal and the hundreds of miles covered.

The desk clerk took my credit card and returned it with the room key card and the number, 121, carelessly written on its cover. Yen was outside, stretching, passenger door open, its interior light a puddle in the empty parking lot, her tongue licking her lips and teeth like a cat cleaning itself.

I shook away my irritation, grabbed our bags from the trunk, locked the coupe, checked its doors again, and led her through the lobby, to the right as directed by the clerk, through another entrance for which I had to key ourselves in, down a corridor which was neither dim nor brightly lit, to our room, at the end of the building. The brand name had brought me to the motel, but clearly it was the brand's anonymity that sold it to travelers. The room was bland to the point of vertigo. Beige green speckled wallpaper and beige blue speckled carpet. Two mass-produced art works — paintings that looked like faint paper prints or paper prints that looked like paintings — on the walls. The desk and tiny refrigerator were so battered as to assume some kind of unsavory character, as if they had been banged, dented and scratched by a series of enraged guests.

Yen found the television remote immediately, beside the bed table, and turned on the television. The large television and small double bed were the only new things in the room. Yuks and guffaws from a laugh track bounced off the wallpaper. I was desperate for some quiet.

"I'm going to take a shower. Want to use the bathroom first?" Soon as she went to the bathroom I turned off the television.

"Hey, I wanna watch the show!" Her voice, muffled behind the bathroom door, was energetic and insistent. I had hoped she might have wanted to go to bed. She had been sleeping for the last two hours of the drive.

"Tell you what. Let's check the telephone book to see if any Wings live here in this part of California!" I looked for the telephone book, found it in the chest drawer beside the bed, lying side by side with a book stamped in large gold print, "The Holy Bible."

Yen came charging out of the bathroom. "I look, I look," she yelled.

"Tell me what you find." I grabbed my pajamas. "I'll be in the bathroom for a while."

And wonders of wonders, resting my dizzy head on my hands as I sat on the toilet, feeling the hot piss flush out of my body, no laugh tracks crept in under the bathroom door. For once, Yen had found something else to occupy her than the blaring voices and colors from the picture tube.

Twenty Two

Swee asked me to look up "Wing" in the telephone book. Such a thick book, so many pages with names, addresses, and information on so many offices, businesses, restaurants, motels, and what-not. When Swee was driving up north after San Francisco I saw America was empty. Only big, big green trees, too many to count. Trees the whole way, whether highway going up or down, curving right or left. Also, fewer signs. A few names of towns. But many, many roads, only now, the road signs just numbers. Exits also numbers, as if now we entering a world with few people, numbers must fill in for people names. Where were all the people, shops and businesses that appeared in the telephone book? Must have been hidden among the green trees, where I thought was only empty land.

I was surprised to find four Wings in the telephone book for this empty looking place! One was the name of a business. "Wing Company, Cloverdale Rd." On the other page I read the ad, "Learn to fly in six months with Wing Company. Experienced pilot instructors." One was "Wing, Scott Tall Mountain." Didn't sound Chinese, not a name like our Singapore brothers, although in America I almost forgot their names. Wanda's wedding so long ago and mine in two more weeks, so much happening in two years I almost forgot about Malacca and Mama and Ah Chee! One other Wing name also did not sound Chinese. Jesus Perez Wing. But this one, "L L Wing," I thought maybe a Chinese lost in Northern California. The name said "MD." Chinese doctor disappeared in the green trees. I felt sad for this doctor.

So I turned to happier thought, Wayne's name, "Stanhope." No problem. I counted thirteen Stanhopes. "Stanhope,

J," three times. One "Stanhope, Abramowitz," very strange name, like two different names in one. No Wayne, no Patrick Stanhope here, but others with nice easy names. Mary, Robert, William. Easy capital letters. "G" for "George," I guessed. "N" for "Norman"? Maybe relatives of Wayne? How nice to have a name that gave me so many relatives, even in a nowhere town so far away from Long Beach, California.

Swee left the drawer open where she found the telephone book. I took out the other book in the drawer. I see "Holy Bible" on the brown plastic leather cover, and "Placed by The Gideons." Who were the Gideons? Perhaps the motel owners? Why they're so generous? Or maybe Gideons some American version of Bible?

At Buenavista, one English professor told us about different versions of stories by different translators. How one story became many kinds of stories. None the same although the first one never changed. I never liked Bible study at Methodist school. It was very boring because the Bible teacher, Miss May Chu, was a dragon. Everything for her must be learned by heart, word for word. I wondered if the Gideons Bible had the same words as in Miss Chu's Bible and if she dare get mad with the Gideons if their words not the same as in the Methodist Bible. I forgot the verses she forced us to learn, but still, curious, I opened this motel Bible to see if it was the same as Miss Chu's.

Aiyah, I could not tell! Like Miss Chu's Bible, this Gideons Bible also hard to understand. Supposed to be English, but not real English. I flipped the thin pages afraid to tear something. Only now I noticed the foreign names. Genesis, Exodus, Leviticus, Deutoronomy. Not pronounceable.

Only one name I recognized. Book of Ruth. One nice simple woman's name. Must be a girl story.

I tried to read it but it was very confusing. Why did Ruth have to follow her mother-in-law? Made me think of Wayne's mother in Kansas too far away to come for our wedding. Mama also too far away to come. Maybe I have no more need for mother. But this Ruth story ended very well. Her mother-in-law gave her good advice, she got pregnant and married a rich man.

I didn't have to worry about money, Swee told Wayne. But reading about Ruth, I felt sorry for myself. When Wayne and I marry, I have only Wayne, no nice mother-in-law like Naomi. And no sister, not even Swee, because she said she'd soon be leaving California for New York.

Swee was in the bathroom a long time. I tried not to fall asleep until she came out. In the car, I tried to sleep, be quiet, not be a nuisance.

For a long time, Swee was the smarter sister. I teased her, "Sister Swing," swing higher than me. Her school grades so good Mama always nagged me because I could not keep up with younger sister. For a very long time Swee believed Mama, she actually the older sister. Whenever I told her what I knew, Swee acted like she knew better. She didn't believe what I said about Ah Kong, but then she had the nightmares. She didn't trust me with Wayne, but Wayne was a better person than Sandy. Wayne and me like that song, "Love and marriage, love and marriage, go together like a horse and carriage." Except we got together first, like a horse and carriage, and that brought us to love and marriage. Sandy kept secrets from Swee. He left her alone every Sunday, hiding the day and himself from her.

The thing I knew about Swee was she was more timid than me about some things. Sometimes I got confused, got bad marks in exams, but I was not afraid to say whatever was on my mind. I knew my mind. Swee may be too smart, end up with more than one mind. Always careful, must say what was right. Could not bear to think she made a mistake, got things wrong. Could not stand to be stupid. She must think and think. Must analyze and analyze. Everything must have more than one side, more than one story. Like when she was a little girl, stay on the swing for a long time. Swing up, swing down, swing up, swing down. Different perspectives, she said, when she learned this big word, explaining why she liked playing on swings so much. Mama told Pastor Fung Swee was one moody girl, one time smiling, another time bad-tempered, one time brave, cannot wait to fly away, another time screaming because she dreamed about frightening birds.

Swee was just like that with Sandy. One day "Sandy no good," another day she said, "Sandy has potential." For her to spend time with Sandy, he must already be more interesting than what he really was. She wanted Sandy to help make her at home in America, like Wayne helped me. But Sandy was just a rat. He shook her so hard she was blue black for days. "I say Sandy a nasty rat," I told Wayne. "I don't swing backward and forward like my sister."

Swee didn't know I knew her inside secrets, her trouble was no longer about me. We both changed. She now truly the younger sister. She stopped worrying about me because Wayne take her place as my guardian. But she didn't know yet it was my turn to worry about her. Today she told me where we were going. Some town in Washington State.

I didn't want to come with her on the trip. What for? So boring. Just drive and drive. She said she wanted to see where Sandy ran to hide from FBI. She said the house burned down. So I asked, why drive so far if no house left to see? But she didn't answer.

"Why?" I asked again.

"Because Sandy. . . . " She stopped, moved her hands on the steering wheel.

I opened my mouth, closed it again. I wanted to repeat, "Why?" but I couldn't see what was in her eyes. They were fixed on the road. She had told me to look out for a motel for the night but I forgot to do so.

Why look for Sandy now when she wouldn't open the door to him the times he came knocking after the last fight? She wouldn't forgive him then.

Wayne asked me about it. Sandy had talked to him about Swee, if she was ever going to make up.

"She's like that," I said, "since a little girl. 'When she was good she was very, very good, but when she was bad she was

199

horrid.'" Wayne looked at me like I was crazy. I tried to explain Mama's poem for Swee. Swee's mind swing two ways, until bingo! one way got decided. She accepted Sandy, even when she didn't like his friends. She was willing to take the bad with the good. But then she decided Sandy out, so no Sandy, no matter what. "Swee too smart," I said. "She thinks too much, more hard to be satisfied. I think not so much but I know what makes me happy." Wayne was grinning at me, also happy.

So now I was trying to understand why she was chasing Sandy all the way to Washington State. Like in detective story, maybe the end was only a trick. Maybe Swee not so finished with Sandy as she thought. Love or not? Maybe Swee herself not know. Or maybe she still swinging, her heart not yet come to a rest.

Now I was the one to feel sorry for my sister. Now I keep quiet. I played the telephone book game she asked me to and waited for her to come out of the shower.

"No TV? What are you reading?" Steam followed Swee, her face shining and hair wet, out of the bathroom.

"The Holy Bible."

She burst out laughing and collapsed on the bed.

"This Naomi is very nice woman," I said. "Mama would never do that for us, and she is our own mother, not mother-in-law like Naomi! Mama probably prefer to make us just like herself and Ah Chee, two Buddhist nuns. When Ah Kong died, only man in their life is Buddha, with fat belly and laughing face."

"Like Wayne?"

I leaned over and punched her arm. "Buddha is not a male body. Buddha's figure is smooth, more like woman than male spirit. Wayne is a warrior. He's getting round, but he has a strong back. When I put my hands flat. . . ."

"It's alright. I don't need more description."

But Swee didn't understand. It was OK for me to be soft because Wayne was hard. To be young because he was older. What that woman's book called orgasms Wayne called loving kindness.

I closed my eyes and thought of Wayne's loving kindness.

Maybe a baby after we marry. A baby with Wayne's strong back and my soft hands. An American baby.

Twenty Three

*D*riving did strange things to me. It kept me focused, yet it set me free. Free to think the strangest thoughts, to slip in the slip wind of the car's speed and flow with the miles, like a particle returned to the state of pure energy.

It was only after we had passed Solvang, in that pang of remembering this was Sandy's town, his own country, that I considered how I had moved from planes to buses to motorbikes and now to my coupe. I had gone through dependency — leaving my life in the hands of unknown pilots to giving it over to Sandy. Sandy rode his bike with his whole body, not just his hands. His thighs gripped the metal like it grew out of his groins. His entire body leaned, bending the bike to his will, and I was merely a carry-on, surviving on his mastery of the machine and road. At any moment, had his attention wavered, his judgement failed, I could have been killed. It was thrilling to give myself over so completely to Sandy's power, and I knew he appreciated me for that trust.

But with the coupe, my life was now in my hands, in my grip on the steering wheel, my pressure on the gas pedal, the quick turn of my foot to the brakes. It was this nervous humming of energy through eyes, hands, thighs and feet that kept the car running, rounding corners, that made it stop in time before a fallen eucalyptus branch near Santa Barbara, and so kept me and Yen from death.

I could not imagine myself ever again giving my life over in the same way I did to Sandy, now I had my license, my own vehicle. The coupe was not as safe, as connected, as a town to live in, like Solvang, but it would do until I decided where I should go next. Right now I was on a trip to Trinity Cove, to where the United States ended and Canada began. It was like a school trip, to learn something, although what the lesson would cover I still did not know.

Yen, humming to country western music, left me alone on the first day of driving to observe my thoughts, and they were as much about Malaysia as about the land we were driving through. Perhaps because so much of the land was flat where it was not mountain. Flat agricultural fields with sweeps of water irrigating in narrowing circles. It was March and none of the fields were bare. The land was organized in long furrows running to the horizon. I was driving too fast to take in much of the vegetation, which seemed all low green plants stippling loam the color of Sandy's hair. The landscape was different from what we had known in Malaysia, seen driving to Singapore, the lush plantations of short fat palm trees, fronds so thick they meshed like family. If I had to choose between the two, I'd pick the plantations, offering shade, where one could hide. I wondered how illegal immigrants could be working in broad daylight in the clear rows of these fields. Sandy had talked about California going downhill because of Mexicans taking over the state. These corporate farms did not seem to be where they could be hiding. The heavy foliage of rubber plantations kept rushing into memory as I pedaled down on the gas past Salinas, even as the flat open fields fled past like the shapes in my bad dreams, minutely sharp and repetitious.

Yen sat up after we passed Marin County. I wondered what she was thinking as she stared blankly at the thick strands of evergreens and sequoias that came down right to the edge of the highway. This overgrown green reminded me of Malaysian jungle. I thought of Sandy and Keith practicing whatever they were practicing in those protected national forests Sunday after Sunday. Like a mass religious meeting, a gathering defense against a national nightmare. It was the illegal immigrants he kept sounding off on, while Yen and I were legal, paying tuition, paying rent, paying our dues, he said. Here in these northern woods that could conceal whole armies of men like Sandy, paying dues didn't seem so important. Who would be collecting them here anyway?

The second night we stopped also at a Vacation Inn. "Oh let's! Let's!" Yen begged when I asked where we should spend the night. The familiar was very big with Yen, always had been. That was why she was constantly surprising me in California. As much as she needed to be with the familiar, she seemed to want the new. It was amazing how she took to Wayne and biking. Every ride was to some place new, yet she never whined about strangeness when she was with Wayne. He was her security blanket. And I gave him credit for this new Yen. Even the music player, the tape recorder, took her inside, perhaps to a noisy place, but at least a noisy place inside her head. Yen now seemed capable of talking to herself when she had been distracted all her life.

We had been eating at fast food places and gathering garbage from Long Beach to Eureka. It was all-American garbage. Take-out containers with smiley faces, shiny foil wraps for hot burgers, cardboard containers for fries, candy wrappers and crackly bags once filled with chips and assorted orange and yellow snacks. Yen helped me pick them up from the carpet and stuff them into the plastic shopping bag she had filled with goodies at the supermarket where we had stopped to buy more soda, the goodies now gone, leaving only trash.

It was night and beginning to rain. We were many miles north of Eureka in Oregon and I was not going to drive any further. My hands were cramped from gripping the wheel tight, especially in the last fifty miles or so as it was getting dark.

I had to agree with Yen. Fatigue made the familiar welcome. It was almost the same motel as last night's. The channels on the familiar television set were the same. Yen turned up the volume to the same shows she watched in Long Beach with Wayne.

It was the same country, but it was also different. Long Beach seemed bright, colorful, almost like Malaysia, while this country was dank green in late winter, foggy sullen, icy. Instead of the vast Pacific, all kinds of waterways showed up around every other bend. Long narrow tidal flats. Ponds. Metal grey lakes. Rivers with stony banks and with reedy banks. White birds fluttered in the distance. Gulls. I preferred imagining them as ospreys. For sure, herons and egrets, wings and beaks like fine calligraphy in the ink-washed drizzle.

Long Beach was where we saw all colors of people, whites, blacks, Asians, browns, all forms of mixtures. The further north we went the less color there was. Every supermarket checker and fast food cashier, every gas station attendant and motel desk clerk, was white. Bun Jon didn't know what he was talking about. Once outside of Southern California, his Asian time was nowhere in sight.

I called the front desk to complain about the cold. I had missed the knob for the heating unit. It was by the window, under a metal cover, under the beige and dark green curtains. I could start up the heat myself.

"I'm hungry!"

Yen had devoured every snack we had bought in two days.

"Let's try the vending machines." I was in no shape to drive further. The wet had been only a mist. I had to turn the windshield wipers on every few minutes when the water fuzzed the glass enough so I could not make out the road ahead for more than a few yards. But the mist was too light to keep the wipers going continuously. As soon as the glass dried the wipers squeaked abominably, like a dying cat, a sound that had the skin on my arms rising in pin dots of protest.

Outside the door I hesitated. Did we have the door key? Was the door locked securely? Taking care of Yen I had grown an armor of worry. Worry took me through each day, double checking on her courses, whether Wayne was dropping her off in time for her classes, having the doctor prescribe her pills in case Wayne forgot his precautions. Thinking for two was complicated, and secretly I was looking forward to the wedding, when the two of them would be taking care of the one of her. Yen was steadier now, but she would always need another to keep her whole. I didn't think she had been wounded by Ah Kong's rejection or Mama's impatience. I hadn't, had I? It was just her nature, born incomplete.

As for me, I was constantly anxious about locking myself out of the apartment, out of a room. I didn't assume like Yen did that there would always be someone to let me in. Perhaps needing another made for an easier mind.

The vending machines were in an annex at the end of our corridor, two as bulky as soldiers and painted red, white and blue, the colors of the logos of the popular soda brands. A prominent sign in red and white read, "ALL MONEY REMOVED FROM MACHINES DAILY." My fingers twitched on my purse heavy with coins. Too many choices and only one money feeder, one way to feed the dollar bills, the stern face of George Washington up as it sped out of sight. The sodas clanged down the chute. The other machine with its clear glass door was packed with small bags of chips dusted with onion flakes, cheese bits, barbeque powder.

The candy bars had names of celestial bodies. Mars and Milky Way. Lifesavers. I stared at the names. Exhaustion made me think there was a message in these offerings. Four different flavors of Lifesavers. Not colors but flavors. Peppermint, fruit, cherry, pineapple. They seemed to approximate to colors, everything but black. No wonder Mrs Butler was mad at the world, mad at the United States. Everything was alphabet and number coded, but there were more letters and numbers than there were selections. Yen could not understand what buttons to press and in what sequence. I fed the quarters into the slot, checked her choices, punched in letters and numbers for her. But even after our dollar bills and coins ran out, the haul was meager. A handful of super mingy bags of chips, a few candy bars, four cans of soda. We needed to find a place for dinner.

A national franchise was just on the other side of the parking lot, the desk clerk said. We could brave the dark and wet and run across to the restaurant.

It seemed a number of others had the same need. Perhaps something about late hanging-on winter or about the continuous wet and cold drew people out to eat. A half-hearted attempt at Easter decorations made the restaurant look even blander. Some tinsel, a cardboard bunny and yellow paper chicken cutouts, curly lines of green foamy plastic suggesting spring grass. A window dressing that said it was safe to approach the building.

The large brightly lit room was divided into booths, and in most of the booths were couples, chiefly white-haired and heavy set. The youngest diners were well over middle-aged. They tried not to stare when Yen and I came in and waited for the manager to seat us. The Vacation Inn must have attracted many kinds of travelers and conditioned diners to strange company and to general politeness for strangers. The waiter was suave, at ease with us. We were young, Asian, but after all, we were two. The couples looked at us and turned to their meals. Something about being two made everything safe, for them, for us. Being paired, the minimum number for coming in under the radar, cloaked in the costume of two-ness, Yen and I settled in at our table, ate the peculiar green leaves passing for vegetables in America, swallowed enormous heaps of fries and beef patties oozing fat and mayonnaise on soft tasteless buns. We could have had chicken, pasta — but knew after almost two years that hamburgers were what these restaurants did best.

The dinner made me feel braver. I woke up next morning for the first time since Wayne had told me Sandy's story without the feeling of bad dreams still lingering. The coupe was again filled with bags of snacks and sodas from the grocery store down the road. This time the rain came down quicker, with a hard rattle. Yen took the audio plugs out of her ears to listen.

"Hail."

"Hail?"

"You know, freezing rain that comes down as ice?"

The bits of ice drummed on the window shield like grit thrown in a sandstorm and the sun never seemed to have come out that third day of driving. The din went on for miles. I worried the hail would turn to ice balls, come crashing down and crack the glass as I had read in newspaper accounts of bad weather. We were driving north and north into an extreme of climate. My fingers tingled with the urge to turn around and return to warm sunshine in Long Beach, but I knew I would not give in to this impulse. Nothing outside our contained habitat hurtling at over sixty miles per hour down the gray slick highway was as heavy as the sensation in my chest, misery one moment like inert iron and the next, for no good reason, hot and rolling, like a kettle overflowing with superheated fluid.

It was almost four when we came toward Trinity Cove. We had outrun the hail and even the rain. The skies cleared as the signs saying "20 MILES TO CANADA" came into view. I had plotted the road leading to Trinity Cove, which turned out to be a recent development with similar looking two-storied, sloping-roofed houses, beige, green and grey. After a dozen of these, I could see how remarkably unremarkable they were, pre-fab siding and concrete, glass and fake wood, half-posed around long winding unpaved driveways, on little bits of cleared land planted with half-grown pines and trees now bare of leaves. And everywhere was wilderness. These homes made no real incursions into the thick shadows of ancient pines packed close together. Only an open garbage dump gave some clue to human intrusion. A dump with fire pits, a pile of white porcelain turning into toilet bowls on closer approach, bits of pink and white plastic bags caught in the shrubs by the side of the road. Even here plasticized cups and beer cans were planted on the ground, testimony to someone's careless presence.

Wayne had talked about the house on a ledge above giant boulders and the stormy ocean but had given no address, no road name. I could see lights in some homes but didn't stop for directions. I could not imagine these northerners would welcome my interest. Instead I steered the coupe toward the sunset, driving carefully around bends and sudden turns to where the sky was reddest.

The north Pacific sprang up unexpectedly before me just as

the road swerved as if to avoid plunging down the cliffs. I slowed down in time to see blackened ruins where the road began to run parallel to the waves below. I braked, reversed, drove the car back and stopped. Yen was silent, watching me, her earphones plugged in.

The evening felt damp but there was no rain when I stood by the side of the road. An updraft blew from the water and whistled in my ears. A narrow driveway led from the road to the dark stained tumbled walls, scorched timber, collapsed roof, metal twisted and melted into lumps and odd shapes. I imagined a smell like old ashes, something burned to inedible grossness. The horizon behind it was blazing with deep orange and coral, tropical colors in a freezing evening.

I shrugged on my oversized sweater, tucked my fingers in the sleeves, and turned to tell Yen I was going to walk down the driveway where a yellow tape still divided the burnt-down house from the rest of Trinity Cove. She had her window down and was talking to a stranger bent down to listen. I had not heard him with the wind loud in my ears.

He straightened up when I approached, perhaps the tallest man I had ever met, rising thin and stringy like the star basketball players Wayne cheered on the television screen. But he was old. His head was full of white hair, thick tufts handsomely stirring in the wind. For a few minutes I thought he was blind. Dark glasses with elegant thin black rims covered his eyes.

"Thinking of jumping off?" Perhaps it was the blank glasses producing an impression of threat.

"We're. . . ." I was breathless, my lungs seized by timidity.

"You're not from here." His voice came from above my head, the words carried off by the blowing air.

"No, we came to look at the ruins."

"I can see that. It's private property. In fact, the place belongs to me."

I could see his eyes now behind the darkened lens, large irises restless and suspicious.

"But you can't possibly be living there. . . ."

"My residence is right next door. I own many of these houses. Rent them out to summer people. You're not rental folk."

"Someone told me my friend might have died here."

"Adolphus Weinberger? I don't believe you."

The anger in his voice shocked me. Yet it reminded me of Sandy's anger when it came from what I had thought of as nowhere, directed towards people I couldn't see, who appeared all too real and close for him. That anger had bruised me, directed again toward me now.

"I have macular degeneration. Blind spots in my retina. So there are areas in my point of vision where I cannot see a thing. But I can see well enough as long as I move my head around, and I can see you are not the kind Adolph would have had as a friend."

Tears came to my eyes. It might have been the blustery air stinging my cheeks and eyes.

"Adolph had problems, but foreign women was not one of them. Didn't care for any of that kind."

I had not noticed his walking stick before. Now he pointed it at me, a long cane with a plastic handgrip and a metal tip like a tiny horseshoe.

"You're Hong Kong people, aren't you? People from China. I was in the Merchant Marine in the Japan Sea, '44. We beat you people then. Now you're all over Canada, north of us. Bought over Vancouver. Just one big Chinatown, I've been told. Well, I'm not selling to you. No point checking it out."

"We Malaysians, not Hong Kong, not China. You're stupid! Who wants your burned down house anyway? My sister only want to see where Sandy die. Poor Sandy. No funeral, no *pai-pai*, for him. We come say *pai-pai*, make sure he not go to hell." Yen had come up behind him, was urgently waving me to leave.

The stranger seemed to remember I was not alone. He took off his glasses and immediately became an elderly man in a brown winter coat, even if towering extraordinarily and distinguished with silver hair. The sun was almost gone —

streaks of color remained only above the horizon line. It was too late now to stay and argue, far too late to try to explain what I had shared with Sandy.

"Sandy tried to love me," I said, "but he couldn't. That should make you happy. What I want to know is why I tried to love him. I know why I couldn't love him, but why did I even try?"

He was walking away rapidly even as I spoke, as if to prove his identity, walking down the pathway that connected the ruins to the neighboring house, beige, green and brown, almost hidden among grown pine and dense rhododendrons.

"Thank you!" I shouted to the disappearing figure, my tears evaporating in the chilly air. "Thank you!" I would thank him even if he didn't want my gratitude. The words would grate on him. He'd remember them later at night, sitting in his brightly electrified home with his wife at his side, and think of how much I must have benefited from him, from people like him, despite their menace, their rejections, to insist so on thanking him, and he would become angrier, more helpless.

"Swee, come on, time to leave." Yen's voice was softer than the wind that had picked up, roaring and bending the tips of the pines.

I looked at the wreck on the ledge and further down toward the Pacific where the icy waters from Alaska were mixing up with the Humboldt currents and where the waves had brought down bluffs and cliffs through the centuries. Perhaps Sandy had scrambled down the ridges. There were patches in the fading light that looked like trails down to the rocks below. Even with a round white moon lighting up Trinity Cove, a man could appear a shadow and escape among scrub and clefts. I didn't want Sandy to die. I didn't want Sandy to be only a memory of meanness, to be remembered for hatefulness. No one deserved to be hated for hating. No one deserved to die for hating another.

Then I thought of the two men, tired from working all day in some one's yard or factory, who had been killed while sleeping at the Mission under the still unformed cross, who might have crossed themselves before falling asleep. They hadn't escaped. I had not until now wondered what had happened to them. I hoped they had not died hungry, that they had eaten well that evening at Pearl's feast, remembering with a burn in my throat hearing the echo of Sandy's angry voice, "Freeloaders!" when I had first watched the hungry eat at the Mission. Like Sandy's lost self, where might they be buried? Were they like the Chumash at the Santa Barbara Mission, unidentified bodies tumbled into a pit, undocumented also in death? I thought of Mrs Butler's deep rich voice lecturing me sarcastically on the art of closing one eye. "That's no way to understand the history of racism in this country. You rich folk, you new-come-latelys, you have not known the whip and the chain. All you know is the art of closing one eye." Perhaps that had been my problem as Mrs Butler's student, my absence of full attention, full sightedness to the kinds of history Sandy carried with him.

I opened my eyes wide and stared at the darkening hulk, the charred walls still standing. Where had Sandy died? Under the beams lying collapsed like massive matchsticks? By the bathtub whose purine white porcelain still gleamed despite its immersion in flames? I could see the place yards ahead of me, the physical geography where he had perhaps last been. But I could not see him. His faint smile whenever he saw me across a room, a parking lot, like a recognition of who we were together — I had lost its sweetness when he had shaken me so hard I thought my neck would snap. But, no, I had not abandoned him. Sandy had left months before I discovered his fury; checked out for a different road that lead him to the house on Trinity Cove.

"Swee!" Yen's voice rose to a whine, above the wind's thrashing.

The evening was biting, burning raw on my cheeks. I felt the weight shift in my chest. Yen was right. We couldn't stay here out in the open.

Twenty Four

*I*t wasn't just the reporters, detectives and LA police who aggravated me. I didn't leave Father's mission because it had suddenly become sticky. "Don't let them hassle you," Mr Leong said in his uncle manner when he caught me sitting down-in-the-mouth in the annex, airless, windows shut to keep out the rubber-burnt smells, the heavy metal particles, after yet another interview, this time with a bulked-up sergeant who asked stubbornly, over and over again, why I had left Malacca for Los Angeles. What was I doing with these Mexicans coming to the Mission? How many Mexicans did I know? How many illegal immigrants had come through the Mission? What was the Chinese connection? Hassle. A strange word, used only by Americans. Sounding like what coolies did to sacks of rice, snagging a pick into the mesh, throwing hundred kilo loads from lorries onto pallets. Or flinging them onto lorries. I was a sack of Chineseness he was hassling, digging sharp, chucking me again and again onto a train out of LA.

But these interrogations were a simple matter in contrast to my meeting with the Council of Elders. The Christians I had thought my sisters and brothers bothered me the most. Of course, no one blamed me, they said. At the first congregational prayer gathering after the bomb, so many took the time to assure me that I knew they were blaming me. Whose idea was it to put up the monstrous cross, who thought the Mission needed such an extravagant structure, and, of course, it would have attracted enmity, where had all that money come from, and did anyone stop to point out what a waste it was with so many real needs unmet? When the news came out that the unknown donor was me, the elders were even more unhappy. I appeared deceitful, even if I had good intentions; the path to hell was paved, and some one remarked the money could have gone to expanding the pre-kindergarten morning classes for the working mothers. Or more vocational summer courses for the teenagers who couldn't find jobs because they didn't read and write English well or because they were dark-skinned or both. No one said it, but everyone, including me, probably thought it.

The elders gently chastised me for wrong thinking, for a proud spirit and misplaced priorities. Worse, the council noted in its Mission Bulletin, those construction funds were now lost, and the salvaging of the wreck added to the Mission's final costs. At the Council, I was made to acknowledge my youth, and, except for Mr Leong smiling kindly at me, I felt my difference. I had tried to change the Mission's administration to fit Father's multicultural vision, but after the bombing and the deaths of the two men on Mission ground, the elders wanted to be safe again. They elected long-term white parishioners. Even the Hispanic members were white. How could Father wish to continue as pastor in this old Mission? But he was oblivious, his multiculturalism was in his head, not in the elders.

Submission. This was the Gospel's message for the ages. But it was hard to submit. My spirit groaned, like grain thrown under a millstone, losing its seed shape, the inner kernel from which can sprout a new root and green stem pounded close to extinction. My eyes closed again and again in prayer, but my faith in the Mission was mashed to powder, ground down by the elders who knew better and were wiser than I.

In the weeks after the destruction of the cross, communal sharing no longer lifted me up. All through childhood I had never cared for the kind of eating my sisters craved — sweet cakes, spicy meats, strong salty plums, and sticky drinks to wash all the masticated glop down into their gullets. Here at the Mission on many Sundays, I had learned not only to endure but to stir tenderly over the chewing, gnawing, munching, sucking, slurping, of hundreds of gallons of food stuff. After the elders' rebuke, I felt myself corroding in the presence of worshippers, each Sunday, eating, sharing their communion, even as I knew they must if they were to live.

    Submit. Digest. Disgust. The joyfulness went out of my body.

Mama's arrival offered me an excuse to leave: a daughter's duty to family, to parents, to mother. Everyone understood this universal commandment. The third of the tenth. Honor thy father and thy mother. I was third of three, the Holy Ghost was the sign of my birth, and I would be directed by his Great Spirit, I told Father and Robert in explaining my wish to return to Malacca.

    Of course, in a Chinese family, it would have been difficult for a husband to follow his wife; the man's father was the small god of their world, and Father could have called on his Chinese birthright to insist I stay in LA.

    But we were a Christian family, and Mama's soul was in need of salvation. To honor her, I must save her soul, baptise her in the blood of the Lamb; but Mama would only consider conversion, she said, from her home, never among the throngs of brown, black and white in the Mission. Mama was scratching around for any excuse to escape baptism while saving her daughter's father-in-law's face.

    For once we were in harmonious agreement. Los Angeles would not do for the Wings. Mama and Ah Chee left almost immediately after Yen's wedding; and Robert and I followed a few months later, after we had trained alternative assistant pastors for the Mission.

    Korean, Mexican, Thai, Salvadoran, Vietnamese, even white Americans — Anglos, Father calls them, a name so close to "angel," so haloed by associations with divinity Father never questioned their authority in the Council — everyone accepted the reason I gave.

    One of the three daughters should remain home to care for Mama — and because I was willing to return to Malacca, I left with victory snatched from death, an American-returned, bearing all I had learned in Los Angeles. Exuberant clapping, clasping of hands, swaying as one chain swinging in God's breath, salsa music, percussion, guitars, there being always some men happy to play for the congregation. Sharing of clothing and food, from those with plenty to those with little; it never being certain who has plenty and who less, for the rich ache to give from the hollows in their lives, and the poor dance and sing, laughing like the cricket in the fable, whose scratch-it, fetch-it, scratch-it, fetch-it tells everyone the world is warm and bright. Yes, no one said I had failed in the United States. It was there I learned my true mission, ministering to Christians at home, not in a foreign church.

Twenty Five

OK, I get to tell the story last. Because I am in California. Everyone else has gone away. Peik went back to Malaysia. She said she also had religious calling, so no need to simply follow father-in-law, and Robert must go with her. She feels sorry for heathen people like Mama and Ah Chee, she can no longer ignore their souls. In Malaysia so many Chinese are going downhill to PAGANISM. Pearl is afraid they are condemned to ever-lasting fire. She says LA got many, many problems, many, many souls to save, but she must save CLOSEST TO HOME. Mama writes letters to Swee and me, complaining like anything about Peik. Peik saying Mama and Ah Chee must be BAPTIZED. Cannot go to temple any more. Cannot give alms to Abbot Narasimha or monks. Mama wrote she was surprised Ah Chee never mind to change religion. Ah Chee says one god just like another. Jesus as good as Kuan Yin. She don't care if Peik says God man or woman, white or Chinese. All prayers are the same. Ah Chee thinks she and Mama already visited so many temples everywhere, Penang, Bangkok, Hong Kong, Japan, even Burma! Now, just as good to become Christian and find new places to visit, churches, ca-the-drals! Ah Chee wants to fly to Manila. The neighbor tells her Philippines has lots of old ca-the-drals. Also Macau has one big old church half-standing. I don't understand. Mama complains, say no way she can change just like that, but Ah Chee, she's so funny, never complains!

But Swee was a different story. That time we drove back from Trinity Cove! She was so tired and I couldn't help her. She was like a robot. I never worried she would crash the car because I saw everything for Swee was under control, her face tight like when she studied for exams. Concentrate, concentrate!

I told her about the rude man. "He asks what we doing there, looking at his house, and I say, where got house? Only burn down junk. He says we come to buy land, like buying Manhattan Island with beads. Even I know that old story. Wah, so bad, as if we are like his kind, cheat Indians and steal land!"

Swee wasn't listening to me. She only wanted to get as far away from that house as possible. But outside it was very dark, the road was narrow, narrow, and too much curving, every minute was dangerous. She had to slow down, no more seventy, eighty miles speed. She drank two cans soda, for caffeine, she said, then had to find a bathroom, quick quick.

We stopped at a rest stop, bright lights, with a coffee shop next door. "Better safe than sorry," Swee said, locking up the doors and pushing me in front of her. The toilets had stinky urine and chemical smell. Chemicals to kill germs made me want to throw up. The floors were slippery wet, toilet paper everywhere on floor and nothing on roll in the toilet. I was so happy to leave.

When we got back into the car, Swee said, "I'm going to give the car to you and Wayne for your wedding present." She promised no more restroom stop until we find a nice motel.

I was afraid to speak. I thought anything I said would make her sadder. I listened to Wayne's music and dreamed of house and baby and Wayne. No choice, lah, because nothing to see. Everything was so dark outside, the world was like no world, and Swee was only driving like demon, not talking, not drinking. Then I didn't know what happened, I fell asleep.

When Swee woke me for the night at the motel, I forgot what day it was anymore. "You have a rehearsal wedding a week after we get back to Long Beach," she told me. I remembered thinking, "Only a few more days, then Pastor Fung make us man and wife!"

Swee talked and talked all through second day of driving, third day of driving. She talked about what she wanted to do.

She was going back to New York, but this time she was moving to the city. She was no longer afraid of Sodom and Gomorrah, she was a big girl now. She was going to study journalism — going to be a reporter. Going to be Asian American reporter. She said the city was the right place for someone like her.

"What you mean, someone like you? You're like what? You're like no one! You're only like you. You never find another Swee in New York!"

I was hoping she'd laugh, but she was too serious. Wah, when Swee was serious she became very talkative. Said so many things I could not remember. "Heart-to-heart talk," she said, but this time she did the talking and I the heart must listen.

"I'm not like you," she said, as if I didn't already know. "I'll probably never marry. I don't know why I'm in such a rush. I'm tired of sitting around Long Beach waiting. I don't know what I'm waiting for. See, Ah Kong's money hasn't done me any good. I don't feel motivated to do anything. Trying to work just to make money doesn't make sense. Those months at the pharmacy, a waste of time! I think I did it to pretend I was like all the immigrants coming to California. Being one of the others. It's safer to be one of the others than a solitary you."

"Huh?"

"I don't mean you. You and Wayne are a natural couple."

I smiled at that. "Natural" for Swee I know is big compliment.

"I mean a legal immigrant. It was important for me to feel like we were legal, even if legal meant being bad. You know, those thunder rides, drinking at Pete's Bar and Sandy and his motorbike gang."

"You say you pretend all that?"

"I don't know. A part of me enjoyed it. I knew Sandy was wrong about many of his attitudes. He didn't like black people, brown people. I didn't approve of his attitudes. But I also didn't want to be someone he didn't like."

Too confusing! Big headache trying to understand Swee. I was trying to be a big sister, but now I gave up!

I put on earphones and listened to Beach Boys music again

because now we were back on Highway 1, coming down toward Monterey!

The last two hundred miles I looked at the map again and again to see how close we were getting, how many miles more before we turned into the exit for Long Beach. I was no longer interested in eating chips, eating peanuts, eating Mars and Milky Way. I only wanted to hurry back to Wayne. One time I believed Swee was blood of my blood. That was never going to change. We were forever sisters. But what changed was my body. It was too bad Swee found someone bad like Sandy. Now she's alone. But it was good I broke away from Swee. My body was happy, hurrying back to Wayne.

Twenty Six

*N*ovember 21, 1983

Dearest Yen,

 I hope Wayne has fixed the postbox and my letter will find its way to your address in Venice Beach. Please write down this new New York address. I have just moved to Brooklyn, and I still like to think of myself as a New Yorker, although my classmates tell me Brooklyn is nothing like living in Manhattan.

 You won't be interested in these classmates. They're all career-bound. They'll find you and Wayne limited, while they believe they have arrived at the center of the universe. They are smart, no doubt, but they are shallow. Even their depths are black-white-and-gray. I like them. They are all I have in New York, these smart, professional-type students. They think they know everything about different cultures and races, but they have too few demons. They enjoy most of all to shop, to make money and spend it, and to be with others just like themselves. My journalism classmates who are Asian American never worry about pai-pai. They do not keep altars in their apartments.

 Thank you for that long phone call last night. I'm glad Wayne likes the car and has decided to garage the motorbike. Tell him I think he should consider selling the Harley someday. I have signed all the papers transferring car ownership to him and I include them here. As I told him last night, he only has to pay for the car insurance, which will now be in his name. You must not worry I miss having a car. I have learned to take the subway and buses, and where they don't go I have been walking. I am tired of driving and will never buy another car.

Is it a sign of adolescence or of aging that I am using the word 'never' more often? 'Never' is like closing doors behind me. No, not doors, because you can backtrack, you can go back and re-open old doors. Although why one would want to do that I don't know. You open an old door and you might find corpses. Mummified but dead. When Beauty was woken up, she must have screamed to find herself in a mausoleum among mummified bodies of her family who had died the day she fell asleep. Prince Charming was only a partially successful wizard. Which woman could trust a man like him? 'Never' is like burning down a house. That long drive to Trinity Cove, I thought I had something, control, my life in my hands. But after smelling that ruin, after six days of driving, I never wanted such speed, such distances, again. I may never buy another car.

 I didn't have time to tell you yesterday I'm wondering whether I should continue my journalism studies. After writing as I wished for *Asian Time*, I find it difficult to absorb the theoretical readings the professors assign. The courses seem so abstract, not like real life. I know you will laugh at this, but I am afraid I seem to have grown stupid. Either that or all this academic work is truly dull and lifeless, and I am sure my professors will not agree!
 In fact, last week as I was walking up the 42nd Street subway exit, a woman gave me a card and asked me to come and see her. Her card said "Crystal Readings by Theresa." She is a psychic consultant who gives palm and tarot card readings. Her card says she gives advice on all problems, including love, business, marriage, etc, and that she can help where others have failed. What do you think of that, Yen? She looked directly into my eyes and said, "I can help you, you look like you need help." If you were there, you'd probably push her away and call her cheeky. But I took her card, which is bright pink cardboard paper, and I am looking at it now as I write to you.

Of course I don't plan to go to a gypsy psychic to have my fortune told. My nightmares may have returned, but at least they are changing rather than repeating themselves loop after loop. Taking public transportation — being public — that is part of what I like about not driving a car. Theresa, the psychic consultant, would not have been able to talk to me if I had been driving with windows shut against the cold dirty New York air. Maneuvering a car past the slag of slushy and brown-black grainy ice banks I would not be able to study city signs and city people the way I do each day from the uptown bus, some days thinking I can see Manuel with his black nubby hair uncovered standing by a sidewalk.

On Fifth Avenue and 111th Street, such an auspicious address, someone had spray-painted in bold letters large enough to read fifty yards away, "DEAR RICH AMERICA." The first time I saw it I was thrilled. A public letter to the country! But here we Wings are, richer than many in America, richer than most in Harlem, and what are we doing in America if not for money? The letter-graffiti must be carrying a message from an immigrant who had heard those slogans in his original home, blaring out from television set and radio. "DEAR AMERICA! RICH AMERICA!" Who had followed father, mother, brother, uncle, neighbor, through desert, sea borders, etc, to DEAR RICH AMERICA, and now, in Harlem, can only send letters to this America, not found in Harlem, not in New York state, not even in California. DEAR RICH AMERICA. With my bank accounts flushed with Singapore dollars and Malaysian ringgit, am I looking for another America, rich not in dollars but promise? Looking for myself in America. Whatever it is I cannot be in Malacca. But after Sandy, I am no longer so certain what this promise is.

I search for more signs on the streets. WE BUY AND SELL GOLD. Shop after shop with this declaration. At least, it's no longer WE BUY AND SELL SLAVES. Above a restaurant a sign reading MOFONGO: CHINESE CUBAN FOOD. Leaning by fire hydrants, clusters of colored men at 3 pm, smoking, bottles at their feet, in their hands, held to their mouths. And down by Central

Park, a child stands by the pavement looking into the park. He is standing there as the bus approaches and is still standing in the same spot when I look behind.

I read the city streets like I used to read books, and wonder who I will become here.

I think Theresa, whoever she is, is probably right and I need help deciding what I wish to study. But there is no college for psychic consulting where I can register to learn how to give crystal readings to myself! So I am thinking of switching from journalism to psychology. I've checked the requirements and I will need only two more years of coursework to complete a degree in psychology. Then I can make up my own cards to give out to people like me who need help.

If you ever visit me, I'll probably take you shopping and eating. After classes, that's what I spend most of my time doing. A giant city like New York, you can shop and eat in a different place every day and pretend you are living in a whole big world, not just in twenty or so blocks. The city doesn't appear as real as Malacca, maybe because even with seven or so million, I know fewer people here than in little old Malacca. Everyone seems like a shadow, not even clouds but the shadows of clouds passing. I am beginning to feel not quite real myself.

Yet New York welcomes me with food and shops. Red Apple Supermarket doors steam open every three street corners. Doors to the subway trains slide open with a loud sigh. I step in, look around, walk to the middle of the car, and sit beside the woman who is clasping two brown paper bags on her lap. I look for women to sit next to — not just in subways and on buses, but in class, the cafeteria, library. Walking out of the station I look for signs of women's bodies under their nylon padded winter jackets. I walk briskly behind, pretending a casual ignorance of their presence, a fixed preoccupation with the pavement. I pass by swiftly, and gulp down their scents — lotion and perfume, hairspray, toothpaste breath, sweaty wool, pungent whiffs from menstruating bodies. It's my sister I am missing. I pretend the city is full of Yen — her loud voice, awkward body shifts, her life flung with mine in America, and I comfort myself with the women I accidentally meet each day. The Puerto Rican sales clerk at the Union Square discount store. I stop there twice a week, buy a couple boxes of Kleenex, a cheap thin towel — she smiles as she rings up the register. I shun the men, seeing Sandy in their brown hair, their quick furtive glances, like Sandy's, checking out who I might be to them.

Wasn't it good of Mama and Ah Chee to surprise you on your wedding? I was really grateful to Wayne for taking their visit so well, especially as none of us except Pearl knew they would be arriving on the day before the wedding. Pearl is very good at keeping a secret! The church photographs turned out well. Pearl finally sent them, all the way from Malacca! Did she send you copies as well? I must say Wayne looked rather startled in the first few shots.

In fact he looked totally freaked out. Too many Asians for one wedding, he'd muttered. It was Ah Chee who unmanned him most. Ah Chee refused to wear anything but her usual black pants and blue samfoo top. She was like an alien invading from another planetary system. But I thought Wayne recognized her, or someone very much like her. Someone from that personal past he never wanted to talk to Yen about. He kept looking at Ah Chee from the corner of his eye like he was expecting her to morph into his personal monster. You could see that freak fear in his face in a couple of the candid snapshots. But Wayne must have realized at some point Mama and Ah Chee were nothing like the bar mama-sans he had met at a different time in his life. He grew calmer as the ceremony proceeded. Then, a church dinner with Pastor Fung, Robert and Mr Leong saying three different graces and Mama seated beside the church elders in her regal purple floral frock — that is the only word for her outfit — like the Queen Mother, and with a strand of real pearls even. Her very first color dress marking her coming out of mourning, just a few more days to the third anniversary of Ah Kong's death. "For Eldest Daughter's marriage, the abbot said, it was permitted." Probably more respectably dressed than Wayne's mother might have been had she come to the wedding. And Ah Chee kept silent throughout the dinner. Nothing in broken English or in Hokkien. Nothing to embarrass.

The two of you were a beautiful couple and that wedding cake that Mama ordered was enormous! I am sure the church parishioners were grateful to have so much leftovers. Too bad Pearl and Robert have left the Mission Church. I don't know how the pastor will manage without them.

I'm not going to write to Pearl the Mission doesn't seem to miss her at all. The communion lunches she had made such a fuss about has gone from her handiwork to that of a number of Mission regulars. Women are good at picking up pieces. When I dropped in to say goodbye in August to Mr Leong and Melody, Mrs Leong was in the annex working on a computer program to keep the accounting books for the Mission. All those five-dollar entrance fees have finally to be audited now the Federal Government is keeping an eye on the Mission finances. The church elders have dropped the idea of the cross and are working on providing more services instead. "Christ made flesh, not steel," the Los Angeles Times *had reported Pastor Fung preaching to the congregation.*

Perhaps Mama's dropping in at your wedding influenced Pearl's decision to leave LA. Mama looked like a nice Christian woman in the Western dress Pearl had bought for her from the Glendale mall, don't you think? Pearl must have been shocked to see Mama look so converted, it must have made her think again about whether she wanted to stay in the United States or do her church work back home.

I was surprised she was able to persuade Robert to follow her home to Malaysia, even though Pastor Fung agreed it was more godly to take care of the soul of one's own mother than of needy Angelenos! I've only received a couple of letters from Pearl since.

Nothing you'd be interested in. Pearl is the mystery in our family, don't you think? You're settled in California, I am looking for myself in New York, and Pearl is looking for God in Malacca. Now, who do you think will be the first to succeed? Aside from yourself, that is? She wrote she's begun a new mission with Robert, using her money where it was made: already about sixty parishioners, including some of her teachers from the Methodist School. They like the gospel border music that she'd learned in Los Angeles — she'd brought back lots of tapes.

Pearl was the most shocked by the collapse of the cross, the deaths of the two men sleeping by the portico, crushed under the steel. "It was vanity," she'd said, after the salvage company had cleaned up and left the Mission Church looking almost the same before her big vision came along and began building upward. I could have told her California geography dictates nothing tall except mountains and sequoias. But Pearl believed in the kingdom. It didn't matter to her where she was in the world. Everything was for God anyway. For a moment I thought she would lose faith. That blank look of guilt as the white ambulances pulled away screaming. If not her, who was responsible for those deaths? And I suppose she did lose faith, faith in the church in America. Back home, she could do her mission without seeing those Mexican American ghosts every Sunday in the faces of their countrymen.

At least one of us is staying on in California. It isn't quite a defeat for the whole Wing family, is it?

The other afternoon, during a big bad snowstorm, I saw a bird flying in the snow outside my window. I figured it was one of the passenger pigeons that Luz, the Cuban woman who lives up on the top floor of my building, is breeding. It was shying off the lighted windows on the different floors, from my fifth floor to the fourth, the sixth and then down to the street. It looked like it was trying to find a way into the building.

A pigeon in the blizzard. What would it say to me? I am cold.

Sister Swing

I am hungry. *It was warm and blue, and now it is icy and gray. It doesn't understand time. It's come from a coop on a Brooklyn rooftop where the Cuban woman in love with pigeons has been breeding generations of them. She has been in New York for almost as long as I have been in the US. Came over on a shrimp boat from the port of Mariel — a small-time crook who had only stolen a wallet from a pair of trousers on a chair by an open window. She'd been a young girl following her father, a gardener, in his work at one of the hotels for visiting Soviet military men and their wives and mistresses. Who'd know the colonel was in bed alone taking care of business when she'd snatch the pants, snatched the fake leather billfold, found only rubles worth hardly anything on the black market? Who would know the colonel was a spiteful man, a strong man who jumped out of bed, penis still red and swollen, to grab her hand, his hand still sticky wet. "But perhaps," Luz had continued, in the stuck elevator, confiding her entire life in the half hour while we waited for the elevator to move or the world to end, "perhaps that was the blessing my grandmother had promised me when she sent me away, crying, from the village to stay with my father in Havana, on the grounds of the Maximillu Hotel." Because, if she had not been sent to jail, she would not have been shoved on to the rotting boat. She would not have braved a wave-tossed passage to land on a sandy strip in Florida, and she would not have made her way from Miami, where the other Cubanos spat at her, to New York, where she has found respect as a cook of prized plantains and empanadas, all the dishes her Tito had taught her in that long ago village, and where she could now spend time and money breeding gray and blue birds, trained to fly with messages unread to no particular place before returning to their sky-high coop.*

 Luz likes bright colors — the elevator always seems to sing with yellows and pinks when she's there. She asked me how long I had been in mourning. When I answered three years, she said it was a strange culture that required such a long period of grief.

 I watched the gray blue wings fluttering over the snow bank. So close to home it had lost its way, and no wonder. The heavy all-day arctic blast had obliterated familiar landmarks and the sun behind the thick cloud cover was merely a sick yellow cast and no help for orientation. No, it was only in my dreams the creature took on Ah Kong's beaky nose, a sad comedown from the proud man he'd been. Messenger pigeons come and go, but they always turn to return home. Not to swoop into a human's sleep, roost in her dreams flapping sorrow and pity, and wake her up, face drenched in tears.

Watching the faint movements, I knew how it felt. I felt frozen and tired also, like I had been through a long journey, longer than when I had first traveled all the way from Malacca, stopping in Kuala Lumpur, Amsterdam, and London to New York and then to Albany where a white van took me, the lone passenger, to the college. Longer than my return flight after the first year, all my bags repacked, reversing directions, back to the house that appeared shrunken, browner for all the scrubbing Ah Chee did every day, shabbier. Longer than the flight with Yen from Singapore to Sydney to Los Angeles, and then the bus to the mall where Sandy had picked us up in yet another van. This time I had not followed Pearl home to Mama. This would be the winter when I give up my feathers and lie in a nest of ice. But no, even as I watched, the blue gray colors were flapping up and up. It had discovered some rooftop antenna, it was swirling toward the skyline. Then I lost sight of it, hoped it had found its Cuban mistress and rooftop coop.

Last night, I dreamed about Ah Kong again. He was no longer a fierce beaked shape but a pigeon. He wasn't even trying to get in away from the ice on the dirty sill. He was just sitting there, feathers all puffed up like a down jacket to keep warm, but I recognized him because of something in his bill.

Poor bird father! I tried to open the window to coax him in, but the lever had been painted too often and was bonded, painted into its wedged position. I tried to be quiet and unobtrusive, but because I was banging the lever to free it, Ah Kong took fright and flew away. In my dream, the window looked out into an air shaft and I watched him spiral up and up, looking for a way out, then he was gone, one tiny gray feather in the night. Ah Kong was no falcon peregrine in New York City. He'd shrunk into a common ghost bird, all his past colors leached out. No longer afraid, I wanted to get him into my shelter. In my dream I was asking, which one of us is American? I'm not sure what my question meant, if dream questions can have meaning. I guess it might have referred to Ah Kong or me. Or perhaps it meant all the new strangers I am meeting in New York, so many from places Ah Kong would have found difficult to fly to. Ethiopia, Gambar, Niger, Turkistan, Tibet, Bhutan. New Yorkers with stronger wings than he ever sprouted.

It was a nothing dream, but when I woke up I found my face was wet. The dream must have made me cry. I'm still thinking of Ah Kong wandering over New York in the winter, so small and cold and alone. Remember, Mama warned me Ah Kong's ghost would follow me to America if I do not wear black for three years? The three years have passed and I still have not gone shopping for new clothes because in New York my classmates are always dressed in black and I fit right in.

I'll come and visit you and Wayne when the baby arrives. Do people wear black on Venice Beach? I guess I will have to find myself some new aunty clothes.

An American aunty. Or an aunty in America. I thank Yen for this new role. She will be more interesting than me, my niece, who will only know about being a Wing second-hand. She will have to be the promise of America for all of us, the littlest one, bearing the dreams we have left standing.

Your loving Sister Swing,

Swee